ALGONQUIN LEGACY

THE ALGONQUIN QUEST SERIES

I Am Algonquin

Algonquin Spring

Algonquin Sunset

Algonquin Legacy

An Algonquin Quest Novel

Algonquin Legacy

Rick Revelle

DUNDURN PRESS

First published by Crossfield Publishing, 2021

All characters in this work are fictitious. Any resemblance to real persons, living or dead, is purely coincidental.

Publisher: Meghan Macdonald | Cover designer: Lawrence Stilwell

Library and Archives Canada Cataloguing in Publication

Title: Algonquin legacy / Rick Revelle.
Names: Revelle, Rick, author
Series: Revelle, Rick. Algonquin quest novel.
Description: Series statement: An Algonquin quest novel
Identifiers: Canadiana (print) 20250180057 | Canadiana (ebook) 20250180081 | ISBN 9781459756304 (softcover) | ISBN 9781459756311 (EPUB) | ISBN 9781459756922 (PDF)
Subjects: LCGFT: Novels.
Classification: LCC PS8635.E887 A62 2025 | DDC jC813/.6—dc23

We acknowledge the support of the Canada Council for the Arts and the Ontario Arts Council for our publishing program. We also acknowledge the financial support of the Government of Ontario, through the Ontario Book Publishing Tax Credit and Ontario Creates, and the Government of Canada.

Printed and bound in Canada.

Dundurn Press
1382 Queen Street East
Toronto, Ontario, Canada M4L 1C9
dundurn.com, @dundurnpress

Dedicated to:
James Favel and Susan Chief
and
the Rest of the Winnipeg Bear Clan Patrol,
Protectors of the People

In Memory of:
Willie Bruce
Oshkaabewis
Aboriginal Veterans Autochtones

AUTHOR'S NOTE

FOLLOWING THE PUBLICATION of *I Am Algonquin* in 2013, *Algonquin Spring* in 2015, and *Algonquin Sunset* in 2017, this book will be the last in the Algonquin Quest Series. The series follows the evolving migration of the Anishinaabe from the east coast of Turtle Island to the vastness of the prairies. During the time of this migration, you have followed how they survived and prospered through hunting, loss of life, making alliances, and warding off the great nations of the Haudenosaunee, the Lakota, and the powerful Blackfoot.

The Anishinaabe people are many nations. In my novels, they are Mi'kmaq, Omàmiwinini (Algonquin), and the confederacy known as the Three Fires: Potawatomi, Odawa, and Ojibwe, whom I call the Anishinaabe. Through the guidance of the Seven Prophets, they made the great migration west and split off along the way, becoming the Three Fires communities around the Upper Great Lakes at the end of their journey. Their last migration was west of Lake Superior, where they became the Saulteaux, or Plains Ojibwe.

This last novel will introduce you to two new Native nations and their languages: the Blackfoot and the Cree. These tribes were traditional enemies who were trying to live and survive on the vast lands of the western prairies, competing for the huge buffalo herds that roamed from the southern grasslands to the northern prairies. Pre-contact, these herds numbered sixty to seventy-five million but, by the 1890s, European buffalo hunters, killing for buffalo robes, reduced the great herds to less than five hundred animals. This slaughter was also encouraged by the governments of the day to deprive the "Horse Cultures," the Nations of the Great Plains, of their traditional food source and drive them off their lands onto desolate reservations. During the time of the buffalo, the Indigenous people were a formidable foe to the U.S. Army, and the only way they were defeated was by killing off the buffalo and slaying their immense horse herds.

I wrote about a Lakota buffalo hunt in *Algonquin Spring*, and you will read about another here, this time by the Blackfoot. Each tribe went about it in different ways but always for the same result: survival. A story cannot be written about a Plains Native nation without them hunting this great mammal.

I would like to thank the website All About Bison (allaboutbison.com/natives/blackfeet/) for supplying the story about the Buffalo Rock, as told by George Bird Grinnel in 1920. Miigwetch.

Today, all these aforementioned Native tribes survive and retain their cultural links to the lands they still live on. They are trying to rescue their heritage and languages from the painful experiences of the residential schools era, which became a brick wall in our cultures. My books are historical fiction about real Native nations and how they lived. The culture, hunting, and warfare that you read about in these novels are based on hours and hours of research. I have read over 125 nonfiction books and visited every major museum between Newfoundland and Manitoba and in the Midwestern United States. You can travel to every single place I talk about in my novels.

Now sit back, grab a berry tea, and read my final book of the Algonquin Quest series and enjoy. Miigwetch!

PROLOGUE

AFTER THE BATTLE of Crow Wing River, fifteen summers ago, most of the Anishinaabe warriors and their women, led by Zhashagi (*sha-sha-gee*: Blue Heron) and his brother Omashkooz (*oh-mush-goes*: Elk), made the decision to go towards the setting sun and live with their friends the Omashkiigoo (*oh-mush-key-go*: Cree). It is here that the surviving family members of the brothers, Mahingan, Kag, Wàgosh, and Mitigomij, made the decision to part ways.

Anokì (*uh-noo-key*: Hunt), his dog Nij Enàndeg (*neesh en-nahn-deg*: Two Colour), his sister Pangì Mahingan (*pung-gee mah-in-gan*: Little Wolf), and her husband, Ki'kwa'ju (*key-kwa-ju*: Wolverine), were the only ones from their family unit to make the decision to go with the Anishinaabe. Elue'wiet Ga'qaquis (*el-away-we-it ga-a-gooch*: Crazy Crow), the fierce Mi'kmaq warrior, also went west, followed by his Mi'kmaq friends Jilte'g (*jil-teg*: Scar) and E's (*s*: Clam).

The ones that returned to the Omàmiwinini homeland along the Kitcisìpi Sìbì (Ottawa River) were Anokì's last remaining uncle, Mitigomij (*mih-tih-go-mesh*: Red Oak) and his black panther, Makadewà Wàban (*ma-ka-de-wa wah-bun*: Black Dawn); his mother, Wàbananang (*wa-ba-na-nang*: Morning Star); and their chief, the two-spirited woman Kìnà Odenan (*key-nah o-de-nan*: Sharp Tongue), who was still mourning her female partner, Agwanìwon (*uh-gweh-nee-won*: Shawl Woman). Kìnà's lifelong male friend and guardian, Kànìkwe (*kaw-knee-kwe*: No Hair), and Anokì's twin cousins and their pregnant wives — Makwa (*muck-wa*: Bear) and his wife, Àwadòsiwag (*uh-wa-dow-she-wag*: Minnow), and Wàbek (*wah-bek*: Bear) and his wife, Ininàtig (*e-na-na-dig*: Maple) — accompanied the group going back to the eastern lands of the Omàmiwinini.

Never before had the family split up like this. It was a sorrowful time when they parted ways, but the future always holds surprises.

Since the Battle of Crow Wing River, the dead warriors from that day are gone with the mists of time, with their names no longer mentioned. Along with Zhashagi and his brother, the aforementioned parts of the family unit accompanied them towards the western sun, along with another 130 Anishinaabe men, women, and children. During the first three summers, they had lived near the Omashkiigoo people. They became valued allies and taught the newcomers how to hunt the animal they called paskwâwi-mostos (buffalo), ᐸᐢᑳᐏᒧᐢᑐᐢ. These huge animals kept them fed, and their carcasses supplied the people with hides to make lodges and clothes, as well as bones for weapons and utensils, along with everything else that helped the Anishinaabe survive. The Omashkiigoo also took them out on Sâkahikan (*sag-a-he-gan*) Wînipêkohk (Lake Winnipeg), ᓵᑲᐦᐃᑲᐣ ᐏᓂᐯᑯᕽ, and showed the travellers from the east the best places to fish.

After the first seven summers, the Anishinaabe community had grown to over 100 lodges and 421 people, of which there were 83 warriors. The decision was then made to move away from their allies and create a community between the two big Omashkiigoo communities. The one who lived west of Sâkahikan Wînipêkohk called themselves the Nēhiyawēwin (Plains Cree), ᓀᐦᐃᔭᐍᐏᐣ, and the ones who lived below the big salt water bay called Wînipekw (*win-a-peg*: James Bay), ᐑᓂᐯᐠ, called themselves the Nīhithawīw (Woods Cree), ᓀᐦᐃᖬᐍᐑᐤ. This gave the Anishinaabe powerful allies on both sides. They also inherited a powerful enemy of the Omashkiigoo, whom the Cree called the kaskitêwaýasit (Blackfoot Tribe), ᑲᐢᑭᑌᐋᔭᓯᐟ, a foe as powerful as the Haudenosaunee and the Lakota.

During the summers after their battle with the Lakota on Crow Wing River, they had now become a strong nation of western Anishinaabe. Built up after fifteen years of relative peace and plenty in this new country, the Omàmiwinini, Anishinaabe, and Omashkiigoo now numbered over 600 strong and could easily field 130 warriors. The Blackfoot were a constant threat, and there had been a few skirmishes with them over the years, but never an outright war. Their hunting grounds intersected at spots, but between the plentiful buffalo and the surrounding lakes to keep them in food, there was plenty enough for everyone. The Blackfoot would not eat fish, so the lakes were a peaceful place. Trade with their allies gave them other types of furs and items that they did not normally have access to, and life was good for the time being.

The language spoken by the community had evolved from a mixture of Cree and Anishinaabe (Ojibwe), which they called Oji-Cree. Since they would talk in both Cree and Anishinaabe, the reader will have to distinguish who the speaker is and what language they are using. When an Anishinaabe person speaks, it will be in their own language, and the same goes for a Cree or a Blackfoot person. Glossaries are at the back to help you along the way, Miigwetch. Many times, when they *do* talk to each other, it will be with hand language, unless the tribe had a captive that spoke Cree or Blackfoot and could translate.

1

THE STORM

ANOKÌ

We started out on the morning of binaakwe giizis (*be-nack-que-we gesus*: October Moon). The sun shone brightly and the sky was as blue as I have ever seen: no clouds and just a whisper of wind. The occasional grasshopper that had survived the early morning frosts jumped up and cast its tobacco-coloured spit at our feet as we rustled through the long prairie grass. The fall chill had already eliminated the biting insects that buzzed around our heads a few weeks earlier. The melting morning frost dampened the slowly dying grasses, and the mustiness of the aging vastness before us was the only aroma on the whispering winds.

I thought back to when we had arrived in this flat, vast area towards the setting sun. With Zhashagi and Omashkooz's leadership, our small group had grown and flourished. Three years after arriving here, I had married an Omashkiigoo woman called Osk-îskwêw (*os-kee-is-kwee*: Young Woman in Cree). Osk-îskwêw had been brought up by her grandparents; her mother had died at childbirth, and her father had been killed in a battle with the Blackfoot shortly after her birth. By marrying her, I also took on the responsibility of her grandparents. They were wonderful people, and both have passed away in the last few years.

Osk-îskwêw gave me two wonderful and healthy children. During the first year of our life together, a girl was born. Her grandmother gave her a Cree name, Wâpikwan (*wah-pi-kwan*: Flower), and then a boy was born the following summer. He was so large when he was born that his grandfather also gave him a Cree name, Môso (*moo-so*: Moose), because the old man said he would become as big and strong as a moose.

It was impossible to leave the village without the two of them wanting to come along. They were constantly at my side, always wanting to learn the ways of the hunt and the lands around us. Both of them were tall for their ages, lean and sinewy. Wâpikwan was approaching twelve summers and becoming a beautiful woman. Long-haired and almost as tall as me, she was skilled in hunting and in tanning the hides of what she slew. Osk-îskwêw had taught our daughter all she needed to know about making clothes, cooking, and the duties of the women, but she was also skilled in the world of male responsibilities.

Môso was big for his eleven summers, already taller than I was and among the tallest boys in the village. His sister watched over him like a mother dog over a young pup. She taught him the skills of the hunt that she had learned from me and Elue′wiet Ga′qaquis (*el-away-we-it ga-ah-gooch*: Crazy Crow). Even though Môso was larger than the other boys, they sometimes tried to see how far they could push his easy-going demeanour. When this happened, his sister was quick to show them a smouldering within her that no one in their right mind would want to ignite. The older children soon realized that she was someone you wanted on your side as a friend.

Even though Môso was shy and not aggressive, the other village boys came to understand that his sister was looking after their well being more than his. This occurred one summer day when Crazy Crow gathered all the young boys together and organized running, archery, wrestling, and swimming competitions. To the amazement of all the others, Môso won every event. Wâpikwan won all of the same events that Crazy Crow had organized for the girls and likely would have embarrassed the boys if she'd been allowed to compete with them. I think he sensed that this would happen, so he ran two separate competitions.

After that day, Wâpikwan and Môso had a following among all the young children who looked up to the siblings. Those close to Wâpikwan and Môso in age considered them to be leaders among their group.

I awoke from my daydream as my daughter said to me, "Where do you want to spend the night, Father?"

Amazed that I had walked so far lost in my thoughts, I stood there, wordless.

"Father, did you hear what I just said?"

I could hear Môso laughing and saying, "I think he was sleepwalking, Sister. Jab him with your bow to get his attention!"

"Okay, children, no need to make fun of your father when your mother is not here to defend me."

We all started to laugh, and I grabbed both of them and squeezed them around the shoulders. "I became lost in my thoughts of how the two of you have grown and become so respectful of your Elders, so do not disappointment me!

"And, yes, I heard you, Wâpikwan. This is as good as any place to camp. We have some cottonwoods to shield us from the elements and the Asinii-bwaan Ziibi (*ah-sin-nee-bwan zee-be*: Assiniboine River) here for water. This spot is also shallow enough to let us cross in the morning."

I have found myself losing my Omàmiwinini language, talking more Anishinaabe and Cree and mixing everything together. When I talk to my children, I try to talk to them in the language I grew up with.

With no bugs and our enemies, the Ayaaj-inini (Blackfoot person, people), out hunting buffalo on their ranges west of here by two or three suns, this was a wonderful time of year for us to hunt. We had already had ours a few weeks ago, and it was very successful. Our people have been in this land for fifteen summers, and we have learned to use the buffalo hides to make our lodges. We now had thirty of them, which sheltered one hundred and fourteen people. When we split off from the summer gathering to go to our winter camp, our community was the smaller of four. Out of this number, we had thirty-two warriors who fed and protected our village.

The Ayaaj-inini have never attacked our village, because of its seclusion and also because we are surrounded by our Cree allies. Every seven or eight moons, one or two hunters will disappear from a hunting party, which we attribute to running afoul of a small Ayaaj-inini warrior group on the prowl. The Blackfoot are a dangerous and powerful enemy that we try to give a wide berth to. Our Cree friends, though, have been continually fighting this powerful nation long before we appeared, and I predict that our future will hold larger skirmishes with them.

When we left, the women were still tanning hides and drying meat. Wâpikwan had worked very hard with her mother, and Osk-îskwêw gave her permission to leave with Môso and me to seek some antelope. We had six dogs with us, and my children were as skilled as any of the adult hunters. My wolf dog, Nij Enàndeg, had passed on many moons ago, but these six were his five sons and a daughter. These loyal, fierce war dogs were also great trackers and relentless hunters.

As I looked at my children, I knew that my father would be proud of his offspring. Môso was the image of his grandfather, Mahingan. Possessed of the demeanour of her grandmother, Wàbananang, Wâpikwan was quick and decisive when it came to defending her loved ones. It was good to be alive and see my ancestors in my offspring!

We weren't long in making a makeshift lean-to for that night's shelter. Once this was done, I watched as a grinning Môso took the pack off one of the male animosh (*an-ney-mush*: dog) and retrieved a few chunks of buffalo meat. Using some dry grass and twigs, he soon had a fire going. Wâpikwan then turned to another animosh, removed his pack, and then emptied a very big pile of buffalo chips onto the ground. As she fed the fire with the aromatic buffalo dung, Môso drove three sharpened sticks into the ground at a slant over the fire and hung the meat on it. Meanwhile, I went down to the river's edge and filled our buffalo bladders full of water. While there, I collected some fist-sized river rocks as well as some raspberries and blueberries that the birds had not yet devoured.

When I arrived at the fire, I tossed the rocks into the flames and filled a rawhide skin container with water. After the rocks had turned red from the heat, I took two sticks, one in each hand, and used them to retrieve the stones from the fire. I dropped the heated rocks, along with the berries I had collected, into the skin container of water. In a short time, we dipped our clay cups into the vessel and shared a very tasty berry tea.

We sat in silence, watching the flames licking up against the meat, hearing the dripping grease sizzle, and enjoying the mouth-watering aroma that tickled our senses. Added to this was the sound of cracking buffalo bones as the dogs feverishly sought the delicacy of marrow hidden within their white, protective coverings. The wind gently picked up as it crept over the open prairie and made its way through the encircling cottonwoods. We were nestled in and enjoying the whispering voices of all that have gone before us.

We tossed some tobacco into the fire to thank Kitchi Manitou for what we were eating. Sitting around the fire, the children asked me about my past battles. I told them the story about the battle with the Haudenosaunee in the Land of the Tattooed Warriors and how their uncle Mitigomij had slain their grandfather's killer, the great Kanien'kehà:ka (*ga-ni-en-ge-ha-ga*: Mohawk) warrior, Ò nenhste Erhar (*o-noss-tay air-har*: Corn Dog).

After that, we went into our lean-to and looked out of the opening at the bright stars in the expansive sky overhead and the ground, which was dappled with beams of moonlight. We made clicking sounds with our mouths, and the dogs came into our little branch enclosure to keep us warm, and we slept the night away.

I woke up at sunrise to the smell of boiling tea and a couple of aagask (*ah-gust*: grouse) cooking over the dung fire. I looked out onto the long prairie grass, reddened by the rising sun along the horizon and gently swaying with the morning breeze. I watched as the six dogs jumped and pounced in the long grass as they chased down moles and mice for their early morning meals.

I looked up as the children were preparing everything and asked, "Who is looking after whom on this hunting trip?"

They both smiled and giggled, "Father, you did tell us to respect our Elders and look after them."

"Yes, I did," I answered with a chuckle. "Who hunted down the aagask?"

"We both did," replied my son. "We had the dogs walk through the grass ahead of us to scare them up, and then, to make sure we didn't tear the birds apart, we used our blunt arrows just like you taught us. Wâpikwan shot the first one and I shot the other one."

"I am impressed!" I answered. I then arose from my sleeping spot and went behind a tree to relieve my night's build-up. Looking around, I chuckled to myself; the six dogs were in the process of doing the same thing.

Then, after they were done, they rolled in the grass and wrestled with each other. The six of them were all from the same litter and were very close, with the one, big female acting as their pack-ruling leader. She had to be strong-willed and tough to control her five male siblings, who were all powerfully built and very fierce but totally devoted to her. With Nij Enàndeg, my wolf dog, I was used to just one canine companion, but this group followed me and the children everywhere. They were excellent hunters and defenders. Because they were inseparable, none of them were given names. Whenever they were called, the pack came to the caller like a rolling river rapid, moving swiftly, smoothly, and with a hidden power beneath the surface.

The sun was above the horizon when we started our trek. Once again, the sky today was as blue as the day we set out, with just the occasional wisp of a cloud, but we also knew that the weather in this area could change in a heartbeat.

We pointed ourselves towards the ningaabii'anong (*nin-gah-be-a-nung*: west) in search of the fastest animal we hunt, the gibichii-adik (*gah-bich-e-ah-dik*: pronghorn antelope), hoping that, between some good luck and our dogs' keen sense of smell, we might stumble on a herd of these swift animals. Our dogs have hunted these animals before, and they work well together. It takes a well trained pack of animosh to run the gibichii-adik down, giving the hunters a chance to make their kills.

After removing our clothes and moccasins, we held everything over our heads and crossed the river at a spot where the water came up to our waists. The river bed was made up of all sizes of stone, so we had to slowly and carefully work our way across to avoid turning over an ankle. Ever since the children were young, their mother had immersed them daily in cold-water plunges, which toughened them up for times like this. Even with their packs on, the dogs never laboured in the strong current. The five males followed their sister's lead, always trusting her to get them to safety. Once on the other side, we ran up the embankment to get away from the pack as they all started to shake the water from their fur.

Looking back towards the sound of the shaking dogs, I watched as the flying water droplets and loose, wet, airborne hair shone against the light of the morning sky. It was a magical show of reflecting colours. Bending over to put my clothes back on, I glanced over at the children, who were standing in awe of the same magical light show that I had just witnessed.

"Father, look on the horizon," whispered my son.

At that same moment my daughter quietly said, "Father, the dogs!"

Taking a quick look at the dogs, I saw that they were all crouching down in the grass as if they were stalking prey. On the horizon, I could see the heads of numerous gibichii-adik. We were downwind from the herd; a lucky break because the dogs had caught the scent of the animals, and they could not smell our presence. The animals stood looking in the distance, not a sound emitting from any of their throats. Except for blowing occasional gusts of air from their nostrils to scatter the few grasshoppers and flies that were circling their heads, they were completely motionless.

"Okay, each of us will take two dogs. I will come from the giiwedin (*gee-wid-en*: north), Môso from the waabanong (*wah-ba-nung*: east), Wâpikwan from the ningaabii'anong (*nin-gah-be-a-nung*: west). Stay downwind as long as you can. With only three sides covered, we will have to rely on the skill of the dogs and hope that our prey will not run towards the zhaawanong (*sha-wah-noon*: south).

Bent over in a crouch, we silently made our way into position. As soon as we were within bowshot to the animals, we all dropped to the ground and started to crawl. Gibichii-adik are constantly on alert, and it is very difficult to get close enough to them to get a killing shot. Once alerted to danger, they are very swift and agile runners, so the dogs would be used to tire the gibichii-adik out during the resulting rundown.

Wâpikwan loosed her two dogs first, and they charged towards their prey. As I lay there, I could see the dust and grass chaff they stirred up floating over the waist-high grass, silhouetted by the sunlight. They started off with a slow growl, and then the wolf yip of their ancestors broke the morning silence. The antelopes' ears perked up and they immediately took off. After Wâpikwan's two dogs cut five of them from the main group, they skillfully chased them towards Môso. His dogs then took up the chase, and, once again, the wily animosh maneuvered the frantic antelope towards my hiding place.

The hurtling antelope and dogs stirred up dust and insects, the latter of which were quickly picked off in mid-flight by groups of soaring birds. Clearly, we were not the only ones that were hunting their meals this day. The first two dogs were now lying beside Môso, resting and watching, drool dripping from outstretched tongues onto their lazily crossed front legs and the surrounding grass.

I waited patiently, listening for the snorting of the animals hurtling towards my place in the long prairie grass. At the very last moment, I stood up and yelled, "Go!"

The dogs took off like an arrow shot: heads out, bodies in a straight line, ears pinned back. The wide-eyed fleeing animals turned so suddenly that one of them threw grass-interlaced froth onto my face with a wet splat. I reached up and wiped the warm and sticky, pungent-smelling spittle off my forehead.

The female dog with me was an expert at this deadly game of tag. I pointed to Wâpikwan and her dogs and said, "Go!" because we needed dogs running at these labouring animals from all directions. As they were driven back towards Môso, I watched as two of the older animals started to weaken.

With another quick hand signal, I motioned for Wâpikwan and her dogs to close in on the antelope opposite from where I was standing. It was now time for the kill. Môso's dogs were able to turn the two slower animals back to where Wâpikwan and I stood. As they came towards us, we each shot two arrows off in quick succession, which made dull *thud* sounds as they struck the frantic animals. Both of the gibichii-adik somersaulted towards us with loud gasps of air. They crashed at our feet, stirring up the dust and the earth, scattering birds, and parting the long grass. Flying spittle, foam, and a cloud of dirt and earthy chunks settled on our hair and clothes.

Not wanting the pack to rush over and tear away at the felled antelope, my daughter yelled, "Stop, dogs!"

Môso rushed over to the downed prey and finished them both off with accurate lunges to their lungs and hearts with his lance.

I kneeled by the carcasses and gave a gift of tobacco for the fallen gibichii-adik so that their spirits would know that we appreciated their sacrifice for our well being and survival. Then we quickly started to butcher the animals while the dogs sat patiently nearby for their reward of intestines and necks. We worked in haste, knowing that there is a monster on these flatlands that can smell death from many footsteps away, a creature that towers over the tallest warrior when it stands on its haunches.

Gichi makwa (*gich-e muck-wa*: grizzly bear), the big bear of this land, is a fierce and dangerous killing machine. I had no desire to lose any of our dogs to this monster.

I have seen men left scarred, bloody, and missing body parts after a battle against this makwa. As such, the title of "bear killer" brings great honour to any warrior, and wearing a necklace of gichi makwa teeth commands tremendous respect. By wearing the bear's teeth around his neck, the hunter takes on the spirit and power of the bear. Very rarely do we ever find a warrior who loses a battle with this giant, since they usually end up spread across the land as bear dung.

While we skinned and cut up the animals, I looked to the west as the sun started its descent to the earth. My stomach knotted, and a bitter taste flowed up to my mouth, making me flinch. The sky was turning as black as the morning coals of a dead campfire. Below this blackness was a rolling white blizzard coming swiftly over the flat horizon.

"Môso and Wâpikwan, we have to hurry. Wâpikwan, please hasten and finish skinning and butchering the animals!"

Handing Môso a shoulder blade of one of the dead antelope, I said, "You and I must quickly dig a hole with these and make it deep and wide enough for us and the dogs."

Luckily, the ground was soft from the fall rains, and we were able to dig at a rapid pace. In no time at all, both of us were standing in a hole up to our waists. We then lengthened our makeshift shelter and, as we did this, I could hear Wâpikwan pulling the final skin off. Taking a quick glance, I watched with pride as she cut away the last hinges of meat clinging to the pelt and then hastily cut off the legs and head. Her mother had taught her well, and I was glad that my daughter was a fast learner.

Looking up out of our hole, I noticed the dogs lying in silence, staring off towards the rapidly approaching prairie storm. The sweat of my labours had soaked through my shirt, and moisture was running down my face. I could feel the temperature dropping, which cooled my body sweat and sent a shiver through my clammy skin.

Many unprepared, roving warrior and hunting parties have lost their lives in a blizzard. They have been found frozen stiff, with an arm or a leg sticking out of a snow bank or, when the snow melts, they are discovered half-eaten by roaming animals looking for a meal. I was determined not to be that hunting party; we would survive and make our way back home in the end.

My arms were starting to ache from all the digging and scraping, and my hands were filthy from picking up the soil and throwing it out of the hole. I stole a look at Môso, who was doing the work of a man and easily keeping up with my labours. This was a life-and-death struggle to survive and, so far, we were staying ahead of death.

All of this was being done in silence. None of us spoke, and the only noise that broke the eerie tranquility was our breathing, our digging, and the sounds of a knife cutting through the meat as it was being butchered. Even the dogs were silent. Clearly, this was the calm before the storm.

Just in time, we managed to make the hole deep and long enough. The wind started to pick up, the air temperature dropped like a stone off a cliff, and the sweat began to freeze to my body.

When my daughter said, "Father!" with a worried hint in her voice, I quickly responded.

"Yes, I see. It is time … in the hole! Dogs, come!

Once my children were nestled in among all but the female dog, who refused to leave my side, I began to spread the animal skins over the hole. Using chunks of meat to hold down the sides, I soon had everything in place. I took four of my arrows and pierced them through the two skins to attach them in the middle. Then, holding up an end, the female animosh and I crawled into the dark hole. I pulled a flap of skin down and pushed the blade of my knife through it and into the side of the dirt hole, shutting off the opening. With all the body heat from three people and six dogs, our little shelter quickly started to warm up, to the point where you could remove some clothes if you wanted to.

"Father, hold out your hand," said Môso.

He placed two things into my outstetched palm: a chunk of meat and something else that turned out to be a zhingibisiwashk (*shing-ibisi-washk*: turnip).

"Son, where did the zhingibisiwashk come from?"

"I dug them up today while waiting for Wâpikwan to send her dogs on the chase towards me," he replied. "There was a huge area dug up by a gichi makwa where I was sitting. He must have eaten his fill, because there were still a few turnips left over. I left a bit of asemaa (*as-say-maa*: tobacco) there for thanks, Father, just like you taught me."

"Well done, son," I answered.

After I heard my daughter start to laugh, I joined her, and pretty soon laughter was echoing through our dirt shelter. Being so close to death had created a nervous tension, and the laughter released all of our stress.

With meat and zhingibisiwashk, as well as buffalo bladders filled with water, I knew that we could survive this ordeal.

"What's that gnawing sound I hear?"

"I gave each of the dogs a leg to keep them occupied," replied Wâpikwan.

Again, I started to laugh, "My children, you never cease to amaze me. Well, unless one of you brought a pebble game to play, I think I will have a sleep. This heat is making me drowsy!"

I do not know how long I had been asleep, but I woke up in a sweat. It seems I had overachieved my goal of sealing up our shelter, because the hole was stifling hot. We needed air to circulate, so I crawled among the sweaty occupants of our makeshift shelter and created a small opening at either end of the hole.

As I lay down again beside the female animosh, I felt a pile of buffalo dung under me.

"Why are the buffalo chips in here?" I asked to no one in particular.

"Well, Father, after this storm is over, we still have to eat and stay warm on the trail back home. Frozen buffalo chips do not burn as quickly as the thawed-out ones do," answered my daughter.

Laughingly, I replied, "What would I do without the pair of you? If I had gone out alone, I might have starved or been frozen in the snow by now! I am proud of both of you and how you are always thinking ahead."

"We doubt that you would have died without us, Father. You are too skilled a warrior to let yourself be caught without food or shelter," replied Môso.

The storm howled and blew all night. Every once in a while, the dogs would whimper because of the loud winds. Throughout all this, we were warm and well fed.

Wakening again, I caught a glimpse of light coming through our air holes. Rising from my sleeping area on the ground, I got on my knees and swept the dirt off my clothing and stretched as best I could. I needed to relieve myself and check the weather outside. The opening of the two air holes had brought the temperature down in our hideaway, and my clothes were no longer sweaty and stuck to my body. This was good because wet clothing would hasten the effects of getting a cold chill and increase the chance of getting sick.

I pushed the skin covering open and climbed out, followed by the dogs. It was not long before there were yellow streaks in the snow everywhere. As I started to walk away, the canines kicked up clouds of snow around their urine paths, dousing me with a layer of fine powder. The snow was up to my knees, making it difficult for the dogs to course their way through it, and the air was so thick with snow pellets that I could barely see past the length of my arm.

"Môso and Wâpikwan," I yelled through the wind. "Do not stray more than five paces from the shelter. You will get lost in this whiteness and freeze to death if the dogs and I cannot find you."

"Yes, Father," they said in unison.

Taking my other knife from its sheath, I hacked away at some meat and threw the frozen chunks to the dogs. We would need them at full strength when the storm was over. I still had enough meat in my pouch to keep us nourished until a fire would be needed. I smiled to myself, thinking that the two of them probably also had ample food.

Grabbing a pair of fur mitts from my belt, I scooped up snow to put in one of the empty water bladders to melt. I did miss making a fire for tea, though.

"Dogs!" I yelled, "come in."

With that command, both dogs and people crawled into our sheltered hole for warmth and protection.

As we entered the hole, I grabbed some buffalo chips and made a small fire. I wanted tea and was willing to suffer some smoke for a short time in order to get it. To my surprise, the winter storm gusts quickly sucked the smoke out through the exit holes. After heating some small stones in the fire, I used two sticks that I had found to pick them out and drop them into one of the water bladders, along with two or three handfuls of berries that I had.

Soon we had our clay cups full of steaming berry tea, a nice treat from all the mayhem surrounding us.

"Father, when will be able to head for home?" asked Môso.

"My guess is that this storm will last another sun or so, and then we will have a three-day walk back to the village. Even though we are only one-and-a-half suns from there, it will take twice as long to return, because we did not bring any snowshoes. This return trek will not be easy. We will have to take turns breaking the trail. The skins will be frozen enough to pile the meat on, so we can hook a couple of the dogs up to each one and have them pull their loads through the snow like a sled. Without any fuel for warmth, we will have to burrow into the snow, make a snow cave, sleep with the animals, and rely on our body heat to keep us from freezing. What buffalo dung we do have will only last long enough to make a few cooking fires."

"Sounds exciting, Father," replied Wâpikwan.

Again, I could not help but smile at their eagerness for the task at hand.

"Will anyone come out to look for us?" Wâpikwan asked.

"It depends on how many of our people were caught away from camp during the storm and who is available to search," I answered.

"Father, Crazy Crow will never leave us out here. He will come for us. I know he will!" shouted Môso above the winds.

"Yes, Kitchi Manitou will guide someone to us if he thinks we are in trouble. We gave him thanks for the turnips and the antelope with an offering of tobacco. We have done nothing to upset him, and mother Nokomis will also have Nanabozho watch over us. All will be fine, my children."

"Father, we also have each other," said Môso.

"Do not worry, Father, I will take care of you and Môso," chirped in Wâpikwan.

"Yes, I believe that, my daughter. Now, we have to cut up the dogs' pack bags and make harnesses for them to pull the frozen skins. This will keep us occupied in the darkness. We have made these many times before, so we should be able to do it from memory and feel and not need a lot of light. If you are having trouble, just go outside once in a while to look at your work. Instead of sewing, we will make knots to connect the leather strips. When the packs are all used up, I have an extra pair of pants in my bag that we can slice up."

I paused for a moment before remembering something important.

"One more thing: here are a few handfuls of cattail down. Put it in your moccasins to keep your feet dry and warm."

The next morning, I awoke to a wonderful stillness. The storm had blown itself out, and wisps of snow were entering through our two air holes, reflecting the sun's rays off their whiteness.

I was in a celebratory mood as I started up a small fire, heated up water for tea, and hung some meat over the modest flame. The grease from the meat dripped onto the fire, sending quick, jumping sparks away from its flickering flame. A couple of these hot grease projectiles landed on some dog fur, making a sizzle and a sharp, pungent smell of burning hair. The sound of the spark snapping on its hair caused the animosh to bite at the irritation.

The heat of the small fire and the warmth of all the bodies created an almost unbearable swelter. *Enjoy it while we can*, I thought to myself, knowing full-well that the next three or four suns would bring with it intense cold and a near-death experience if we were not careful and aware of our surroundings.

Survival would be a challenge.

2

THE JOURNEY

SPENDING TWO FULL suns and nights in a hole with six dogs and two young adults creates a closeness that only the people involved can appreciate. Getting to know the hind end of an animosh, along with all the assorted smells, is the sort of experience one hopes will only happen once in a lifetime.

As I peeled back the overhead skins that had provided refuge from the raging storm, we were immediately showered with brilliant sunshine and a dusting of snow that had been lying on the flaps. As soon as I brushed the powder off my body, I was immediately covered by the white residue again as the six dogs shook off the snow that had blanketed them during the opening of our hideaway.

Reflecting off the surrounding white landscape, the sun's light was piercing. Looking out to the horizon, I watched as small snow crystals floating in the air became illuminated by the sun's reflective rays, creating a scene not unlike a summer's gathering of waawaatesiwag (*wah-wah-tea-see-walk*: fireflies).

"Father," Môso said in a breathless whisper, "look over to the west!"

Following the line of his pointed finger on the horizon, I could see what looked like walking snow drifts. After doing a double take, I smiled and said, "Môso, that is the famous lost herd of the waabishki mashkode-bizhiki (*wah-bish-key mush-ko-dee-bish-eh-ka*: white buffalo)!"

"Father," Wâpikwan quickly interrupted, "do not fill my little brother's head with such foolishness. Môso, watch the animals closely. They have been lying down during the storm. Soon they will start to shake and their true colour will reappear. To see one waabishki mashkode-bizhiki is a gift from Kitchi Manitou; a whole herd would be a miracle!"

Môso looked at me and said, "Father, you are silly."

Turning back to the task at hand, I called out to Môso and Wâpikwan, saying, "Watch me," to get their attention.

I sat down and started to cut a strip of leather from the bottom of my shirt, long enough to tie around my head and wide enough so that it covered my eyes. I then cut two slits in it to see through. Reaching into the cold embers of the fire, I grabbed some charcoal, smudged it into my palm to make a soft paste and then smeared it under my eyes to help reflect the sun's brightness. I then tied my makeshift sun blocker around my head.

"Father, why are we doing this?" Wâpikwan asked.

"To keep our eyes from burning. The sun's reflection off the snow will cause us to go blind without this. Mitigomij taught me this many moons ago. I once saw a man who had been caught out in a storm. He had come back with his swollen eyes frozen shut because they were constantly watering. He only made it back because he had tied a leash to his dog, and the animal led him home. When he finally opened his reddened eyes, they had developed a white film over them. He had to stay in a dark lodge because the daylight caused him too much pain.

"The village shaman used moss to remove the white film from the suffering man's eyes and breast milk from a nursing mother to help him recover. Even with all of this, it took several suns before the man was cured. During his time of recovery, his eyes were constantly itching, so they tied his hands together to keep him from rubbing them and making them worse."

I handed them my leather strip to copy, and they were quick to cut out their own masks. After I smeared the black under their eyes, we all put on our masks. As we left our refuge, I looked at my two offspring and smiled, amused by the thought that we would surely terrify anyone we came across.

Between the heat from our bodies below and the insulating snow covering from above, the hides did not freeze as I had hoped they would. Regardless, the dogs would still have to pull the skins as we had planned. Turning the hides hair up, the meat was spread onto them. Coming into contact with the cold air and elements, the hides would eventually freeze and make them easier to pull. We would rotate the dogs that were getting tired with fresh ones.

Môso and I harnessed the dogs and attached them to the makeshift sleds. While we were doing this, Wâpikwan got a buffalo chip fire going to make tea and roast some meat. She also gave the dogs some bones to gnaw on for the precious marrow inside.

Wâpikwan came up to me and handed me some furry pieces of hide. Unbeknownst to me, she had taken the time to make boots for the dogs while we were holed up.

"Here, Father, I made these! You and Môso can finish the job by putting them on the dogs … and here are the leather thongs to tie them on their feet."

"Daughter, again you amaze me," I replied.

Without these little moccasins, the dogs might cut their paws on the hard snow, or the soft snow would clump between their toes, forcing them to stop and chew it off.

It was fortunate that we had left the village prepared for the cold. Not only did we have fur hats and gloves, we were also wearing knee-high moccasins, which would help us in the deep snow.

As I felt my cheeks start to chaff from the brisk wind, I reached into my medicine bag, took out some buffalo fat, and smeared it on my face to protect it from freezing. I turned to offer some to the children, but they were already smearing fat from the slain gibichii-adik onto their own faces. Bending over, I cut some strips off one of the hides, which I then handed out to Môso and Wâpikwan. We used these makeshift scarves to cover our mouths so that our hot breath would reflect off the fur and keep our faces warm.

After eating, we started off. Intending to walk through the night, I hoped that the skies would be starry and moonlit enough to help guide us in the darkness. By following the stars and their sky positions, we would be able to reach a distant grove of woods that I knew of. With nothing but a scant supply of buffalo chips to make a fire for heat, freezing to death was a very real danger.

The first day of walking was easy. Still strong from eating well and staying warm from the exertion, our small group made good time over the barren, snow-covered land. Luckily, the night was clear and moonlit. The heads of everyone in our party, dogs included, were constantly surrounded with wisps of fog from our hot breath meeting the brisk, wintry air. The steam rising from our bodies reminded me of looking out onto the river in our village on a crisp, early fall day and seeing the swirling mists rising from the warm, gently flowing waters. We had been walking almost a full sun since our departure, and it was now rising in the east.

"Children, are you tired yet?" I asked.

"Not yet, Father," they replied in unison.

The dogs were strong, and the males would not falter as long as their sister kept going and did not show any weakness.

Although no more whiteness came from the skies, the wind would sometimes blow unhindered across the prairie and stir up clouds of drifting snow. When this happened, our surroundings became a complete whiteout. Because of the flatness of the land, we could see the tumbling white havoc developing on the horizon. To keep us all together, I passed a long piece of leftover leather through our lines. After positioning one of the children between each sled and myself at the front, we held onto this strap to keep everyone together. This prevented any possible separations during one of these deadly whiteouts.

Just before one of these snow squalls, I thought I saw a rabbit and a huge black cougar standing side by side on the horizon. As quickly as I spotted them, they suddenly vanished in a swirling eddy of whiteness.

Turning to the children, I asked, "Do you see anything on the distant horizon ahead of us?"

"No, Father," they replied. "Did you see something?"

Before I answered their question, I looked at the dogs. With their keen sense of smell, any strange odours on the wind would stir their senses, but none of them seemed to be tensing over anything out of the ordinary.

"No, children. It must have been my imagination."

It had been many years since I'd last seen the image of those two beings, so it was hard to believe that they were both still alive and living in these lands close by. I decided that the lack of sleep, strain of walking through the deep snow, and not stopping enough times to eat was causing my mind to see things.

The snow swirls ended, and I looked again to the horizon, where I watched as two disappearing shadows cast by the eastern sun vanished before my eyes. Granted, what I was saw was unlikely but, if it were true, I felt assured that we were now safe from death!

We walked for the rest of the day and, that night, arrived back at the cottonwoods grove. This was at the same river we had crossed during the start of our journey. After letting the dogs loose, we dug two holes in the side of a huge snow drift that had gathered around some trees. The resulting two-doored snow cave would be our shelter for the evening. Wâpikwan and Môso gathered enough wood to make a fire, and I peeled the bark off some trees, which I used to make some good, strong tea for us.

After feeding the dogs and eating some cold, roasted antelope that we had cooked over our last fire, we crawled into our snowy cave with the animals and slept for the first time since leaving our previous hole in the ground. With all of the tightly packed bodies, the cave quickly warmed up and I soon fell asleep.

"*Grrr!*"

Waking to the sound of the female animosh emitting a deep-throated warning, I looked outside our snow shelter, squinting in the bright sunlight. It took a few moments for my eyes to adjust, but when they did, I saw several fur-clad figures among the trees, along with several dogs.

"Osk-îskwêw!"

"Anokì!" she replied.

"How did you find us in this barren land?"

"A man came to me in a dream two suns ago and said, 'Follow the tracks of Wàbòz (*wah-bose*) the rabbit and Mishibizhi (*mish-a-bish-e*) the panther. They will lead you to your loved ones.'"

"Osk-îskwêw, are you sure it was a dream?"

3

THE ORDEAL

ELUE´WIET GA´QAQUIS

As I turned the meat on its cottonwood branch spit, the flames of the small campfire, irritated by the dripping grease, hissed, jumped, and licked at the buffalo hump like an agitated rattlesnake. Beside me, boiling in a bark container heated by red-hot rocks, was a bloodied buffalo tongue while ode´iminaniibiish (*oh-day-eh-men-an-e-bish*: strawberry tea) steeped in another bowl. At my feet lay a huge black and white male imu´j (*all-mooch*: dog), gnawing on a bone that snapped with each grinding motion of its teeth.

During this time, I kept a close watch on the surrounding skies. This country had a habit of springing sudden storms on you without warning. Many times, I had seen a violent thunder storm off on the horizon with nothing happening around where I stood. This time of the year, there could be sunshine where we are camping and the worse kind of blizzard just a half-morning's travel away.

Even after spending almost twenty summers with the Anishinaabe and becomming adept at speaking their language, I would occasionally mix my words up. Often times I would think in Anishinaabe and Mi'kmaq, like just now when I used the Anishinaabe word for "tea" and the Mi'kmaq word for "dog."

I still had opportunities to speak Mi'kmaq, the language of my adoptive people, whenever my friends Jilte'g (*jil-teg*: Scar) and E's (*s*: Clam) were around. After marrying Cree women, the two often moved back and forth between the two nations, which gave me an opportunity to speak the Cree language as well. Unlike my friends, I never married. I enjoy the freedom of having only my own mouth to feed in times of need, and, even when alone, I always have the companionship of my Ga'qaquis (*ga-ah-gooch*: crow) friends to talk with.

As I tended the meat, I slowly pushed the ends of the firewood into the fire. A Mi'kmaq Elder taught me how to do this when I was young, saying that only stupid people piled their wood and burnt it quickly. By placing the wood in a circle and slowly tapping the ends into the flames as they burnt down, it made for less waste of precious fuel and more control over the fire. As such, I always made my fires this way.

Since I did not want my lone good eye to start watering and stinging from the smoke, I kept my distance from the fire. My left eye had been taken from me by a Haudenosaunee arrow many summers earlier while Jilte′g and I were out hunting near our Mi′kmaq home. Our capture and escape from the running of the Haudenosaunee warrior line will forever stay in my memory.

The warmth of my small fire and the aroma of the cooking meat began to make me drowsy. As I started to nod off, my leg suddenly jumped, kicking the dog and startling him enough to drop his bone and give a quick growl. My twitching leg, and the sudden movement of the imu′j, snapped my head back, and I was now wide awake. Fearing that the five young Anishinaabe warriors seated nearby had seen this and were going to laugh and tease me relentlessly, I glanced over at them. Fortunately, they were completely engrossed in a game of Makizin Ataagewin (*mak-e-zin a-tash-win*: moccasin game) and did not notice what I was up to. All they seemed to care about was that I was cooking a meal for them.

Three suns ago, these five young Anishinaabe warriors of Zhashagi's group and I had left our camp from the south of here, one sun after Anokì and his children had gone hunting to the west for gibichii-adik. As we made our journey in the suns of the binaakwe giizis, we had to be wary of the weather because it could change in a heartbeat. The flat lands here had no defence for bad weather.

Beyond the fire lay the other five dogs, their tongues hanging out, dropping intermittent balls of slobber onto their crossed paws with every other breath.

Being as close as we were to Ayaaj-inini (Blackfoot) territory, I decided that it was time to break up the game these young warriors were playing. I sent two of them out from our hastily made camp to keep watch on each side, and I put the others to work completing the task of cutting up our day's kill while I finished preparing the meal.

Earlier that day we had come upon a mashkodebizhiki (*mush-ko-dee-bish-eh-ka*: buffalo) stuck in a muddy wallow. The cow had walked into the water to get a drink, but the bottom did not support her weight, and she sank in above her knees. By the time we got to her, she had been struggling so hard to escape that she was near death from exhaustion. I considered ourselves lucky to have beaten the wolves and the bears to her. After ending her misery, we gave thanks to Kitchi Manitou for their gift to us with an offering of asemaa. This would also help the animal's spirit leave its dead body and show that its sacrifice was appreciated.

We had to wade into the muddy wallow and cut her legs off so that we could drag the rest of the carcass out. After we tied the animal up with ropes, we used a collective effort between ourselves and the dogs to pull it out of the water hole. By the time we were done, the six of us were covered in mud that quickly became dry and caked-on in the midday sun.

As my thoughts drifted back to the meal I was preparing, I thought I heard my name slurred by one of the young warriors. At the same time, the dogs started to growl, and I looked up to see Mindido Animosh (*min-di-dough an-ney-moosh*: Big Dog) staggering towards the fire with an arrow lodged in his throat and blood spurting from his mouth. The young man fell into the fire, sending sparks flying into the air and flipping the spit end-over-end towards the dogs.

Everything came to a head like a clap of thunder. As the growling dogs rushed towards the buffalo meat, all the flying embers in the air landed on the nearby grass, and it instantly caught on fire. The stench of Mindido Animosh's hair burning as the flames started to lick at his body nauseated me. As I bent over to pull the dead Anishinaabe warrior from the fire, a lance whistled by my head, catching the inside of my right ear on its twirling flight. It ripped the outer part of my ear off and thudded down in front of me, the spear-point pinning my torn ear to the ground.

With blood dripping down my shoulder, a sudden rush awakened my senses to the danger all around me. Turning to face an assailant, I grabbed my lance staff and swung it with all my strength at a charging painted warrior. The violent swing caught him in the face and the collision between him and my staff sent a vibration down my arms and into my shoulder. As the staff collided with his face, I could hear bones break and a muffled scream emit from his throat. The Ayaaj-inini warrior fell to the ground with blood flowing from his eyes, ears, and mouth.

Closely behind this dying warrior came another of his fellow tribesmen. Dropping down low, I swung my war staff again, this time aiming at the rushing man's bare knees. Upon contact, I simultaneously heard a loud crack as the joint exploded as well as the tormented screams of my foe. As he writhed on the ground, I thrust the spear end of the staff into his throat with a short, powerful lunge.

I tried to quickly disengage the weapon, but it had lodged in the ground as it exited the man's throat. I heard an eerie guttural yell and saw a fierce warrior with a large yellow hand imprinted on his red-painted face attempting to impale me with a large lance. In one motion, I stepped aside and grabbed my war club from its case on my back. I used this weapon to turn aside the lunge and, in another motion, brought it forward with a mighty swing, breaking both the attacker's collar bone and his shoulder. After he fell to the ground in a painful heap, I finished him off with a smashing blow to the head.

In the background, I heard the snarling sound of the attacking dogs turn to sharp yelps as the charging foes killed them with well placed arrows.

With a powerful jerk, I retrieved my spear and hurled it through the air and into the chest of a charging warrior. The man tried to fall forward, but the butt end of the spear jammed into the ground, balancing him in a suspended forward position with his arms dangling at his side.

I grabbed my knife from its neck sheath and held it in one hand and my war club in the other. I stood my ground there, defying anyone to come and take my life. Two young Ayaaj-inini, with their faces painted half red and half black and red hand prints on their chests, rushed at me, screaming their names to let me know who was about to end my life. Before they reached my position, a large hand on my shoulder spun me around in a half-circle. A stone axe hit me in the stomach, knocking me backwards onto the hard ground.

When I landed, every breath of air in my body left in a huge gasp. As I lay there, I thought that I might die from the lack of air in my lungs alone. Gasping and coughing up blood, I rolled onto my left side, waiting for the final blow to send me to the afterlife, where I would meet my fallen friends and family. But the final strike did not come. Instead, a group of enemy warriors gathered around to strike me with their weapons and coup sticks.

After taking their coup, they grabbed my arms and roughly jerked me to my feet. I bent over, gasping and coughing, watching as the blood flew out of my mouth and onto the legs of a warrior standing in front of me. After he dropped a noosed leather rope around my neck, the two young warriors that had tried to slay me a few heartbeats earlier jerked my hands behind my back and tied them there.

My captors wasted no time stripping the weapons and clothes from the bodies of my fellow fallen warriors, all the while mutilating their bodies. After their blood lust was fulfilled, four of their warriors hoisted their dead comrades onto their backs. My breathing slowly started to return to normal, but blood still trickled out of my mouth, dripped onto the prairie grass, and reddened the yellow stalks. As we walked through the killing field and stumbled over the dead dogs, I counted the bodies of my Anishinaabe warriors and noticed only four bloody scalps on the end of the attackers' lances.

That's when I realized that Oshkiniigii Gookooko'oo (*osh-kin-eh-gee goo-koo-koo-oh*: Young Owl) had escaped the slaughter. My imagination instantly had him running swiftly through the long prairie grass towards our village. If he ran at a constant lope, drinking just enough water to keep his body and mind alert, and did not stop to eat or sleep, he would arrive at our lodges in little more than two suns. Once there, he would gather up a group of warriors, return to this place, and bury what was left of our dead, after the wild animals had gotten their fill. They would notice that my body was absent and either follow the trail of the Ayaaj-inini or go back home and leave me to my fate.

The Blackfoot called themselves Niitsítapi (*knee-tisit-ta-pee*), and I had been captured by one of the Blackfoot Nations called Siksiká (*six-sah-ka*). Their homeward trail led to the southwest. I counted seven warriors, two of whom had wounds from the battle. In a short time, we came upon two young boys tending about twenty dogs. The deceased warriors were laid on the ground, wrapped in buffalo skins, and then placed on their own travois, along with food and the captured weapons. Each travois had two dogs to pull the bodies. The young boys came around and handed out dried buffalo meat to each of the men, who ate the sparse meal as they walked.

One warrior took a dog and watched over our back trail, while two others took dogs and spread out to either side of the small column to watch out for danger from man or beast.

The column was quiet, with barely any conversation. The only exceptions came from the young boys, whose occasional sharp commands to the travois-pulling dogs broke the silence whenever the animals lagged behind. These tall, silent, constantly smiling men ushering me across this endless land had strong, chiselled features. The Ayaaj-inini people were known as great hunters and warriors. They depended on the buffalo for their sustenance and were very good at hunting this animal, which kept their villages well stocked with hides and meat.

I noticed that one warrior walking a few steps away from me struggled with a broken shoulder. Although he was clearly in excruciating pain, he never uttered a sound. To keep his shoulder immobilized, they had bound his arm to his body with a leather sling made from strips of buffalo hide.

It looked like a lance point had grazed the shoulder blade of the other wounded warrior, exposing the whiteness of bone beneath. The wound was seeping blood and running down his arm. I watched as he took the bloody piece of moss that had been bound to his wound and tossed the poultice to the side of the trail. He then took some chewing tobacco out of his mouth and applied it to the seeping wound to stop the blood flow and help heal the gash. He then took some fresh moss out of his medicine bag and bound it with leather to the torn skin. During all of this, he kept up with the rest of us and never once winced or asked for help.

Throughout that fall day, the group moved in silence, and the dogs were so well trained that only their panting could be heard. The only time that these dogs had been spoken to was at the beginning of the trail. Shielding my eyes from the sun, I peered up into the sky and noticed a couple of my crow friends following us. As long as I was alive, they would not abandon me.

The surrounding prairie gave off a musty smell of dying grass and dust. In the area we now walked through, the lack of fall rain had turned the ground hard underfoot. After the midday sun, the wind slowly started to pick up, and soon loose chaffs of grass and dust were swirling around, covering my body and hitting my unprotected face. With my hands bound, I could not shield my eyes from the airborne particles. Squinting helped, but I could not close my eyes completely for fear of tripping and then being dragged by my captor along the rough ground.

The warrior at the end of my noosed leather rope was slightly taller than me. He had a red scar running diagonally from his left shoulder blade to his waist. The scar was dotted with needle entries where the healer had closed up the gash, and then someone had painted a black streak alongside it, highlighting the wound in a most frightful way. His hair was tied up in two braids wrapped with a white weasel skin. The Ayaaj-inini never gave out eagle feathers for bravery; they gave out waabiski zhingos (*wah-bish-key ching-gwas*: white weasel) to signify bravery. My leash-mate never spoke a word, but I heard someone call his name in their Ayaaj-inini language once, and he just grunted an answer. His name was Ki'somm Áwákaasii (*key-som ah-wah-ka-see*: Moon Deer).

My understanding of the Ayaaj-inini language had come from a boy the Anishinaabe had captured a few years back and adopted into their tribe. I taught him Mi′kmaq and he taught me Ayaaj-inini.

Ki'somm Áwákaasii gave a short, quick tug on the noose and we started off at a trot. The wild Ayaaj-inini dogs pulling the dead warriors followed a lead warrior and an animosh that looked to be the matriarch of the pack. With a huge head and short ears, the female animosh looked like a cross between a mahingan (wolf) and a makwa. Her fur was a mixture of greys and browns, her paws were as big as two of my hands put together, and her chest was wider than my shoulders. She looked like she could take a wolf by the neck and shake the life out of it.

We kept this easy loping run up until dark. Given that my hands were tied behind my back, I was thankful that all of the biting flying insects had died off, because they would have feasted on me. Running bound up like that was hard enough without any other distractions.

Even after stopping for the night, they made no fire. I suspected that they were still concerned that my people, or some other enemy, might be close and did not want to attract any attention with the smell of smoke and the cast of fire-light.

After laying me face-first on the ground, they tied my feet together and then bound my hands to my feet, arching my back in a very uncomfortable position. Thankfully, they did not pull my fingernails out, like the Haudenosaunee were prone to do in order to keep their prisoners from working at the bindings.

I prayed to Kitchi Manitou to keep me from getting a muscle cramp, which would be excruciatingly painful lying on the ground in this position. Eventually, I drifted in and out of a fitful sleep. Even though the flying biters were no longer around, many ground bugs took bites out of my exposed skin. At one point, I could feel the scaly skin of a snake crawl over my arched back and felt its tongue flick up against my wrist. Since there were no distinctive sounds, I could not tell if it was an alarmed zhiishiigwe (*she-she-gway*: rattlesnake) or not. Its senses were probably locked in on a waawaabiganoojiinh (*wa-wa-big-a-no-gee*: mouse) in the grass beyond my body. To take my mind off the uncomfortable position I was in, I played out the step-by-step process of skinning and butchering a mooz (*moans*: moose) in my mind.

I woke up early the next morning with a desperate craving to scratch the itching from all of the ant bites. As I lay there in the early morning warmth of the sun, I tried to drive the burning sensations of my bite-ridden body from my mind and wondered what these men might do with me. I had slain friends of theirs and they would not let that go unpunished. Would they be like the Haudenosaunee and let the women of the village decide my fate? Ever since we had moved towards the western sun after the Battle of Crow Wing River against the Lakota all those years ago, I had found that the Ayaaj-inini were just as powerful a warrior society as our old enemies, the Lakota and the Haudenosaunee.

Just as the sun completely broke the horizon, I felt my bindings being cut. Someone jerked me to my feet and shoved a buffalo bladder full of water and a good-sized chunk of meat into my face. I was so stiff, sore, and bitten that I could hardly straighten up, but I hastily grabbed the food and water. I took two long pulls from the bladder and stuffed the meat into my mouth, trying to get down as much of it as I could before he changed his mind and ripped it out of my hands. At that point I raised my head and watched a large, muscular warrior approach me.

"Elue′wiet Ga′qaquis!" he shouted, calling me by my Mi′kmaq name. "You are a long way from home, but your reputation precedes you as a fearless warrior who, I am told, can talk to the mai′stóó (*may-stew*: crow) who fly near him. Our people call you Mai′stóó Nínaa (*may-stew knee-nah*: Crow Man); we do not know if you are crazy. We captured a Lakota warrior many moons ago, and he told a story of you and your Anishinaabe friends. Like I said, your exploits precede you."

I looked at this warrior, a head taller than his companions, and immediately knew who he was. His lance and shield had white weasel pelts hanging from them, proving his bravery. He had a bow and a cougar skin quiver slung across his back, a knife around his neck in a sheath, and another stuck into his left knee-high moccasin. Two red handprints were painted on his chest, signifying that he had slain enemies in hand-to-hand combat. He had painted his face black with red circles around his eyes and mouth. The black meant victory and the red, blood. His chest bore a slashing knife wound that he had painted yellow, which meant that he would fight to the death. His hair was long and braided. Clearly, this powerful-looking man was a great warrior.

I addressed him by his Blackfoot name, "Ííksspitaawa Kiááyo (*iik-sspitaa-wa key-i-o*: He Is Very Tall Bear), I have also heard of you. You have slain many enemies!"

"Very good, Mai'stóó Nínaa," he replied. "Now we know each other. I know that you have also fought many battles and that you lost your left eye to a Haudenosaunee arrow, then ran a gauntlet, saved your friend, and escaped. But now we have the great Mi'kmag warrior Elue'wiet Ga'qaquis, whom we call Mai'stóó Nínaa, at our mercy! I also see that one of my warriors has added to your good looks by taking part of your right ear off."

"Why did you not kill me when you had the chance?" I asked.

"We have plans for a great warrior like you," he answered.

Ki'somm Áwákaasii then walked up to me with a smile, slipped the rope noose around my neck again, and tied my hands behind me. Trussed up like this, my biggest fear was falling. With no hands to protect me, my face would take the brunt of a sudden meeting with the ground.

We ran until the sun was high in the sky before stopping along a small river with trees for shade. The day was unseasonably warm for this time of year. Two of the warriors left with a dog and soon came back with several kíítokii (*key-toe-ki*: prairie chicken). They soon had them on spits, and the smell of the birds cooking made my dry mouth water. I watched as Ki'somm Áwákaasii walked to one of the spits and sliced off a good chunk of meat with his knife. He came towards me with the meat in his hand, dripping grease, and shoved it at me, along with a bladder of water.

"I am told that I have to keep your strength up for what you have to face when we get back to our village. So eat, drink, and enjoy what little time you have left in this life."

He sliced off my leather bindings and, once again, I quickly ate what was given to me. The meat was so good, and the juices ran down my chin onto my legs. I wiped my hands in the grass and then used a clump to clean off my legs.

After I finished eating, Ki'somm Áwákaasii came towards me and said, "Get up! You will not be tied or noosed anymore. However, you will be guarded by two of our war dogs. If you run from the column, they will tear you apart!"

My new guards were huge, but nothing when compared to my friend Mitigomij's big mishibizhi. As big and mean as these dogs appeared to be, I smiled knowing that they would not slow Makadewà Wàban (*ma-ka-de-wa wah-bun*: Black Dawn) down for a second and the panther could kill both of them in a heartbeat.

Just before we got up to leave, one lone warrior ran off in the same westerly direction we were headed in. I knew that he would be announcing our arrival and that my entrance to their village would not be a welcoming occasion for me.

The warriors picked up their pace and ran at a distance-eating lope. It was so much easier to run now without my hands tied behind my back and a noose around my neck. The two war dogs ran beside me with their tongues sticking out of their open mouths. Every time they turned their heads to look sideways at me, they threw gobs of animosh drool onto my chest and legs. Between their slobber, my sweat, and all of the dust and chaff being kicked up into the air by all the runners, I looked as if I had gone swimming and then rolled around on the ground. If anyone who knew me could see me now, they would think that I'd become a wild man in need of a good washing.

Just as dusk set, we crested a small hill. Down below was a river that I heard the warriors call Ponoká'sisaahtaa (*ponoka-si-sahta*: North Saskatchewan River). On the west side of the river, I saw many campfires and teepees made of buffalo skins. The village looked like it had around three hundred to four hundred inhabitants.

Upon entering the village, I smelled rancid, rotting meat that a pack of dogs were fighting over, burning buffalo chips, and roasting buffalo meat. I also caught the sweet scent of burning sage and sweetgrass, which almost masked the other smells.

Then I heard it: the agonizing wailing of women in mourning for the fallen warriors. The sound gave me a cold chill and made my skin rise up in bumps. As I neared this group of crying women, I noticed that their arms and thighs were bloody from slashing at them with their knives. They had also hacked off their long hair, which lay in clumps at their feet.

Whack, a chunk of dirt hit me square in the side of the head. Then rocks pelted my body, followed by buffalo chips and children running up and hitting me with switches and rawhide ropes. A few of the rocks cut my skin, and the switches caused my skin to welt up. I was now covered with sweat, blood, dirt, and grass chaff. I walked straight ahead and looked neither to my left or right. The abuse and projectiles rained down upon me.

This went on until Ííksspitaawa Kiáàyo raised his arm and barked out something in their language, but his words failed to stop an old woman from coming up and delivering a stinging strike across my neck with a sturdy stick. I looked sharply at her and smiled. She was a short, wrinkled woman of many winters. She returned my stare, opened her toothless mouth, and screamed at me in a voice that pierced my ears, causing my inner hearing to vibrate from the high-pitched sound.

"You killed her son two suns ago," said Ííksspitaawa Kiáàyo. "She wants you dead."

I was then taken to a lodge in the middle of the village. There, I found a robe, water, a chunk of meat, and some turnip, which the Blackfoot called *ma's*. I ate my fill and lay down to sleep on the robe. I would need all my strength for whatever slow death they surely had planned for me. Given half a chance, I would try to escape. The only friends I had in that camp now were my crow friends, and together we had suffered worse fates in the past and gotten out alive.

As I lay on the ground, bemoaning my fate, I sensed another presence in the lodge.

4

THE DOG MAN

HOTAMÉTMÂSÊHAO'O

"Boozhoo (*beau-show*: hello)." I directed my words in the Anishinaabe language to the dark corner of the teepee, where I thought I sensed a presence of another person.

"Haáahe (*haa-aah*: hello)," came the reply, in a language I had not heard before.

Following this sound to the source, I watched as a tall, lithe warrior with black, waist-length hair emerged into the shimmering light that filtered into our space through the opening of the flap. The light caught him flush in the face just as he neared me. He had glistening black eyes and rugged, weathered facial features. In his hair were two eagle feathers, denoting that he was a respected warrior. He was dressed in only a breechcloth, and his chest showed recent wounds from several knife slashes, and he had an ugly-looking bump above his left ear. Someone had sewn the more serious slashes shut with rawhide and smeared honey on all the cuts.

He sat across from me and pointed at himself. Through sign language, and talking his language at the same time, I understood his name to be Ókȯhkevó'omaestse (*oak-key-whoa-a-mast*: White Crow), and he was a Tsétsėhéstaestse (*tih-dis-dus*: Cheyenne person).

I offered him my portion of meat and water, and we sat there talking back in forth with sign language and our own languages. Through all this, I listened to his story unfold and how his journey ended up here in this teepee with me.

"One moon ago, two of our hunters who had been sent out to look for the great buffalo herd came back to our village with news that they had found the beasts. They said there were so many that the dust from their movement across the land hid the sun in the sky and covered them both in a thick layer of dirt as they neared the herd. This was good news to our people, since the meat from the hotóá'e (*ho-toe-why*: buffalo) would keep our people from dying during the lean winter months, when the cold winds blow and starvation lurks in all our lodges.

"The members of our village became very excited, and immediately the women started to break camp, taking down our lodges to move near the great herd. While all this was happening, one of the scouts, Éháesenove (*e-has-a-nuff*: He Has a Temper), approached me and said, 'Ókȯhkevó'omaestse, the herd was heading into Mo'ôhtávêhahtátaneo'o (*mo-a-taf-a-tet-a-knee-o*: Blackfoot) territory. They will not be in a very accepting mood if we enter their hunting grounds.'

"'Éháesenove, that does not worry me,' I said to him. 'We need the food, robes, and all the other things that the hotóá'e will supply us with. The very real threat of starvation is a lot worse than the fear of dying under the war club of the Crow or Blackfoot!'

"'Having said that, the Mo'ôhtávêhahtátaneo'o are indeed dangerous and very protective of their hunting grounds. They will defend these grounds if we enter and they discover us. We will also have to pass through the lands of the Óoetaneo'o (*ooh-ooh-ten-yah*: Crow). With so many enemies lurking around, it will be too perilous to travel with the whole village.'

"We stopped taking down the lodges and called a meeting of the people. We were only a small village of forty-two lodges with one hundred and forty-one women, children, and Elders, plus thirty-eight warriors. Of these, eleven were of the Hotamétmâsêhao'o (*ho-dam-map-saw*: Dog Men) warrior society.

"After consulting with all of the Elders, we decided not to put the whole village in peril. The Dog Men, one hundred dogs, and sixteen women would leave the next day. The plan was to attack the rear of the herd when we came upon it. Since the Crow and the Blackfoot would have many more hunters at their disposal, they would likely be hunting at the head or the sides of the herd. As the animals passed through their territories, they would cut out large swaths of the beasts to either corral or run over a cliff to make their kills. By attacking the stragglers and the weaker animals at the end of the herd, our only competition would be the wolves and bears. These herds were often so huge that it would be a half-day's travel from the front to the back. So, while we were doing this, we hoped that the dust and the thunder of thousands of hooves would hide our small band.

"Our summer village was on the É'ometāā'e (*eh-oh-my-da*: Missouri River), where we were able to fish and grow mȧhaemenȯtse (*ma-mints*: corn), monėške-ho (*mons-skech*: beans), and mȧhōō'o (*ha-ah*: squash). Even though it sounds as if we have lots to eat, we need all the hotóá'e has to offer for our survival. Ma'hēō'o (*ma-hay-oh*: Supreme Being) has given us many things to live our lives, but the buffalo is the most important, since the meat and robes keep us alive and warm.

"The next morning, we left our village at dawn. I can still remember the smell of the sweetgrass in the early morning dew as the sun rose in a cloudless sky. The group went into a single file trot, with a scout and several dogs at a distance in the lead. On each side, and at the end of the column, we positioned several warriors to guard our group. Each of the women and warriors had a couple of favourite dogs carrying packs that contained their food, extra arrows, and other necessities. Sixty-four of the dogs each pulled an empty amėstó'eeseo'o (*um-stow-as-see-oh*: travois) to carry meat on the return trip.

"Our hope was that we would find the herd within ten suns. We left our own hunting grounds and, after two days of travel, entered the lands of the Óoetaneo'o. From there on in, we had to travel at night and sleep during the day to ensure our safety. During the first two nights of travel, we could see far-off campfires, which we kept our distance from.

"One breaking-dawn morning, before we stopped to rest, we came upon a small group of vó'kaa'e (*vok-ah*: antelope). After some well placed arrows quickly brought the animals down, the women immediately butchered them. Thankfully, several of the women travelling with us were experienced in making a smokeless fire; otherwise, we would have been forced to eat the meat raw.

"After filling our stomachs, we lay down to sleep in the long prairie grass, listening to the dogs emit deep-throated growls as they cracked open the vó'kaa'e bones that had been cast to them. No guards were put out during any of our resting times, since the dogs would warn us of any danger. During our daylight rests, we stayed away from places that enemy warriors might seek out, such as rivers or other fresh water areas. Only once in the first five days did we see any Óoetaneo'o people, and they were far off on the distant horizon.

"The dogs we brought along were used for the heavy work of pulling travois, carrying packs, and guarding camps. They were very highly trained in this last duty and did not give away our position by barking at everything they considered dangerous to our group. They were not ordinary camp dogs, which barked at their own shadow when scared. These dogs would lie down and emit a low growl if they sensed something out of the ordinary, allowing others to take up guard positions when the alarm was sounded.

"We had left our village late into our Oenenéeše'he (*on-a-nay-shea*: Harvest Moon, August). The bugs were still biting and attacked us in swarms. We used mixtures of goldenseal and bear grease to keep them off, as well as mud when we had access to water.

"During the sunrise of our twelfth day out, we noticed a huge cloud of dust and swarms of birds on the distant horizon; sure signs that the great herd was near. The dogs stood with their noses stuck in the air, gathering in the smell of the buffalo in the distance. Happy now that we had found our prey, we lay down to rest, knowing that once dusk came, the final leg of our trip would begin.

"We headed towards the herd at nightfall and, by the next morning, came to within striking distance. As the sun rose over the land, it highlighted the immense dust cloud of the hotóá'e as they started moving. As the animals rose from their sleeping positions, the biting odours of urine and buffalo dung made our nostrils quiver from the rankness of it. Some of the dogs even put their paws over their noses to try and keep the smells at bay.

"After awakening from their sleep, some members of the herd rolled on the ground, adding to the dust cloud. The immense flocks of birds accompanying the herd rose into the air, creating a din of flapping wings and chirping. Our dogs lay on the ground beside us as we watched the herd start to move. We needed the old, weak, and lame members of the herd to lag behind, since they were our targets that day. Fortunately, the women with us were as skilled at hunting buffalo as the warriors and, between the twenty-seven of us, we hoped to quickly bring down the sixteen beasts that we could handle on this trip.

"As the herd slowly started to move, we immediately picked out two lame bulls that had likely been injured in battles during the rut with other males. I and four other warriors put wolf skins over us and crawled up on the prey. With well placed arrows, we downed the bulls quickly, and our people came from their hiding spots and started the butchering. Thanking Ma'hēō'o, we offered up a gift of tse'némoo'o (*set-knee-moor*: tobacco) for the first kills. Before the sun reached the midday sky, we had downed fifteen animals. We placed four warriors on lookout, and the rest of us worked together in five- and six-person groups, making quick work of skinning and dividing the animals upon the travois.

"Now that we were deep in Mo'ôhtávêhahtátaneo'o territory, we needed to do all of the killing and butchering before the sun set. Since we were all intruders in someone else's hunting grounds, all of our lives were in danger here. Battles big and small are forever fought over game territory, food, and the protection of family. When women and children are captured, their absence can result in starvation and even the demise of a community. As the lifeblood of every nation, they are needed to grow and prosper, and every warrior will fight to the death to defend them, as well as their food stocks.

"As the hunks of meat were hauled from the carcasses, the travois would be quickly loaded. Each of the dogs was capable of carrying close to a quarter of one of the butchered beasts on their travois. They were big, strong animals and used to pulling heavy loads. Once eight travois were filled, a warrior and two women started off towards our homeland.

"The decision was made that we would meet at our second-to-last-day's resting place and then go home as a group. We did not want to be caught all together here if the Crow or Blackfoot stumbled upon us. By sending groups back once they were loaded, we stood a better chance that a few got home than none getting home. After the first group left, the remaining eight groups would each have seven travois to take home.

"Drawn towards the killing field by the smell of death, one hó'nehe (*hoat-nay*: wolf) appeared, then another, and then the rest of the resident pack from this area. Then a vóhpåhtse-náhkohe (*whoop-say-knock-a*: grizzly bear) showed up, the most dangerous carrion eater there was. It would kill anything standing in the way of its meal. Any warrior wearing vóhpåhtse-náhkohe claws around his neck was the bravest of all hunter warriors. To engage in a life and death fight with one of these beasts and survive, or to slay one and live, was the bravest thing a warrior could do in our world.

"Fortunately, there were enough carcasses scattered around the grounds that these beasts paid little heed to us. The wolves went about their work, tearing away what meat was left on the bones, emitting low growls and snapping at any of the lesser members of the pack that came too close to their meal. The wolves dared not approach where the grizzly was eating, since one swipe of its paw could kill or severely wound a wolf. These imposing killing machines stood taller than a man and outweighed us by two to five times, depending on the sex of the animal. We, the Cheyenne, did not eat bear meat, since we consider them to be ancestors. To us, eating a bear is like eating a relative.

"Only three of our number now remained: a warrior named Ho'néhevotoomáhe (*hoat-nay-a-doe-ma*: Wolfrobe); his wife, Vóhkeesá'e (*wak-is-saw*: Crooked Nose Woman); and myself, along with eleven dogs, seven of which had a travois behind them. Vóhkeesá'e was hastily finishing the butchering of the last animal, and neither I nor her husband could keep up with piling the meat on the travois and securing it.

"I was loading the last of the meat when I noticed the four dogs beside me rise up with the hairs bristling on their backs and emitting low, throaty growls. The dogs with the travois nervously started to pull away from us.

"'Ho'néhevotoomáhe', I whispered, 'Weapons!'

"My lance and bow had been leaning up against the travois, but the two weapons were now being scattered into the long grass by the spooked dog. I quickly grasped my two bone knives, one from the case around my neck and the other from inside one of my knee-high moccasins.

"At that moment, I heard a bone-crushing thud and a bloody gurgle from where Vóhkeesá'e was. I quickly stood up and felt a slash across my chest from the point of a spear. I turned and swung my left hand in a sweeping motion, cutting a warrior across his cheek. Except for his white-outlined mouth, his face was almost completely painted black. The blood spurted out from the wound, reddening the side of his face and neck, and he dropped to one knee without saying a word.

"A knife cut my chest, deeper this time, which was quickly followed by another slash. I was being cut to pieces by knives and lances, but none of them were killing blows. During this time, I heard a few of the dogs yelp as they were put down by our attackers. Battling for my last scrap of time on this land, I glanced over to my left and caught the final moments of Ho'néhevotoomáhe as he went down in a bloody mess from an onslaught of war clubs. I fought for my life: slashing, cutting, and even using my fists as the enemy closed in on me. Then the last thing I remember was a violent strike to the left side of my head, ringing in my ears, and blackness.

"When I woke up, I did not know how much time had passed. I found myself in a hunting camp, where the women were drying buffalo meat. The smoke from the fires and the smell of the raw meat gave me a headache, and my chest felt tight and sore. I sat up and looked at my belly. Someone had sewn my wounds up and slathered me in háhnomápano'ėhasēō'o (*ha-toe-ma-pa-no-ha-say-o*: honey), which the flies were constantly buzzing around.

"As I sat there, waving at the flies and vomiting from my headache, an old woman came along with a chunk of meat, and some water. She smiled a toothless grin and spat on my food as she handed it to me. I smiled back, wiped the moisture off the meat, and nodded my head. She mumbled something that I could not understand and walked away. The food helped stem my hunger, and the water was cool enough to refresh my weakened body.

"Three suns later, I found myself here. No one has talked to me at all, except for a few grunts from the woman who brings me food and water once a day. They posted four young boys around this teepee as guards. Two suns after I arrived here, you showed up. I am puzzled as to why they have not put me to death on the fire rack."

"That is a quite a story you have told me, Ókȯhkevó'omaestse," I said as he finished.

He laughed when I tried to pronounce his name. "*Oak-key-whoa-a-mast*," he said while smiling, "*Oak-key-whoa-a-mast!*"

"Okay '*Oak-key-whoa-a-mast*,'" I answered, and he laughed and nodded his head. "I know the Blackfoot, and they are a very proud, fierce, and feared nation of warriors. My thinking is that torturing us on the rack will not be their way for us and that they have something different planned. They want to be known as the warriors who have slain Elue'wiet Ga'qaquis, Crazy Crow, and the Cheyenne Dog Man, Ókȯhkevó'omaestse, known as White Crow, but they will soon learn that it will not be easy to slay two crows."

The sound of footsteps outside interrupted our conversation. The tent flap was thrown wide open and blinding sunlight streamed in. I looked up to see a tall warrior blocking the sun, and his shadow crept across the ground towards us. Two painted warriors walked around him and approached us quickly. One walked behind my back and prodded me with the sharp end of his spear on my right arm, drawing blood.

"*Oak-key-whoa-a-mast,*" I whispered, getting his attention. He turned his head to look, and I quickly hand-signed, "Our time had come, stay close to me."

5

TO KILL A LEGEND

AS WE LEFT the teepee, I hesitated for a quick moment to let my eyes adjust to the brilliant sunlight. This pause was all the excuse my guard needed to whack the back of my legs with his spear. This irritated me and I lost my temper. Spinning on the dusty ground, I recognized my abuser as Ki'somm Áwákaasii, who had been my constant overseer on our trip to the village.

With lightning reflexes, I grabbed the spear out of the warrior's hand and took his feet out from under him in a single motion that completely caught him by surprise. He fell with a thud, a grunt, and an expulsion of air from his lungs. As he quickly bounced back up to his feet, Ki'somm Áwákaasii unsheathed a bone knife. Just as quickly, I cracked his hand with the bladed end of the spear, causing him to yelp in pain. His hand was sliced to the bone and the gushing blood reddened the ground around him. I tossed the spear on the ground at his feet and spat.

No sooner had I tossed the spear than Ííksspitaawa Kiááyo, the Blackfoot warrior leader, walked up to Ki'somm Áwákaasii and started to laugh. This made the bleeding man glare at me with clearly murderous thoughts.

Ííksspitaawa Kiááyo said, "Ki'somm Áwákaasii, you should know that you never poke a kiááyo (*key-i-o*: bear) with a stick unless you want a fight. Go now and find the healer; you need care."

Looking at the Cheyenne and me, Ííksspitaawa Kiááyo called us by our Blackfoot names: "Come with me, Mai′stóó Nínaa. Today you and the Imitáá Nínaa (*e-me-ta knee-nah*: Dog Man) die."

Oak-key-whoa-a-mast looked at me and I just shrugged. Neither of us understood what our captor had just said, but a push from our guards gave us the idea that we were to follow him.

My inner senses always became keen whenever danger was near, and, right now, my sense of smell was overwhelmed by a mixture of odours from within the village. The rancid scent of dog urine, the musty odours of unwashed bodies, smoky campfires, the pungent wafting of food cooking, and the putrid stench of drying buffalo meat all filled my nostrils and rejuvenated my inner spirit. I was now on edge and ready to face what was in store for me. I would not go willingly or easily. I looked to my new Cheyenne friend and saw that he showed no fear whatsoever in his body language. He was a willing ally and a true warrior.

Like on our first arrival, women and children started to emerge from their lodges and shower us with sticks, rocks, clumps of dirt, and feces as we were led through the village. Elders came up to us and hit us with switches, leaving red welts all over our bodies. And although this was not as brutal as a Haudenosaunee gauntlet, it was a demeaning experience.

Ííksspitaawa Kiááyo came up to us and said, "Take off all your clothes and your moccasins!"

We laid my shirt, as well as our leggings, breechcloths, and footwear on the ground. Ókòhkevó'omaestse and I stood there in the dust of the village centre, naked as the day we were brought into this world. Flies were landing on my genitalia and chest, women laughed at us, and dogs came up to sniff at our rears and private parts.

When I looked over at Ókòhkevó'omaestse, I noticed that a few of his wounds had opened up and flies were gathering around the mixture of blood and honey that covered his seeping lacerations. A couple of the dogs were licking the blood off his legs as it trickled down his body.

He returned my look and grinned, and I quickly signed for him to stay close to me when our death ordeal started.

Ííksspitaawa Kiááyo walked up to us and, using a combination of signing and his own language, said, "Our council has spent the past few days trying to decide how best to end your lives. One of our Elders talked about the weasel and how he hunts the áaattsistaa (*aah-tist-ta*: rabbit). He talked about how the rabbit tries to outrun the weasel, but the weasel wears the rabbit down in the chase and catches him. The rabbit's only weapon is its speed, while the weasel has speed, sharp teeth, and cunning. The Elder then talked about how the weasel is a sacred animal to our people and that we should follow its ways in our treatment of you two.

"Since the weasel always trains its young to hunt at a young age, the Elder suggested that we should train our own young warriors in a similar way by slaying two great warriors in a hunt. So, we have decided that our young warriors will hunt you down in a death run. You will be given a head start with only your ability to outrun your pursuers to survive, just like the ááattsistaa. The young men will have their speed and cunning to catch you, and their teeth will be the weapons they carry. Out-distance them and you live. If you do not, then your scalp will hang in a young warrior's lodge, and he will have a fine story to tell to others around the winter fires."

I looked at Ókȯhkevó'omaestse and said in my language, "We are not rabbits, and they will soon find out that *we* are the weasels!"

The Cheyenne looked back at me, nodding his head like he understood every word I said.

Ííksspitaawa Kiááyo looked at us and said, "I will shoot an arrow into the air and wherever it lands, one of our young boys will pound a wooden shaft into the ground and he will stand beside it. This will be your head start. Once you have reached this spot, our warriors will start their chase."

After he shot the arrow, a boy of about eleven summers ran to where the arrow landed. As he sped past me, I noticed that he wore a sheathed knife around his neck, hung by a leather strap. As soon as he took off, the drummers started beating their drums and singing. Looking behind me, I saw nine painted young warriors with intense looks on their faces. Lying beside them were three large dogs. Although they all clearly wanted the honour of taking our scalps, they would soon discover that I would not die easily and, presumably, neither would my Cheyenne friend.

Since the crowd expected us to start out running, we did the exact opposite. We slowly sauntered our way out towards the stick, saving our stamina for what was ahead. When I turned and flexed my muscles towards the onlookers, Ókôhkevó'omaestse started to laugh and then did the same. This inspired the crowd to yell, hoot, and throw rocks at us, so we responded to this by dancing and singing, which made them even more hostile. I looked at the young warriors again, and they were pacing and shaking their weapons at us while the dogs barked and howled amidst all of the collective noise.

Taking a series of deep breaths, I started to think of a plan to keep the two of us alive. I bent down, picked up three round stones, looked up into the sky, and called out a quick "*caw-caw-caw-aw*," which is an "attention call" to summon several of my sky-friends. As soon as they were within sight, I threw the three pebbles high into the air, and immediately three crows swooped in, snatched the small rocks out of mid-air, and then banked hard back up into the overhead sky. No one seemed to notice or care about what I had just done.

When we were close enough to see the young boy's features, we started to run a slow trot into the long grass surrounding the village. This scared the surrounding birds, who rose into the air, noisily chirping and flapping their wings, which, in turn, brought a colourful swarm of butterflies into the air to flit around us as we ran. Rare for this time of year, butterflies were seen as a good omen, signifying change, joy, and life.

Dashing between the boy, the arrow, and the shaft, I reached out with my left hand and ripped the sheathed knife and leather thong off his neck. The boy stumbled towards me before the thong broke, and, when it did, he fell face-first into the ground with a loud grunt. At the same time, my right hand scooped up the stick and the arrow. As we distanced ourselves from the boy, we could hear the whoops of the warriors, the barking of the dogs, and the cheering of the village inhabitants. A slight chill ran over my naked body, not out of fear, but anticipation of what was going to take place. Combat invigorated me, and I knew that my companion could be depended on when needed. The flight of White Crow and Crazy Crow was now on, and our lives hung in the balance!

Running at a less-than-full gait, I unravelled the sinew that fastened the arrowhead and feathers to the gooseberry shaft. Knotting the sinew together, I was able to get enough length to secure the flint arrowhead to the end of the stick that I had picked up.

"*Oak-key-whoa-a-mas!*" I yelled. When he looked at me, I tossed the spear I had made over to him. He caught it in midair, balanced it in his hand, smiled, and said something in his language that I took as thanks.

Quickening our pace, I took the gooseberry arrow shaft, broke it in two and sharpened the ends of both shafts with the boy's knife. Stopping briefly, I stuck both of them into the ground on our back trail, leaving them jutting out by about a half-a-finger length.

Sticking the knife back into its sheath, I picked up my pace and caught up to the Cheyenne. Turning my head, I watched in the distance as the warriors and dogs were trying to close the gap between us. Suddenly, one of the lead dogs yelped in pain. Over the long grasses, I could see it pitch forward, raising up dust as it stumbled and fell. The animal had stepped on one, or both, of my sharpened sticks. Suddenly, men and animals pulled up, looking towards the ground to see if there were any more on the trail. This enabled us to put some distance between us and our pursuers for now.

But one warrior threw caution aside, increased his running speed, and broke into a ground-eating sprint. Leaving his fellow warriors and dogs behind, he was quickly gaining on our position. I tapped the Cheyenne on the shoulder, pointed to our rear, and held out my hands palms-down, indicating that I wanted to slow our pace. I then gestured towards the spear he was carrying, and he nodded. As we slowed down, our now-lone pursuer quickly caught up to us. All he had was a spear in his hand, and he was running at full speed. Guessing that we were unarmed, he showed no fear. Clearly, his plan was to catch and kill both of us with his weapon and gain all the glory. Little did he know that he was about to become the rabbit!

He started to taunt us as he closed the distance. Given his running speed, we knew that there was no way he could possibly throw his weapon. When we stopped to face him, he let out a warrior's attack cry and charged at us. But then, as Ókȯhkevó'omaestse raised his arm and took a stance to throw my makeshift weapon, our pursuer's eyes opened wide. With a sharp grunt, Ókȯhkevó'omaestse hurled the spear towards the young man, and we immediately heard the sound of his breast bone shatter as the arrowhead tip struck him at full running speed.

After the impact stopped his attack scream in mid-yell, he stood and looked in stunned disbelief at what had just happened. A trickle of blood exited his mouth and dripped onto his white-painted chest, creating a faint red stream as it ran its course. He coughed once, spewing blood into the air. The strong midday sun illuminated the starkness of the moment, and the blood seemed to blossom into a glistening, red cloud. He took one look at his crimson-spattered feet and fell backwards. The spear had exited out his back, and, as he fell, the point of the weapon stuck into the ground, propping his body up at an odd angle.

Although we wanted to strip the body and pull out our spear, there was precious little time to do so. Instead, I picked up his weapon and unwound the leather that he had used as a grip. I turned and handed the weapon to Ókȯhkevó'omaestse, and we took off on the run. There were eight more warriors on our trail and two dogs, so the odds were still against us, but now I had the material to make a much more lethal weapon.

Pulling the blade out of the sheath from around my neck, I noticed that it was a skinning knife made out of buffalo bone, with razor-sharp edges and a pointed tip. I tied some of the new leather to the weapon, hung it around my neck, and held the sheath in my hands.

Behind us, we could hear yelling and taunts as our pursuers stumbled upon their fallen comrade. After looking up into the sky and cawing to my three crow friends, I started to make my new killing weapon.

ANOKÌ

We were well received upon our return to the village. The meat that we had brought back was distributed to the Elders in need. After making sure others had enough, my family kept a small portion.

After being back for a day, my wife, Osk-îskwêw, told me, "Anokì, Elue′wiet Ga′qaquis and some young warriors went south to hunt, and they have been gone far too long. I feel that something is wrong!"

"Did you have another dream, my wife?" I asked.

"Yes, this time I saw crows circling in a blue sky and Crazy Crow's clothing lying empty on the ground!"

The next day, we awoke to warm temperatures and melting snow. With the way the weather changes on these flat lands, it could be completely snow-free just a half-day's walk from here.

At dusk that night, the dogs started to bark at an intruder. As the men rushed for their weapons, we could hear a distant voice above the barking dogs.

"It is I, Oshkiniigii Gookooko'oo!"

He loped up to the gathered warriors, stopped, bent over, and dropped to one knee in exhaustion. Taking deep breaths to replenish his strength, he then rose and addressed us.

"Anokì," he said, "Elue'wiet Ga'qaquis has been captured by the Ayaaj-inini and taken away. Babaa-ayaa Animosh (*ba-baa-ay-ah an-e-moosh*: Wanders Around Dog), Niswi Nishkaadizi Ma'iinganag (*nis-we nish-ga-da-zay na-ing-ga-nag*: Three Angry Wolves), Giizhig Animosh (*gii-zig*: Sky Dog), and Wiipem Makwa (*we-pem muck-wa*: Sleeps with a Bear) were all slain. I was only able to escape because I had been watching to the north, the opposite direction that our enemies had approached from.

"When I heard the sounds of battle, I approached our campsite by hiding in the long grass. I could see that the four young warriors and all of the dogs were dead. The Ayaaj-inini also had Crazy Crow on the ground and were 'counting coup' on him with their weapons. When I saw that he was still alive, I slowly crawled away from the bloody field and, once out of sight, stood up and started to run back to our village. Our hunting group originally took three suns of easy walking and running time to reach where we were attacked. If we leave before daybreak, we can reach there in the same amount of time it took for me to return here at a constant run: under two full suns!"

Once the village heard the names of the fallen, the mothers and wives of the young warriors started to wail, cut their hair, and slash their arms in mourning.

Our community was devastated by the news that four young men had been lost and Crazy Crow had been captured.

"Anokì, we have to go and bury our slain warriors," Zhashagi said to me.

"Yes, but we also have to follow the trail of the attackers and see if we have any chance of saving Crazy Crow. Unfortunately, we do not have enough warriors to go on an all-out attack. The Blackfoot are to be feared, and our Cree allies are too distant to call them for aid. I know Crazy Crow would come for one of us, so we cannot waste any time to see if we can help him," I replied.

"The first fifteen men who step forward will leave with me tonight. Since taking fifteen warriors from our ranks here will leave them very thin, my wife, Oskîskwêw, along with our children, Wâpikwan and Môso, will take a gift of tobacco to our Cree friends and ask them if they can spare any warriors to help guard the village."

Jilte′g and E′s, the two Mi′kmaq warriors, immediately stepped forward.

"I owe my life to Elue′wiet Ga′qaquis," said Jilte′g. "If not for him, my scalp would have been hanging in a Haudenosaunee long house many moons ago. My life is his life."

I smiled grimly when I heard this, since it was true for so many of us. I knew this trip to find Elue′wiet Ga′qaquis might end up being the death of us all, but this was a man who always looked after us. We had to try and help him.

My warrior sister, Pangì Mahingan, and her husband, Ki'kwa'ju, stepped out, along with Zhashagi and his brother Omashkooz, the two Anishinaabe men who had led us to this country. Many of the other Anishinaabe warriors also came forward, along with two Cree men who had been visiting, as well as every other warrior in the camp. After counting out fifteen, I had to ask the rest to stay behind in order to protect and hunt for the women, children, and Elders while we were gone. I made sure that the two Cree warriors were among the fifteen, since I did not want to insult them. After instructing the remaining men and boys to remain ever watchful for the enemy, we asked them to keep enough of their numbers in camp to protect our people whenever they went out to hunt.

I turned to my wife, Osk-îskwêw, and said, "Take the children and the dogs; the dogs will protect and warn you of any animals that might seek to do you harm. I am confident that your Cree community will be able to spare some warriors to send them back to the village here. Safe travels, my love!"

We had made friends and allies with the Cree and Assiniboine when we first came out to this land, but this, in turn, made the Blackfoot our enemies. And although we could not ask the Cree to put their lives at risk against the powerful Blackfoot to help us rescue one lone warrior, asking them to guard our village was a favour they would grant.

"Oshkiniigii Gookooko'oo, we leave at sunset. There is a full moon tonight and no time to waste!"

Turning to the rest of the warriors, I said, "Eat and gather food and water for our journey. Place all your food on your pack dogs; we do not want to carry any extra weight. Speed is our ally on this journey!"

AT THE BLACKFOOT CAMP

"Ííksspitaawa Kiááyo, why did you not kill the Cheyenne and the man they call Crazy Crow, the friend of our enemy, the Cree, while they were in our camp? This run of death has never been done before," asked Ki'somm Áwákaasii.

"This man that I call Mai′stóó Nínaa, or Elue′wiet Ga′qaquis among his people, is a great warrior, and trying to slay him will be a challenging test for our young men. But there is more to it than just that. Mai′stóó Nínaa has a friend that our enemies, the Pinaapisinaa (Sioux), have encountered. Although he has a bad leg that makes him limp, he is also a great warrior and killer who travels with a black cougar. If Mai′stóó Nínaa is in our lands, then the crippled one must also be near, and I want his scalp hanging in my lodge. To slay a warrior of his skill and reputation will be a great honour for me. Come, my friend, collect our warriors to travel at a distance and observe this run of death. There is more at play than just two naked men running for their lives!"

6

THE POWER OF THE CROW

CRAZY CROW

We looked back at the remaining warriors and dogs that were strung out in a ragged line and quickly gaining on us. I still hadn't run at a full lope yet, and I knew that my Nii`inaweshiiwii (Cheyenne) friend still had lots of stamina and speed left. After stepping on a small, sharp stone, one of my toes was now bleeding and marking our trail every step of the way. If we brought down another warrior, I would take his moccasins. As tough as my feet were, a good pair of foot coverings would go a long way towards making my travels easier during this trying encounter.

White Crow was not much of a talker. When he did converse, it was in sign, with a few words thrown in. He could not understand my language, nor could I understand his, but the sign language was our common talk.

Taking a look over my shoulder, I noticed that one of the young men and his large dog had started to distance himself from the rest. This warrior carried a shield and a war axe, and his loose hair bounced around behind him as he ran. Occasionally, the wind would catch it and blow it sideways around his neck, forcing him to reach up and brush loose strands of it from his face. He looked taller than both of us, and his running motion was effortless.

While I ran, I made my new weapon from the leather of my knife sheath and the thongs that were hanging from it. It was a difficult task, since the knife was bouncing around my neck with every step I took. Taking the leather I had remaining, I tied the knife tightly around my left forearm where it could easily be reached.

Looking up, I saw that my three crow friends were still flying in the sky above me. As soon as I held out my hand and emitted a low "*caw*" sound, one of them dove towards me, dropped the stone it had been carrying since we left the Blackfoot camp, and I caught it before it hit the ground. It was exactly what I needed: dark grey and perfectly round. I quickly nestled the pebble into the leather pad I'd just crafted.

After snagging White Crow's attention, I motioned for him that I was going to take out our pursuer. Twirling my new weapon as hard as I could around my head, it made a soft whirring noise in the air, like the sound of a strong wind coming through a hollow tree trunk. Watching the young warrior closing the distance between us, I counted his approaching steps, preparing to let fly. But then, all of a sudden, the enormous dog I'd glimpsed earlier appeared by his master's side and rushed towards me with spittle flying from its gaping maw.

If I did not do something quickly, the dog was going to be at my throat! So, I released one of the leather thongs and the slingshot made a snapping noise, like a tree cracking in the winter cold. The dog looked up at the sound, and, as it did, the stone entered his left eye, and its face exploded on impact, causing the beast to yelp and roll into the ground, stirring up dust as it tumbled head-over-heels towards me. I quickly ran towards the animal and cut its throat to put it out of its misery.

Looking up from my bloody task, I watched as White Crow threw his spear at the Blackfoot warrior, who was only five or six strides away from me. The enemy brought up his shield with amazing speed, and the weapon deflected off the hard buffalo skin. The force of the impact caused the shield to turn the man in mid-stride, throwing him into a running stumble. White Crow then leaped into the air and violently collided with the attacking warrior, driving him into the ground with a breathtaking thump. The shield went flying, but his foe tried to take the Cheyenne's head off with a mighty swing from his stone axe, only missing by a hair. In response, White Crow pinned the Blackfoot's arm, clamped his teeth onto his enemy's nose and bit it clean off. The warrior screamed from the pain, dropped his axe, and reached for his face.

Taking advantage of this opportunity, White Crow quickly grabbed the tomahawk and smashed the screaming warrior's head in.

I hastily stripped the moccasins off the dead man's feet and White Crow helped himself to another pair that the Blackfoot had tucked into the band of his breechcloth. Picking up the spear, the axe, and a bladder of water the warrior had in his possession, we started off on our run.

After some distance was gained, we paused to look back at the young warriors pursuing us. We raised our hands and weapons in the air and yelled "*ye, ye, ye, ye, ye!*" at them from the back of our throats. In response, they raised their own weapons and started a dance, like the weasel does before it kills its prey. Seeing this display, I could not help but whoop and bellow back at them.

"The rabbit is not dying as easy as the weasel is today!" I yelled. "Beware that you are not dancing to your death!"

Even after taking down two of our pursuers and two of their dogs, the odds were still against us. But there was one big difference between them and us: we were fighting for our lives, and our pursuers thought that this was nothing more than a sport without repercussions. The Dog Soldier and I certainly had much more invested in the outcome of this fight, and, with death so near, our senses were on high alert. There have been many times when I have been close to visiting my ancestors, but my wits, instincts, and luck saved my life. This day could still very well be my last on Turtle Island, but I was not afraid of death, and I was sure that the Cheyenne felt the same.

This lack of fear made me much more relaxed than the Ayaaj-inini warriors racing behind us. After all, they were trying to prove their worth as warriors to their Elders and everyone in the village. As they ran towards us with pounding hearts and shallow breaths, doubt was likely starting to creep into their minds. Their "helpless," naked quarry wasn't falling under their war axes nearly as easily as they first imagined we would.

I thought back many years ago to when I lost my left eye to the Haudenosaunee arrow and then ran their gauntlet, saving Jilte′g in the process. With the thought of death keening my senses and giving me the strength and desire to survive, things were no different today than they were on that day. Looking at the Cheyenne Dog Soldier, I saw myself in him.

Laughing at the top of my voice, I stuck my hand out again and "*cawed.*" After another nice, round pebble dropped into my hand, I popped it into my mouth and smiled. My nudity had me feeling free and invincible, and now that my feet were covered and protected from the ground, I felt like I could run faster than the prairie antelopes. Looking over at my Cheyenne ally, I burst out laughing. He was running backwards as fast as I was going forward, taunting our adversaries and singing. Was he singing his death song or a song of triumph?

Only this day's future would have the answer to that question.

ANOKÌ

We travelled from the village that night by the light of the moon, a glimmering circle in the sky that reflected a brilliant yellow colour in the land before us. The only sounds heard in the stillness of the night were the brushing of our footfalls on Mother Earth and the faint panting of the dogs. At least twice that evening, I was startled by a ghostly figure in the sky around me and a gust of air as a kòkòkòhò (*ko-ko-ko-ho*: owl) dropped from the sky onto an unsuspecting rodent. The darkness of the night held many surprises, and such encounters never failed to give me goosebumps.

Just before sunrise, we stopped for a quick bite to eat and slept until the bright sunlight woke us. Our camp was in an area of long prairie grass that came up to our shoulders. I rose from my sleep area and stretched, watched closely by one of the dogs that had been sleeping nearby. Jilte′g and E′s had slept beside me, and I nudged each of them in turn with my spear as I walked by on my way to relieve myself in the tall grass.

After finishing, I stared up into the morning sky, which now completely surrounded us in a brilliant blue. To the north of where I was standing, I could see a single wisp of a cloud. The tranquility was suddenly broken by a formation of geese jostling for position and noisily talking back and forth between themselves. Their black and white bodies contrasted with the blue sky, reminding me of the lodges that my own people painted in similar colour contrasts.

A sudden gust of wind and a faint smell of body sweat awakened my senses and told me that I was not alone. I could hear murmuring and swishing sounds coming through the long prairie grasses off to my right. It was not the wind pushing the grass tops into each other, but a more distinct sound of the lower stalks being moved ever-so-slightly.

I turned towards the sound, but the brightness of the sunrise blinded me to what or who was approaching. As my eyes gradually adjusted, I watched as five sun-drenched heads appeared above the grasses, walking towards me. Then, in my ancestral Omàmiwinini language, one word was spoken to me: "Nitàwis (*knee-tah-wis*: cousin)!"

Tears welled up and I tried to speak, but no words left my mouth. Visions of my past life ran before my teary eyes, and all I could do was extend my arms out to the first person who came within my reach and embrace them.

"Anokì, you have grown into a fine warrior," said a voice I recognized as my good friend Kànìkwe (*kaw-knee-kwe*: No Hair).

Looking over his shoulder, I watched as my late uncle Kàg's twin sons, Makwa and Wàbek, approached from the grassy forest. Both of these tall, muscular men had the right side of their heads shaved to prevent their hair from tangling in their bow strings when firing arrows. Each carried a spear, a bow slung over their shoulder with a quiver of arrows, a slingshot dangling from these quivers, and knives tucked into both of their belts. They also wore knee-high moccasins to help protect their feet and help them travel long distances.

Following them were their Malecite wives, Makwa's wife Àwadòsiwag (*uh-wa-dow-she-wag*: Minnow) and Wàbek's wife, Ininàtig (*e-na-na-dig*: Maple). The last time I saw them, they were both with child after the

Lakota battle on Crow Wing River. They had since become beautiful, raven-haired women, and I could not help but notice that they were also warrior women who carried ample weapons. Growing up watching strong women like Kìnà Odenan (*key-nah o-de-nan*: Sharp Tongue) and her life partner, Agwanìwon (*uh-gweh-nee-won*: Shawl Woman), along with my mother, Wàbananang (*wa-ba-na-nang*: Morning Star), these two now followed in the path of the three women who had preceded them.

After I recognized five of these people from my past, three other figures strode out from behind them. Their hair was shorn like the twins', and the side that was not shaved was braided. They wore turkey feathers in their braids and were clad in deerskin clothes. Each had weapons not unlike the rest, but their slingshots were loosely looped around their necks in a style similar to someone else I knew from my past. They were taller and fitter than the companion warriors they travelled with, and one of them seemed a bit younger than the other two. In unison, the twins and Kànìkwe said, "Anokì, we present you with our sons!"

I was stunned, not by the news that the twins had sons, but that Kànìkwe said that one of them was his son.

Makwa came forward, pointed to the tallest of the young men, and said, "This is Kigìbigomesì (*kih-gee-bih-goh-may-see*: Lark)."

Wàbek then walked up to me with his son and said, "This is Mashkawizì Mahingan (*mash-ka-wizi mah-in-gan*: Strong Wolf)."

But what shocked me the most was when Kànìkwe stepped forward and said, "This is my son, Kìnà Mòkomàn (*key-na mow-ko-mahn*: Sharp Knife)."

I looked at Kànìkwe and asked him, "How is Kìnà Odenan?"

"She died in her sleep several years ago, mourning her two-spirited friend Agwanìwon until the end, but celebrating the life of her son, knowing that she would live on in him. The last thing that she said to me was that I had to be the bodyguard for the twins, their families, and Kìnà Mòkomàn now!"

With that, everyone broke into laughter, and, in-between belly laughs, I said to Kànìkwe, "Kìnà Odenan had a sense of humour to the end."

That brought back memories of when I was young. Kànìkwe's life had been saved by Kìnà Odenan and Agwanìwon many, many years ago, after he had been live-scalped in a battle with the Haudenosaunee. After they found him bleeding and weak, they nursed him back to health, and he became their constant companion, always saying that he was their protector. Even though the two women were fierce, brutal warriors who could look after themselves better than any man could, the three of them were inseparable, and none of them ever married. The women were two-spirited and became war chiefs of our family unit. Agwanìwon died at the battle of Crow Wing River.

I then looked at the group and asked, "My mother and Mitigomij ... have they gone to live with our ancestors?"

Àwadòsiwag responded, "This spring, Wàbananang was getting weaker and having trouble eating. One day, she got up from her bed and said that she was going to see your father, Mahingan, and walked into the woods. No one followed. She walked away that morning and disappeared from our lives. That was when we made the decision to come and find you, Pangì Mahingan, and the others. We had no reason to stay there, and we knew that our family unit would not be whole until we became one with you and your sister again."

"Mitigomij?" I asked.

Kànìkwe replied, "Both he and that cat are immortal."

"Yes," I replied, "I see that the three young men carry their slingshots just like he always did. Where is he now?"

"Around," was all Kànìkwe said in reply.

Just then, the rest of the group came through the grass, lead by Pangì Mahingan and Ki′kwa′ju, followed by Zhashagi, his brother Omashkooz, and the rest of the party. Hugs and handshakes were given all around, and the two Cree warriors were introduced to the newcomers.

Jilte′g asked, "How did you know to find us here?"

Wàbek answered, "We arrived at the village long after sunset, and the people told us that you had left at sunset to search for a captured warrior. When they told us that the warrior was Crazy Crow, we had to find you and help with his rescue. The boys have heard many stories about him and wanted to see this man in person. The three of them were taught how to track by their Uncle Mitigomij … so here we are!"

E´s then spoke up and said, "We are losing time, can you keep up with our rested group?"

"Try us," came the reply from Ininàtig. "We will lead the way and our boys will track . . . try to keep up with us!"

After a chorus of laughter and hoots erupted from all, the group took off at a lope, following the three young warriors. Seeing us all together again made me smile. The numbers and faces were not the same, but the fond memories of the ones who had brought us into this world were ingrained in our souls, and I knew they were smiling and watching over us.

When we reached the killing ground just before sunset that day, we had to chase off a pack of coyotes and turkey vultures. When the three young Omàmiwinini warriors took off towards the west, the rest of us were left to bury the remains of our fallen warriors. Once the burials were finished, we dragged the battered, chewed, and rank carcasses of the dogs off into the night and left them for the denizens of the darkness to feast upon.

The sun dropped below the horizon and night started to close in. Fires were started and food was taken from the dog packs. The smell of boiling berry tea filled the air with sweetness and mixed in with the sharpness of the cool, early evening.

"*Grrr!*"

Lying on the ground with their legs stretched out, our dog pack suddenly warned us of something or someone approaching. We all stood up and pointed our weapons in the direction of their collective growls.

The tall grass started to sway and we heard the sound of "*Hoo, hoo, hoo.*"

From behind me, Kànìkwe made the same sound in reply.

"It is all right," he said. "The boys are returning!"

Sure enough, the three young warriors emerged from the tall grass, each one grasping a handful of dead prairie dogs. They dropped the collection near the fire and soon had them all skinned. After throwing the insides and pelts to the dogs, they quickly put the meat on the spits that we had prepared for the evening meal.

Sitting around the fire, we passed around buffalo bladders filled with water to drink and refill our tea vessels. The dripping fat from the meat on the spits made the flames hiss, jump, and spark, and the pungent smells brought the dogs inching closer, hoping for a morsel. The prairie dog meat was quickly eaten and enjoyed, along with some turnip we had dug up.

As the fires glowed and the moon rose, we told old stories of battles gone by, which soon turned to talk about how Crazy Crow always seemed to be there for us. We now had a formidible group of twenty-four warriors in our camp, but it was still not enough to take on a strong force of Blackfoot warriors. Assuming that Crazy Crow was not already lying in ashes among the fires of the Ayaaj-inini, we would find him and make plans on how to free him. But, for now, it was time for rest.

Knowing that my family was back together once again, sleep came quickly to me.

CRAZY CROW

I turned to my Cheyenne friend and, through sign and voice, made him understand that our remaining seven pursuers would soon try to end this chase. We had proven that their single breakaway runners could not handle us, and losing two warriors was a devastating blow to them. Losing two dogs was even worse, since they were depending on them to chase us down and then corner and attack us, which would give our enemies a chance to close and finish the job. Their deaths now gave us a slowly increasing advantage. By now, our pursuers had to be thinking that we had powerful medicine, which would cause doubt in their young minds.

We had been travelling now for one full day and night. Running towards the east, the heat from the early morning rising sun was a welcome relief for our naked bodies. With only faint moonlight to guide us, our run through the evening darkness had become a battle to stay awake and warm, especially with the cool night air nearly freezing the sweat to our skin.

Now that they were down to one large dog, they were unlikely to separate the group again. Instead, they would try to run us into the ground and finish us off. When that happened, we would have to make a death stand, with the outcome to be decided only by Kitchi Manitou.

"Ókȯhkevó'omaestse," I said, using his name to get his attention. When he turned to look at me, I said in sign, "We have to run faster. They are going to stick together now, and our only chance for escape is to outrun them!"

He nodded his head in understanding, and we started to pull away from the young warriors.

It was almost midday when we started running along the bottom of a small hill to our left. I took a quick look back and saw that the dog was gaining on us, with the warriors close behind. Knowing that their stamina was better than ours and they would soon be upon us, I decided that it was time to make our stand. I shouted my companion's name, and we stopped in our tracks, determined to bring this ordeal to a bloody end.

The huge dog was almost upon us when he leaped into the air at me, his massive mouth wide open, brandishing a fearsome set of teeth covered with white foam.

7

OLD FRIENDS

ANOKÌ

After we emerged from our sunrise dreams and relieved ourselves, we hastily grabbed what cooked meat was lying around, along with what remained of the turnip. After washing it down with water from our buffalo bladders, we started running away from the rising sun, our footsteps stirring up small clumps of dirt as we went.

We could see a huge cloud of dust in the distant horizon, very much like the smoke of a grass fire drifting in the wind. The cloud was caused by thousands of buffalo migrating through the lands. Intermingled in this rising, powdery haze were the constant companions of these great herds: the cowbird, who ate the bugs stirred up by their hooves. The buffalo and cowbirds travelled as one throughout this vast land.

Off to the distant southwest, we saw the far-off flashes of lightning from an approaching thunderstorm. I envisioned the coming storm overtaking the buffalo and merging into one huge mass of animals, water, mud, and mayhem. Another quick look at the distant storm made me shudder, because the sky was not a deep blue, but black as night.

As we loped through the long grass, we came across blackened areas that had been burnt by lightning strikes this past summer, and these areas darkened our moccasins. The Ayaaj-inini (Blackfoot people) came by their name because they always burnt the prairie grass to bring it back tall, green, and healthy for the great herds to feast on. When they walked through the scorched areas after the fires, their moccasins became black from the soot.

Throughout the morning, we watched as eagles circled overhead. Kitchi Manitou sent these warrior birds out every morning to bring back news of what their people were up to each day. On the ground, well fed pashkwadjàsh (*posh-kwah-josh*: coyote), the name we use in our Omàmiwinini language, were jumping stiff-legged through the tall grass, painstakingly hunting for rodents and rabbits. Many of Kitchi Manitou's creatures were out on different adventures early that morning, and all of us were guided by their spirit.

Our group ran silently and swiftly through the early morning air. After changing direction, the distant buffalo herd was now travelling north at full speed away from the approaching storm, creating a huge dust cloud along the horizon that hid the brightness of the morning sun. Since animals have a keener sense of impending disaster than my people, there were antelope, deer, coyotes, wolves, elk, pronghorns, grizzlies, foxes, and rabbits all following behind the herd. The skies were also blackened by flocks of birds flying in the same direction. Only fire, wind, or moving ground could inspire such a panic in these animals.

Jilte′g came to my side and said, "Our warriors are becoming uneasy about the animals running away from the direction we are going towards."

I quickly held up my hand, and the group behind me stopped.

"We will take a break here. After we have a quick bite to eat and some water, we will resume. Anyone who is concerned by what is ahead of us can stay here to await our return or turn back now. We have to be near Crazy Crow!"

I pointed towards a small group of crows circling around a hill along the horizon. After calming my hunger pangs and thirst, I rose.

"Time to go. For anyone who wants to turn back, now is the time."

As I gathered up my weapons, Jilte′g and E′s came to my side. Looking behind them, I could see that not one warrior had left. It was a sight that did my heart proud.

We all watched as lightning streaked from the ground in the distant horizon. The sky was so dark that the flashes made a pathway of light towards the black blanket of cloud beyond. Given how long all of us had lived on this land, we knew full-well what we were in store for. We used this knowledge to push our bodies to run faster, eventually reaching a nearby hill for shelter. Upon reaching the top, we looked down to what lay beyond, and what we saw on the opposite side caused our jaws to drop in awe.

CRAZY CROW

Clearly intent on maiming or killing me, the dog began his descent towards me. As I stood my ground, knife in hand, and awaited my fate, everything slowed down into a dream-like state. As I braced myself for the jarring impact, a huge, black blur hit my assailant in midair. The collision was soundless until the two antagonists hit the ground, and there was a loud expulsion of air from the dog, along with a sharp, painful yelp. I turned my head towards the sudden but familiar sound of a panther scream and watched breathlessly as these two huge animals rolled into the tall grass, a howling, screaming, roiling black ball of fur, blood, and dust.

Like a powerful wind storm blowing through the land, the tall grass was flattened wherever they tumbled. After one last somersault, the big cat spun free, and the dog stood panting and heaving. A huge chunk of the dog's side had been shorn away, and I noticed that its ribs were partially exposed to the day's air. Now fighting for his life, the dog lunged at the cat with the intent to kill or be killed, but the panther stood his ground. With one mighty swipe of his claws-extended paw, it raked the dog's neck, breaking it in the process. The animal soundlessly fell to the ground, reddening the area around its death spot with blood seeping from its fatal wounds.

Makadewà Wàban stood over his kill and screamed. The shrill announcement of the panther's kill echoed across the open prairie, and the raw emotion in that sound caused my skin to rise and my body to shudder.

Looking at the animal that had saved my life, I could only nod my head. Makadewà Wàban obeyed only one person, Mitigomij, a fierce Omàmiwinini warrior who was also Anokì's uncle. This animal and his master were legends among the Omàmiwinini people as well as among their enemies. The two of them were shape-shifters, with Mitigomij being the "Trickster Hare" and the panther "Gichi-Anami'e-Bizhiw," known as the Fabulous Night Panther.

My friend, the Cheyenne, ran to my side and asked in sign language, "What is that animal?"

"A friend," I replied.

White Crow looked at the beast in amazement. The great cat was now sitting and staring at us, its muzzle red and bloody. Eventually, it stood up, shook its body, and disappeared into the long grasses.

ANOKÌ

Just as we got to the top of the hill, we looked down to see a group of Blackfoot warriors led by a huge, black dog, rapidly approaching two naked men, one of whom was our friend, Elue'wiet Ga'qaquis, and the other we had never seen before. We all stood there helplessly and watched as the dog made a leap at Crazy Crow. Then, from out of nowhere, a large, black blur, Makadewà Wàban, met the dog in mid-air, and the pair tumbled into the long prairie grass together. Everything happened so fast that I could barely follow the action. The big cat killed the dog with one swipe of his paw and then stood and screamed a piercing panther death-cry. He then sat and looked at Crazy Crow, stood up again, shook his body, and disappeared into the grass.

I turned, looked at the twins, their wives, and Kànìkwe and said, "Mitigomij has to be around here somewhere!"

Zhashagi pointed towards the Blackfoot warriors rapidly nearing the two naked men. "We must go now!" he said.

I raised my hand, emitted a shrill Omàmiwinini war cry from the back of my throat, and led a charge at the oncoming warriors. Caught by surprise, the Blackfoot quickly turned off and retreated.

I raised my hand to stop. Omashkooz, Zhashagi's brother, approached and said, "We have them outnumbered two-to-one and can end this quickly."

I pointed to a spot halfway between us and the southern horizon, where a line of enemy warriors lay in wait, ready to reinforce the retreating group.

"This is not over; we must be careful."

Crazy Crow came up to us and hugged everyone, thanking them for their timely arrival. He pointed to his friend and called him by name.

"This is my friend, White Crow, or *Oak-key-whoa-a-mast* in his Cheyenne language. He belongs to a warrior society called Dog Men. He is many suns away from his people and needs to have his wounds tended."

Àwadòsiwag and Ininàtig wordlessly approached White Crow and began to treat his wounds. Between all of us, we also equipped both of them with clothes and weapons. Kigìbigomesì, Makwa's and Àwadòsiwag's son, stepped forward and handed Crazy Crow a lance. Crazy Crow looked at it and immediately embraced the young warrior.

"Who are you?" he asked, "and where did you find this?"

"My name is Kigìbigomesì, the son of Makwa and the grandson of Mahingan. I watched a Blackfoot warrior drop this when he turned to run. I have heard many stories of this weapon and immediately knew who it belonged to."

"Thank you. My name is Elue'wiet Ga'qaquis, and I am grateful."

Now fully clothed and armed, Crazy Crow turned and walked towards the distant Blackfoot warriors. Brandishing his spear, he yelled, "Ííksspitaawa Kiááyo, look at me! Your young warriors could not kill me. I do not die easily!"

ÍÍKSSPITAAWA KIÁÁYO (IIK-SSPITAA-WA KE-I-O: HE IS VERY TALL BEAR)

Standing out in the prairie with twenty other warriors, Ki'somm Áwákaasii (*key-som ah-wah-ka-see*: Moon Deer) turned and said, "Ííksspitaawa Kiááyo, our young warriors have failed. We should have killed the two captives at the village. There will be mothers mourning their children when we return."

"We will not return without the scalps of these men," replied He Is Very Tall Bear. "Let us go and meet our young warriors."

As they made their way towards the retreating Blackfoot warriors, they noticed Mai'stóó Nínaa, or Crow Man, step away from his rescuers, shake his spear in the air, and shout something that was too distant to her. Moon Deer stepped forward and said, "Look he taunts us!"

He Is Very Tall Bear was about to reply to Moon Deer when he heard a distant snap, like a tree branch breaking on a cold winter's day. He turned towards the sound and saw two silhouettes, that of a man and a huge mountain lion in the distance. He also felt a warm liquid spatter onto the side of his face and heard the surrounding warriors gasp. When his eyes shifted back towards Moon Deer, he exclaimed in horror when he saw blood and teeth gushing from his friend's mouth. The back of his head had a gaping exit hole and was oozing the red liquid of life. Moon Deer returned his stare, made a gurgling sound, and then fell onto his side.

The big warrior looked back to where he had seen the distant figures, but they had already vanished. The day had become eerily still and there was no wind at all. Off in the horizon, he saw the giant dust storm kicked up by the running herds of animals as they fled from what they knew was coming. Very Tall Bear watched as the long line of beasts slowly disappeared into the void where the sky met the land.

The silence was broken by someone yelling, "Look to the south west … a miiyíkssopoyi (strong wind)!"

The Blackfoot pivoted towards the direction they had been running from and watched as a long sleeve of strong wind, with lightning shooting out of it, appeared from out of the dark sky. The sound was like that of a huge bull buffalo during rutting season, but many times louder. The huge wind cone from the sky began to tear up the ground and spat it out at terrific speeds, along with any trees it came upon. Then, the surrounding air emerged as a strong, powerful gale, accompanied by heavy rain.

He Is Very Tall Bear yelled to his men, "Get down on the ground and hold tightly onto whatever you can!"

With only clumps of grass and some scattered boulders nearby, the warriors held onto the earth and made themselves as small as they could. In stark contrast, the two Blackfoot Elders retrieved their pipes from their medicine bags on their pack dogs. Sitting cross-legged, they packed the bowls with tobacco and lit them. Shielding the bowls from the pouring rain and winds, they offered their pipes to the storm spirit and asked the miiyíkssopoyi to go around them.

8

DEATH COMES WITH A WIND

ANOKÌ

"Look, âhkolawew (*ah-ko-lo-will*: it is a violent wind)!" yelled one of the Cree warriors.

"Anokì, what is he saying?" shouted Jilte′g.

"Wese′an (*we-say-an*: it is a tornado)!" I answered.

Looking towards where the Blackfoot warriors had been, I could see nothing in the pouring rain except clumps of grassy ground, trees, and rocks being hurled through the air.

Yelling as loud as I could to try and be heard over the roaring winds, I pointed to the hill we had just come down, "There! Run for your lives! Lie down at the crest of the hill and hold onto each other, the ground … whatever you can grab!"

While everyone ran towards the sparse shelter of the hill, the dogs tore past us, heading east towards home.

Looking towards the southwest, I could now see the huge sleeve of wind twisting and turning from the dark sky overhead. Running towards our temporary protection, I could see the strung-out fear in everyone's eyes as they tried to save themselves. The rain violently pelted my skin, and airborne pieces of grass hit me so sharply that they slashed my skin and brought swatches of blood to the surface. My arms were now covered with blood, water, and pieces of grass, making me look like a creature from the woods.

Arriving at the top of the hill, I was finally able to dive onto the ground beside E′s. Taking a quick look around to see if everyone was safe, I caught sight of Omashkooz, Zhashagi's brother, labouring up the small incline through the intense rain and winds. Then, without warning, an arm-sized branch came twirling out of the day's darkness and slammed into his head, turning it at a grotesque angle and slamming him into the ground. I was the only one who saw Omashkooz's death; everyone else had buried their faces in the ground in an effort to survive nature's onslaught.

Mercifully, the strongest part of the wind veered around us. Gusting winds, rain, loud thunder claps, and lightning continued on until close to sunset. Eventually, we were uneasily stirred from our relatively safe protective ground by the mournful death song of Zhashagi, who was kneeling beside his brother.

We buried Omashkooz where he died, a long way from his birth home. When a warrior dies in battle, there is always the possibility that you can avenge their death with a mourning raid on their slayers. A death like this, however, is harder to accept. It is a sign from Kitchi Manitou that we cannot choose the way we die. Starvation, drowning, animal attacks, cold, and even old age can take us. Our lives are a constant part of the natural environment around us, and we live at the will of Kitchi Manitou's calling. That is why it is so important to thank him/her constantly for our time here on this land by laying tobacco down during our morning prayers and when we take one of our maker's creatures for our survival.

As we prepared to leave, we noticed that the Blackfoot warriors had disappeared from where we last saw them. There was also no sign of Mitigomij and Makadewà Wàban; they had completely vanished into this vast land.

Remembering our fallen warrior, our trip home became very solemn. When there is a loss, there is sometimes a gain, and we hoped that Crazy Crow's new friend might take Omashkooz's place in our community. Since Ókȯhkevó'omaestse was now far away from home, Crazy Crow said that it would not be safe for him to make the journey back, because there were too many enemies between our lands and his.

The area around us where the big wind had travelled was now a path of destruction. The grasses lay flat, chunks of the ground were missing, and what trees there had been were uprooted, lying solitary in the vast plains as a grim reminder of what had passed through. There were no animals in sight, nor any birds in the surrounding sky, and even the eyes of Kitchi Manitou's mikiziw (*me-kiz-zee*: eagle) could not be seen. The silence was eerie and chilling, and the surrounding sky was still black from Kitchi Manitou's fury. We were being punished by our maker, but why?

When we stopped that evening, we managed to gather enough strewn wood and buffalo chips to get a good cooking fire going. Everyone pooled their food together, and soon we had soup and tea boiling and chunks of meat hanging over the fire. All of these wonderful smells and sounds caused my stomach to tighten up in anticipation of warm food and drink. As the tea was simmering and the food was cooking, Crazy Crow stood up and thanked everyone for coming to his aid.

"The Ayaaj-inini people are very brave, strong warriors, and, as an enemy, they are to be respected. They are as powerful as the Haudenosaunee and the Nadowessioux warrior nations that we have fought in the past. We were lucky to get as far as we did before all of you came upon us, along with my friend Mitigomij and his powerful cat.

"Thankfully, our pursuers were young warriors, since more experienced men would likely have overwhelmed us early. Their downfall was that they did not think as one and were too caught up in individual glory to attack us in force, so we survived to hunt and fight another day."

Crazy Crow then gestured towards his new ally.

"My friends, I would like to offer to you my new friend and warrior, Ókôhkevó'omaestse, known as White Crow in his language, of the Nii`inaweshiiwii, who fought bravely beside me during our ordeal. Please welcome him into our community!"

A high-pitched "*lee-lee-lee-lee*" rose in a yell from all the throats surrounding the fire, signifying their acceptance of our new-found companion.

That night, we gathered around the fire, told stories, and drank an endless amount of tea, forcing me to get up and and empty my liquids on more than one occasion. With no dogs to warn us of approaching trouble in the darkness, we took turns sleeping, with two always on guard. The night was cool, but I wrapped myself up in my buffalo blanket and slept soundly until I was awakened for my watch.

With our robes wrapped around our shoulders, Jilte'g and I stood together in the starry night. Our breaths came out as foggy steam, akin to the early morning mists rising from the rivers of our lands. Both of us had slept well, so we decided to take all of the remaining watches and let the others rest and dream.

The morning sun broke the sharp lines of the distant horizon in a magnificent ball of bright red and yellow light, revealing the blanket of early morning frost on the surrounding land. Aided by the budding light, we busied ourselves by building a fire and making tea. What corn and meat we could scrounge up were tossed into a vessel full of water, followed by four or five red hot stones taken from the fire bed. Once the water came to a boil, we would have a hot soup.

Soon the aromas of tea and soup drifting through the air woke up our slumbering friends. They quickly shook the frost from their coverings, rose from their sleeping area, and walked off into the surrounding area to relieve themselves. Squatting beside the fire, we took turns dipping our cups into the pots for steaming hot tea and soup. All that could be heard was the noise of lips slurping the warm liquid and the occasional sound of early morning air releases.

After our meal finished with little conversation, we collected our belongings and took off on a trot towards the east. Although we would only have to spend one more night out on the land, there was precious little to eat in the wake of the fierce winds that had preceded us.

Near the end of the day's journey, we started to come upon most of our runaway dogs travelling in scattered groups towards our village, and we welcomed them with quick pats on the head. One of the dogs had a very bad limp, so instead of leaving him as a meal for any roaming wild beasts, Zhashagi put the animal out of his misery and quickly skinned him so we could all have fresh meat that night. Our dogs were many things to us: fighters, beasts of burden, hunters, companions, and, in times of hunger, food.

We sat around the evening's fire beside a small stream, knowing that this would be our last night out in the open. With our village only a half day away, we could take our time, knowing that we were safe from the Blackfoot. Since the dogs were now back with us, we did not have to put anybody out on watch. Two fires had been built and each one was boiling tea. Our group divided up, lying within reach of the heat, talking and sipping the hot liquid. Between the sound of the snapping fire and the dung hissing as the flames penetrated the soft, damp inner core, I quickly fell asleep, breathing in the accompanying smells in the crisp, fall air.

The brilliant rising sun hit my face and woke me up from a wonderful, dream-free sleep. The smell of tea boiling and the aroma of our remaining corn simmering in a watery broth roused my stomach muscles. Reaching out from underneath my robe to pull it away, I found that a dusting of snow had fallen during the night. We quickly drank our tea, ate what little food remained, and then started out on the trail.

Immediately, everyone took off their moccasins to cross a stream. On cold days like that, getting your footwear wet risked frostbite and a loss of toes. As such, it was always wiser and safer to wade barefoot across a cold waterway and then dry your feet off.

As soon as everyone exited the stream, they put some distance between themselves and the dogs to avoid being showered by their water-soaked coats. After climbing the small bank, the twins, Makwa and Wàbek, sat down to dry off their feet. They were so preoccupied with pulling their moccasins back on that they did not notice one of the dogs following them out. The animal sidled up close and shook, showering the pair with huge water droplets and covering them both. Wàbek stood up and swung his bow at the dog, yelling, "Get away from here, you wet dog!"

Crazy Crow started to laugh, followed by everyone else. The twins' wives, Àwadòsiwag and Ininàtig, ran over to them, showing shock on their faces and pretended to cry, saying, "Save our poor husbands!" as they dried them off with fur pelts. The twins now joined in the laughter, and soon all of the dogs were sitting on their haunches, looking bewildered and probably wondering what was wrong with everyone. After draping the furs over their husband's heads, Àwadòsiwag and Ininàtig walked off, laughing and singing. This made sure that everyone had a smile on their face as set off again.

Since there had been no food for them this morning, the dogs roamed the sides of our column, looking for mice, ground squirrels, or rabbits. Occasionally, a dog made a kill of a mouse or mole and then quickly gulped it down to avoid a theft by another dog. But when one of the animals caught a rabbit, a tug-of-war ensued between three dogs, each with a grip on a leg. The unlucky rabbit was quickly quartered and eaten, accompanied by snaps, snarls, and growls.

To our dismay, the weather had turned much colder, and now the wind whipped up, blowing snow around our feet in spinning, white swirls. Everyone had robes draped over their shoulders, desperately trying to stay warm. We were not very far from our village when Kìnà Mòkomàn, Kànìkwe's son, came up from the back of the line and said, "Anokì, there is something wrong with one of the Cree warriors! He keeps falling down as he tries to walk!"

Immediately, I knew what was wrong.

"Kànìkwe, start a fire quickly!" I said. "Zhashagi and E's ... pile up as much snow as you can get! Come, Kìnà Mòkomàn, help me carry this man back."

When we got over to the Cree warrior, he was crawling along the ground, and his friend was desperately trying to get him back to his feet. The young man looked up to us without a sound, but all of us could see the pain in his face. Kìnà Mòkomàn and I hoisted him up by his arms and carried him over to the bank of snow that Zhashagi and E′s were piling up. Soundlessly, his friend hurried behind us, carrying his weapons.

As soon as we set him down, the women started to take off the young Cree's footwear, but they stopped almost immediately. It was just as I'd feared: The young warrior had not taken his moccasins off before crossing the river, and now they were completely frozen to his feet! In response, the women quickly produced their knives and carefully began to cut off the leather, but even they couldn't prevent some of the Cree's skin from peeling away with it.

Once the moccasins were off, both women let out a short gasp when they saw that his feet were frozen white! Immediately, they placed them in the snow bank, trying to use the insulation to warm them up gently. If they had used fire to thaw his feet out, his skin would have suffered horribly from the rapid increase of heat.

After everyone blew into their hands to warm them up, they approached the Cree's frozen feet in pairs and rubbed them gently, trying not to damage the skin. By doing this, we hoped that we could thaw them out slowly, get the blood flowing, and save as many of his toes as we could. The women started up a fire to boil water for tea for the man to drink, while the rest of us started on our second turn of rubbing our warm hands on his feet.

Gradually, the redness started to return to these extremities, and he started to groan from the pain that came along with the unthawing process. He was given more tea to drink to keep him warm and prevent him from becoming dehydrated. Finally, we had done all we could do. His two little toes on each foot did not thaw out, and both were as black as charcoal.

Kànìkwe came up and handed me a red-hot bone knife and a stone war club, both of which he also held. With a nod and a stealthy approach, we quickly set our knives on each of the man's blackened toes, swung our clubs, and cut them off. The Cree warrior immediately spat out his mouthful of hot tea between us, darkening the white snow. After we quickly cauterized the wounds with our red-hot knives, Crazy Crow dropped to his knees and spat tobacco juice on both wounds. Seeing that our frostbitten friend had passed out, Crazy Crow grabbed the two toes and threw them in among the surrounding dogs.

"No sense in letting them go to waste. He is done with them!"

Very little time had elapsed during this quick turn of events, but now we waited for our passed-out patient to rise. Everyone took their drink vessels, filled them up with hot tea, and then sat and drank in silence. The dogs lay close by, clearly hoping that something else might get thrown their way.

During this time, we finally learned the names of our two shy Cree friends. The one who had lost his toes was called Kinepik, ᑭᓀᐱᐠ (*kin-a-peck*: Snake), and the other one was Cahcahkalow, ᒑᐦᒑᐦᑲᓗ° (*cha-chak-a-loo*: Blackbird). Even though they had come to our village two days before we had left, we were only learning their names just now! They were there to visit and bring meat to some Anishinaabe friends, whom they had known for many years.

When the call went out for warriors to join the search for Crazy Crow, they decided to come along for the adventure. As the mission ensued, they kept quiet and listened, which helped them learn what was going on around them. Even though Cahcahkalow told Kinepik to take off his moccasins before entering the water, the young warrior refused. He did not want to walk barefoot in the cold water and hated the thought of cutting his feet on the rocky bottom.

"He is now missing two small toes to remind him of his vanity!" exclaimed Cahcahkalow.

As we sat around the fires, awaiting Kinepik's revival, Kànìkwe spoke up and said, "I want to tell a story about a time just after I met Kìnà Odenan and Agwanìwon Ikwe, and how I became their bodyguard."

Knowing that these two powerful women were just about the last people who would ever need a bodyguard, everyone started to laugh.

"Well, I was their protector!" Kànìkwe protested, sounding slightly hurt. "I owed them my life, and, in return, I wanted to ensure that they were well looked after!"

We all conceded the point, nodded in approval, and told him to proceed.

"Well," Kànìkwe continued. "It was a cold winter, and the people of the village needed warm clothing. Not only would winter wolf pelts make fine coats to prevent our people from freezing, but they would also make a great hat to keep my bald, healing head warm. Our snares had caught a few of the animals, and we had shot a moose, but it was not enough to clothe the thirty-odd people in the winter camp. Only eleven of us were of warrior age, and we were kept busy hunting and patrolling our snares.

"Then, one day, an old Elder by the name of Miskoz-i Wàgosh (*mis-ko-zee wa-gosh*: Red Fox), called me, Kìnà Odenan, and Agwanìwon Ikwe into his son's lodge and told us the story of how he once trapped a great many wolves one winter when he was young. As he told the story, he sketched out the trap that he and his two brothers had made to lure the wolves to their demise. The man also told us that there were many wolves that winter because the snow was deep, making it easier to hunt deer and moose.

"'There will be many wolves this winter, just like there was back then,' he said. 'Follow my instructions and you will obtain all the furs you need!'

"The next day, we found a burnt-out clearing in the woods where a past fire was starting to heal, growing trees just slightly taller than a man. We piled up snow to make a large circle, the width of seven of our bodies laid end-to-end in all directions. We then tramped the snow down inside the circle. We had brought six young boys and girls along from the village, all about ten or eleven summers old, and they were assigned the task of chopping down and then sharpening the ends of as many saplings as they could. This took all of one day.

"We cut more saplings the following day and then stuck them into the crusted, deep snow, taking care to point them inward on a large slant. We then took other smaller broken branches we found on the forest floor and interwove them among the saplings on the ground to strengthen the wall. Finally, we threw many pieces of moose meat into the circle and then left the area. Walking until dark, we made a fire and some lean-tos and settled in for the night.

"The next morning, we left camp at daybreak and walked back to our wooden wolf trap. Upon arrival, we found three wolves circling our big snare, afraid to approach it. Three well placed arrows brought them down. We scaled the side of our trap, looked in, and saw that there were seventeen wolves contained in the wooden fortress. They had no way to jump back out over the inwardly pointing shafts because they would have had to leap twice the height of a man.

"Our arrows made short work of them, and we spent the rest of the day skinning the animals. We made sleds out of the saplings that we could pull through the snow and loaded them down with pelts. Three of the young ones were assigned to each sled, and we took turns pulling two others, while one of us led the column and looked out for any danger. That winter there were lots of warm wolf furs for our village."

As soon as Kànìkwe finished his story, Kinepik awoke.

"Look, Kànìkwe," quipped Makwa. "You have woken the dead."

That brought a hearty round of laughter from the group as they rose, gathered their belongings, and started on the trail.

Cahcahkalow and Kìnà Mòkomàn helped Kinepik to his feet. Once he was up, Kinepik put his hand out and said that he could manage by himself. The young Cree bravely kept up with us, although he had a noticeable limp and walked a bit like a landed shìshìb (*shesheeb*: duck).

Jilte′g came up beside me and said, "I do not think he will ever keep his moccasins on again when he crosses a waterway: a good, but tough, lesson learned."

We had sent Makwa and Wàbek's sons, Kigìbigomesì and Mashkawizì Mahingan, ahead to announce our imminent arrival and tell the village to mourn Zhashagi's brother, Omashkooz.

Around midday, we came to the small river that would lead us to the sheltered valley of our homes. As we drew near, we were surprised to see Kigìbigomesì and Mashkawizì Mahingan squatting with their backs to us, looking down the knoll that overlooked the river and our village site. Since messengers would normally remain in the village to await the arrival of the hunting or war party, it was odd for them to double back like that.

As they sensed our presence, the two of them arose from their positions. We went over to them, turned our attention to the valley below, and suddenly found ourselves standing there in stunned silence.

9

THE NIITSÍTAPI

ÍÍKSSPITAAWA KIÁÁYO

The miiyíkssopoyi left us just as suddenly as it had approached. After the winds died down, the two Elders rose from their sitting spots, put out their pipes, bowed their heads, and smiled.

Looking around, I saw that my fellow warriors were all safe and accounted for, although most of them were covered with grass and dirt. Raising my head up to the sky, I thanked A'pistotooki (*ah-piss-toh-toh-kee*: Creator) and Náápi (*naa-pee*: Old Man) for our lives, which had been spared through the prayers of the Elders.

We collected the bodies of the young men who had died at the hands of our escaped enemies. We laid them alongside Ki'somm Áwákaasii (*key-som ah-wah-ka-see*: Moon Deer), who had been slain by the mysterious shadow warrior with the large cougar, and laid each of them on their own travois to take home for burial rites.

That night, we camped close to the village, and, the following morning, we painted our faces before arriving home. Those who had lost a relation painted their faces black. Since no one had slain an enemy, there were no faces painted black with red lines. The rest of us painted our faces ochre red. That way, the village would know immediately who had lost sons or relatives.

When our arrival announced the deaths of the warriors slain at the hands of our enemy, there arose much wailing among the women. Moon Deer's family had lost both a father and a son, and they were overcome with grief. The women approached the bodies and wrapped them tightly, first in robes and then in a lodge covering. The bodies were then placed on platforms of lodge poles upon tree branches, along with their weapons and favourite personal belongings.

Once they had put their men to rest, the female relatives of the dead mourned them by cutting their hair short. For the loss of a husband or son, they also hacked off one or more finger joints and scarified the calves of their legs. For the next month or so, they would make a daily trip to some place near camp, generally a hill or little rise of ground, to cry, lament, and call the name of the deceased over and over again.

There is no fixed period or length of time that one must mourn. Some will keep this up for only a few weeks, but for others, it is much longer. I once came across a very old woman crouched in a grove of cottonwood trees, sobbing and mourning for someone as if her heart would break. On inquiring who had died recently, she told me that she was mourning her son, whom she had lost more than fifteen winters prior. Life is very precious among our people, and the dead can never be replaced in our hearts.

I blamed myself for foolishly letting the two enemy warriors free and making a deadly game out of it. I now realized that our young warriors were no match for them, especially the one called Crazy Crow. Indeed, his legendary reputation was well earned. Any warrior who could slay him would reap many honours and have stories told about this deed for ages.

The other shadowy outline, the one who had appeared on the horizon and slew Moon Deer with a slingshot, had to be the shape-shifter known as Mitigomij and the panther Makadewà Wàban. I could not help but wonder if this man who walked between worlds and his companion creature were both invincible. I hoped that it would not take many more Blackfoot lives to find out.

The ensuing winter saw many a growling stomach. Food became scarce, and the buffalo herds disappeared into the whiteness towards the south. Dogs, fish, snakes, or bear were all unfit, and we would never eat them, even if we were starving. The snow became too deep to take the dogs out on the trail, and the hunters had trouble wading through the waist-deep white lands without snowshoes. Once in a while, they would come upon a floundering antelope, bring it back to camp, and throw it into a community stew. By the time the Elders and children had eaten, there were just scraps left.

It was now mid-winter during the moon of Sawómmitsiki'somm (*sa-om-mi-tsi-ksi-som*: The

Deceiving Moon, February). Five other men and I were out hunting on a brisk, cold day with thick snow falling. We came upon a secluded valley where a herd of antelope was taking shelter. We were able to slay seven of the animals before they vanished into a massive tree grove on the west side of the ravine.

We quickly skinned and butchered the animals. After that, we cut strips from the hides and then drew them through holes at the ends of the pelts to use as a harness. The snow had been too deep to bring dogs, so we had to carry our own hunting spoils home. After piling the meat on four of the skins, we hooked the shoulder straps up to our bodies. We would all take turns pulling the precious food, with one lead warrior breaking the path back along our old trail, which was already starting to fill back up with freshly fallen snow. Another man would bring up the rear, guarding against any incursion by wolves or man.

We left three other hides and some of the larger bones behind. A wolf pack had already caught the smell of the kill and were sitting on their haunches along the ridge, looking down upon us and waiting for us to leave. Driven by their intense hunger, a few of them were already making their way down the snow-covered slopes, raising up tufts of white powder in their wake as they slid and tumbled forward. Not wanting to make a stand for what we had in our possession, we quickly left the area.

Since the hungry wolves would quickly finish off what we had left for them, our lead man and rear guard had to stay alert. If our offering did not satisfy the wolves, they would soon start trailing us for what we had. The two guards always had arrows notched in their bows, and their lances were slung over their shoulders in case the animals were too quick for the warriors to ready another arrow.

Our trek back to the village was cold and snowy. The moisture from my breath froze the cold air around me, forming ice crystals around my mouth and chin, so I was constantly brushing them off my face. This soon caused my skin to become sensitive to the touch.

As we feared, two particularly brazen wolves tried to attack our precious cargo, but our guards brought them down with a few well placed shots. We quickly skinned them for their warm winter fur and left the carcasses for any who followed. Except for the exertion of walking through the deep snow and the pelting, white flakes that endlessly lashed our faces, the rest of the journey back was uneventful.

Arriving back at the community, we were finally able to fill our bellies. While the biting cold and winter snows circled, the long nights were spent telling stories of past warrior deeds, legends of our people, and hunting trips. An aged Elder by the name of Piinotóyi (*pin-ot-toy*: Wolverine) always seemed to tell the same story every winter.

On a cold night, during the same Sawómmitsiki'somm when we had hunted the antelope, he gathered the children and adults into his lodge. It was crowded, but so warm that even the ones who sat on the outside of the circle did not have their backsides go numb. This was always a possibility, since the howling winds circling the teepee were constantly trying to creep in through the snow piled up against the lodge skins.

After their meal, everyone went silent, and Piinotóyi started to speak.

"It was a warm spring day, and I was out hunting mule deer close to the Aiiyimmikoi (*i-kim-e-kooy*: Cypress Hills) with seven of my best dogs. There was a slight, warm mist of rain falling from the grey sky. I decided to go towards a grove of alders, take shelter from the dampness, and watch the open space beyond for mule deer.

"As we neared the tree line, my dogs started to whine and growl. I looked towards the darkness of the grove, trying to detect the danger they sensed. As a precaution, I notched an arrow on my bowstring and placed three more in my teeth for quick access. I took a couple of steps forward, and suddenly my nostrils flared at the same scent that the dogs had picked up. It was the sweet smell of grass — wet grass to be exact. Immediately my heart started racing and bile rushed up my throat and into my mouth. *Grizzly!*

"As soon as that word entered my mind, an enraged female charged out of the woods with a roar, swatting aside and disembowelling two of my dogs as if they were flies. I pulled my bowstring back as far as I could and felt the feathers tickle my forearm as it left the string. The arrow hit the grizzly square in the throat, which prompted a deafening roar from the beast. Blood spurted from her neck and mouth, but she kept coming towards me. Two more of my dogs felt her wrath as she tore them open with her massive claws.

"I had no time to string another arrow, so I slipped the spear off my left shoulder and braced it against the ground. Enraged, the big sow lunged at me, and the point entered her chest, almost snapping the shaft in two as the impact drove it into the ground. I could smell the sweetness of her breath as she opened her mouth to devour my head, covering me with a mid-roar rain of blood and mucus in the process.

"Lunging to the right side of the charge, I pulled my knife from my knee-high moccasins and drove it into her left eye as she raked her claws over my left shoulder. While I stabbed her again and again with my knife, my last three dogs tore at her quivering body with wolf-like ferocity. Finally, the big bear started to weaken. Her spirit left her, and she dropped into a bright red puddle of her own blood. I collapsed beside her, my shoulder throbbing with pain, and I could see that I was covered in both my own blood and the life essence of this great beast.

"I glanced around and saw that four of my dogs were dead, and the other three were lying on the ground, covered in blood and panting heavily. For the longest time, I just lay there in total silence, with the land around me quietly mourning the death of this brave animal.

"Eventually, I washed my wound with what little water I had left and then reached into my medicine bag to gift the bear's spirit with tobacco. Taking what remained, I chewed it into a paste and applied it to my wound. I then wrapped my shoulder with moss, holding it in place with the leather shoulder strap from my lance. Feeling my stomach quiver with hunger, I rummaged around in my bag for some pemmican and quickly devoured it.

"While I sat there, I heard what sounded like a raccoon chattering. I stood up on my shaky legs and looked over to where the dogs were lying. The one female left alive had whelped a couple of pups almost two moons ago and she still had milk. As soon as I saw her, I started to laugh because a very small grizzly cub was suckling away at one of her teats! Sprawled out in a nursing position, the dog's head was raised up, and she had a stunned look on her face.

"The only thing I took from the bear were its claws. She had fought bravely defending her cub, and, as you well know, our people do not eat grizzly, because we consider the bear to be a relative.

"After spying some nearby trees, I decided to head over there for cover. During our approach to the woods, I managed to kill a small mule deer that was drinking at a spring. We had luckily come upwind to her, so the doe never scented our presence. I was able to skin it with my good arm, and, after eating the meat, both the dogs and I re-gained our strength over the next few days.

"As for the male bear cub, he followed us back to our camp, and the female dog kept producing milk until the cub was weaned. For the next two years, the bear lived in my lodge, sleeping with my family and its nursemaid dog. It never hibernated, most likely because he always had a constant source of food. He always moved with our summer camps and followed his adopted mother like an oversized shadow. When he reached almost four summers old, he was huge. One day the dog died, and, when that happened, the bear disappeared, never to be seen again."

"Piinotóyi," called a small voice from the crowd, "can you show us the bear claws and the scar?"

The old man smiled, stood up, and removed his buffalo robe and deerskin shirt. When they saw the huge claws around his neck and the deep scars on his shoulder, made from the very same claws, the children all "*OOHED*" in unison.

The crowd then stood up and left the lodge, along with the young children, who chattered excitedly about the story they had just heard.

Sadly, such happy moments were fleeting, and the contentment provided by our successful antelope hunt only lasted for a few days. Thankfully, our forward-thinking women had stored away a hidden cache of mòòkimaan (pemmican), which they brought out when our hunger became unbearable. Despite these reserves, and what our hunters managed to bring in, the people were losing weight and their bellies were shrinking. When the pemmican ran out after ten suns, we stayed alive by boiling and eating clothing skins and teepee leather.

Even after resorting to these extreme measures, and dipping into the final food cache, we still lost two children and nine Elders from starvation during the hunger months. Another casualty was a hunting party of three men, who went out one calm winter day and then never returned. Just after they departed, a huge snowstorm descended from the distant mountains and enveloped the village, so we assumed that they were lost in the same squall. The loss of fourteen members of our community left a huge hole in our hearts, so we hoped that new, young voices would soon be heard in the village and our pain would be assuaged.

Eventually, the hungry days of winter slowly started to melt away with the snow. The spring rains started, and I could smell the newness of the world beginning its birth cycle again. As the days got longer and warmer, the sleeping animals began to emerge from their winter burrow, and hunting parties were now constantly coming and going, bringing in rabbits, prairie dogs, and deer.

Although these animals would help to strengthen our hungry bodies, what we really needed were the buffalo. With a village of close to three hundred people, there were many mouths to feed, including almost one thousand dogs. Eventually, the long, tall, green grasses would lure them back to our lands, and there would be much cause for relief and celebration.

The warmer weather also lured the young men out of their lodges, and they were eager to engage in warrior training games. Even though they had been stalked by starvation during the winter along with everyone else, they still had ample young energy to burn off.

One of the first events they embarked on was wrestling. Teams were chosen, and the competitors sat opposite one another. One challenger was chosen from each side, and the winner was the one who threw his opponent on the ground. He then remained on the field of battle until someone beat him, and the team with the last man standing won. It was possible that some did not get a chance to wrestle because their teammates defeated all comers from the other side. When that happened, those who had not participated started first in the next round.

I was among many of the older warriors who sat down to watch the competitions. The first match featured a very tall boy of about eleven summers named O′mahkssa'áí (*oomps-saw-ah*: Big Duck), who was from the east row side. The west side sent out a smaller boy called A's Imitáá (*as-e-me-tah*: Young Dog). The match did not last long. O′mahkssa'áí took one step towards the smaller boy, grabbed him under his arm, threw him to the ground, and then pinned him, all to shouts of encouragement from his team.

O′mahkssa'áí defeated a parade of opponents, who left the competition grounds with bloody noses, scrapes, and dust-covered bodies. Spurred on by the increasingly boisterous cheers and whoops of the croud, O′mahkssa'áí gained more and more confidence with each win. His victories always came from the same move: taking a step forward with his left foot, reaching under his foe's right arm, and then throwing him down. Sometimes he threw them backwards; other times they were flipped forward.

With only six members of the other team left, and a full line of O′mahkssa'áí's team left, the winner seemed inevitable. Then, the smallest boy out of all of them, named Máóhkataatoyi (*mook-ka-ta-toe-aye*: Red Fox), stepped forward to a chorus of laughter from the winning side. He came out into the fighting area doing a side dance and yelling "*leeleeleelee*" to the great amusement of everyone watching.

O′mahkssa'áí moved towards the smaller boy and stepped forward with his left foot. Recognizing the move, Miskoz-i Wàgosh quickly grabbed O′mahkssa'áí's leg and flipped it up in the air, tossing his foe over on his back. The smaller boy then leapt on top of his larger opponent and pinned him. Except for a few gasps, there was complete silence, but after the shock wore off, everyone on both sides started to whoop and cheer. O′mahkssa'áí got up, shook Miskoz-i Wàgosh's hand, and then hugged him. Now O′mahkssa'áí's teammates got their chance to wrestle, all to the sound of the energized crowd.

After three suns, the young men grew tired of wrestling, so they moved on to a popular arrow-shooting game. It involved sticking an arrow in a distant bank and then everyone took turns shooting their own arrow at it. Whoever's shot came closest to the target arrow won all of the other ones shot during the round. The arrows were the blunt-ended ones we used to hunt birds, rabbits, and other small game, so no pointed arrowheads were used.

There was a genuine sting whenever you lost a round, since a lot of time and effort was put into making your arrows. As a result, there were a lot of "*oohs*" and "*aahs*" whenever someone came closer than the previous shooters. Between the fast pace, the wagering of valuable arrows, and the critical practice it gave to the young men for hunting and warfare, it was a very competitive game.

In another game that sharpened the young men's war skills, three or four boys would line up with their shields while the others fired blunt arrows at them. The targeted boys would dodge the arrows by dropping to the ground or deflecting them harmlessly away with their shields. The shields themselves were made out of dried and boiled bison skin and then hardened with glue made from bison hooves. The more layers of skin and glue, the stronger the shield. While all the young boys practiced their warrior skills, the women and young girls diligently worked away at the important task of repairing the lodges.

Meanwhile, the Elders sat in the warm sunlight, smoked to send prayers to the gods, and told stories to the young children, who were either lying on the ground or leaning up against the warm bodies of sleeping dogs. The stories they told would always recount some brave deed. They held a bundle of sticks in their hand, and, whenever they finished a story, they threw a stick down on the ground until their bundle was used up. Then another man would stand up and begin his recital.

Before long, the older boys came over to the storytelling circle to listen. Seeing how respected the Elders were for doing all of these brave things, they talked excitedly among themselves, saying, "That man was once a boy like us, and, if we follow their lead, we might accomplish as much as they have."

Young boys would frequently sneak away from the camp to follow a war party. Since they usually left without the knowledge of their parents, they were often poorly provided for, without food or extra moccasins. But by following the for, warriors and watching their ways, they learned about going to war and how to act on the war trail. They would also discover much practical knowledge about the surrounding country.

Whenever I walked through the village, I came upon a few gatherings of Elders telling stories to children, young men, and some of the women listening. Standing just outside one gathering, I listened as a young boy politely asked one of the Elders, whose name was Áísopowa (*a-so-poe*: It Is Windy), to tell them the origin story of the Blackfoot name. The Elder happily agreed and stood up to address the gathered.

"In the beginning," he said, "it is told that all the people were together at one time, and they called themselves the Piikáni (*pea-con-knee*: Peigan). As winter approached one year, the people decided to divide up into three groups. One group would stay, and the other two would move away to hunt and find food in different places so as not to deplete the supply where everyone was living. So, the people went their separate ways.

"The following summer they came back to the Piikáni camp. One group had passed through a place where they had been picking and eating red berries, and the juice from this covered their hands and mouths and looked like blood. The other group had passed through a prairie fire and the soles of their moccasins were blackened by the soot.

"From that time on, the first group who stayed behind continued to use the name Piikáni. The group that had passed through the prairie fire was given the name Siksiká. The third community that had been eating the berries, giving them the appearance of having blood on their hands and mouths, was given the name Káínai (*kay-nay*: Blood).

"There, my little ones, that's how our groups got our names," said Áísopowa. "Remember this story so you can tell your children!"

Even though I had heard this story many times, it always felt as new as the first time it was told to me.

As I continued my walk through the village, I called out for all the headmen to come to the council lodge. Upon entering the lodge, we sat, smoked, talked, and sent out prayers to A′pistotooki to help guide us in making the proper decisions in the days to come.

It was almost nightfall before we decided on a course of action. We needed the meat of the iiníí (*e-nee*: buffalo), so scouts would be sent out in many directions to find the big herd. Knowing that our enemies would also be looking to replenish their own barren lodges, we had to proceed with caution. Once the call went out for volunteers, twenty warriors quickly came forward and then immediately departed in groups of five in four different directions.

While they were gone, the women started to prepare the lodges to move just as soon as any group came back with news of discovering a herd. The lodges were definitely the heaviest and bulkiest things in the camp to transport. Most of them consisted of thirty buffalo or cow skins all sewn together in as many as four strips, which could then be pinned together when the lodge was set up.

The dogs carried our provisions, tools, and utensils, as well as the lodge strips. Being small, low-standing animals, most of them couldn't be used to transport really bulky burdens, but some of them were large enough to carry a load equivalent to the weight of an adult woman.

Even though dogs could haul babies and infants on a travois, this was a risky means of transportation. When we were moving camp three summers ago, a herd of buffalo stampeded through the column. The dogs immediately ran after the beasts, dragging the travois and scattering their loads everywhere. Tragically, three babies also fell off somewhere in the long prairie grasses and were never found.

Thankfully, the hard-working women of our Blackfoot Nation can take down and assemble the lodges very quickly. While the scouts were out, they packed all of our belongings onto the travois, which could then be easily hooked up to the dogs at a moment's notice. The niitóyiistsi (*ne-toy-yis-seas*: tipis) were left standing until one of the scout groups returned with news of finding a buffalo herd.

During this time of preparedness, the women and their daughters were constantly on the move within the community. Mixed in with the excitement of the barking dogs was the sound of laughter from the women as they swiftly went about their work. The younger girls were expected to keep the cooking fires going and make food readily available for everyone. Since the buffalo were the lifeblood the Niitsítapi, the spring and fall hunts were an exciting part of the year. The men and young boys were busy preparing their weapons, out in small hunting parties looking for game, or diligently searching for a Buffalo Rock.

As soon as they heard about the Buffalo Rock, some of the younger children cornered an Elder known as Sik Makóyi (*sik ma-koy-yea*: Black Wolf) and asked him for more of the story.

He looked at the children and said, "Everyone must sit down and remain very silent as I tell this story. It is a very important legend to our people, and you must remember how it is told so that you can pass it down to your children when the time comes. This is the story of how our people were saved from starvation one winter long ago.

"The iinísskimm (*i-nis-kim*: the Buffalo Stone) is a small rock, usually a fossil shell of some kind, which is strong in medicine and gives its possessor great power with the buffalo. The stone is found on the prairie, and the person who succeeds in obtaining one is regarded as very fortunate.

"Sometimes when a man is walking along on the prairie, he might hear a peculiar, faint chirp, not unlike the sound a little bird might utter. If he thinks the sound is being made by a Buffalo Rock, he may be inspired to stop and search the area. If he does not find it, a wise man will mark the spot and return the next day, either alone or with others from the camp to continue to look for it. If it is found, there is great rejoicing. How the first Buffalo Rock was obtained, and how its power became known, is a great Blackfoot legend.

"One winter long ago, the buffalo suddenly disappeared, and the snow was so deep that the people could not travel in search of them. So, the hunters killed deer, elk, and other small game along the river bottoms, and, when these were all killed off or driven away, the people began to starve.

"One day, a young married man killed a jack-rabbit. He was so hungry that he ran home as fast as he could and told one of his wives to fetch some water to cook it. While the young woman was walking along the path to the river, she heard a beautiful song. It sounded close by, but she looked all around and could not find the source.

"The song seemed to come from a cottonwood tree near the path. When she took a closer look at the tree, she noticed a queer rock jammed in a fork where the tree had split, as well as a few buffalo hairs that had been rubbed off. The woman was frightened and dared not pass the tree. Pretty soon, the singing stopped, and the iinisskímm spoke to the woman and said, 'Take me to your lodge, and, when it is dark, call the people in and teach them the song you have just heard. Pray, too, for the buffalo's return and you shall not starve. Do this, and when daylight comes, your hearts will be glad.'

"So, the woman took the rock back to the village and gave it to her husband, telling him about the song and what the rock had said. As soon as it was dark, the man called the chiefs and Elders to his lodge, and, just as the rock had instructed, his wife taught them the song and they all prayed.

"Before too long, they heard a noise far off in the distance; the tramp of a great herd of buffalo coming. That was when they knew the rock was very powerful, and, ever since then, the people have taken care of it and prayed to it. It is also said that if an iinisskímm is wrapped up and left undisturbed for a long time, it will have young ones. Two small stones, similar in shape to the original one, will be found in the package with it."

Sik Makóyi looked at the children and said, "*Do not forget*."

As the Elder rose up from his sitting position, excited yelling of "*Leeleeleelee!*" could be heard in the distance. The whole village looked to the east, where the sound was coming from. Two young warriors were running towards us, waving their arms.

"We have found an iinisskímm! Tonight, when it is dark, we will sing the song and pray!"

The boys created a tremendous excitement in the village. Everyone started to sing and yell "*Leeleeleelee*" and dance with great joy. With the iinisskímm, we now had hope that the buffalo would be found and our starving days would soon be behind us. That night we sang, prayed, and burned the sacred sweetgrass, hoping that the iinisskímm's magic would prove to be powerful.

The next day, as I lay in my tent, looking out the east door at the rising sun and smelling the sweetness of the early morning air, I heard the dogs start to bark. Rising quickly, I grabbed my weapons, rushed out through the tipi flap, and blew my bone whistle to alert the warriors. Men tumbled bleary-eyed from their lodges, some clothed, others naked, but all ready to defend their families.

We ran to the west side of the village and saw five men maneuver through a horde of barking dogs. It was our scouts.

"Iiníí, iiníí … we have found the great herd!" one of them declared. "They are a sun's travel from here!"

The sacred iinisskímm had not failed us. Re-entering my lodge, I said to my two wives, "The time has come. Take down the tipi, we must move quickly!"

My wives were sisters and got along very well. The oldest one, Iipisówaahs (*ipi-so-wa-ahs*: Morning Star), was with our first child. Her younger sister's name was Soota (*soo-ta*: Rain). Their mother and father had been killed in the buffalo stampede three summers before, the same one in which the infants were also lost.

No matter how many times I witnessed it, I was always amazed at how quickly the women of our community took down the lodges, packed them on travois, and then harnessed up the dogs. The village was ready to move by midmorning. All of the women, young and old, had packs of personal belongings on their backs, the amount of weight they carried dependent on their age. The men did not carry any encumbrance, since it was their duty to guard the column from enemies and wild animals as we made our way towards the Kináksisahtai (Milk River), where the scouts had seen the buffalo.

Even though the other three sets of scouts had not returned by the time we had left, they would easily be able to follow our trail and catch up to our slow-moving group. As you might imagine, it is very easy to track such a large group of people, not to mention over a thousand dogs pulling travois.

In fact, compared to other Niitsítapi winter communities, our group was a rather large one. Four years earlier, when we had first decided to winter together, our two groups had fewer than one hundred people total. Now, after remaining together for the past sixteen seasons, we were almost three hundred and fifty strong, with close to eighty able-bodied warriors.

And the group was getting stronger and larger. The past few falls, it was thought that maybe we should split up for the cold, white season. The community was growing so much that it was getting harder to feed everyone when the game became scarce. After a vote, the decision was made to stay together, but, after the near starvation of the people this past winter, I suspected that the next vote would be quite different. This winter had been a very bad one, and our hunters really struggled to keep all of the people fed.

As we set out, we noticed that the air was slightly crisp and devoid of wind. The morning sun had yet to burn off the dew, and our leggings and moccasins quickly became damp from the wet grass. The dogs' legs and underbelly hair were similarly saturated, and the ensuing wet-dog odour awakened our early morning senses a lot faster than normal. There is nothing quite like the smell of a wet dog to cause a man to move out of their path in search of some sweet-smelling morning air.

After the noon sun reached its peak, the grass started to dry, and both the dogs and our body coverings quickly dried out. The column walked all day until sunset and camped by a small stream. Nothing was unpacked that night; we just bedded down beside our campfires underneath the stars, swaddled up in heavy buffalo robes. Everyone quickly fell asleep from the day's fatiguing walk. Guards were put out around the camp and changed at regular intervals so no one was deprived of necessary sleep. We would need it, since everyone's energy levels would be challenged over the next few days.

I awoke to the sweet smell of boiling tea. Soota handed me a piece of elk meat and said, "Unless we find the herd soon, this will be the last you will have to eat for a while!"

I broke the meat into three small portions and handed Soota and Iipisówaahs each a morsel.

"We are in this together, and the two of you need as much strength as I do. Without your able hands, I would struggle for survival."

They both smiled and slowly ate what was given to them. There was lots of berry tea, and that alone gave us some much-needed strength. As we sat there with the early morning sun warming our bodies, we passed the time watching the dogs scratch, nip each other, and roll around on their backs.

Looking towards the west, I thought I saw a faint cloud of dust and what looked like many birds. As I squinted my eyes to get a better look, I could hear Sinopáá (*see-no-paw*: Swift Fox), the head of the warrior society in charge of the hunt, intruct some of his men to head towards the faint cloud to see what it was.

As they ran off with a few dogs, the remainder of our fifteen original scouts entered the camp from the east. They were covered in sweat from their long run, and each man carried a large piece of meat slung over their shoulders.

The arrival of extra men bearing food made me think that A′pistotooki was watching over us, and all of the good signs that had started the day made me hopeful.

10

THE GREAT BEAST

AT THE BLACKFOOT CAMP

Sinopáá's men were back before the sun set, and Sikapínii (*six-a-pee-nee*: Dark Eyes) gave a report.

"Prepare for tomorrow. The great herd is crossing the Kináksisahtai, and it is so large that we could not see the front or the back of it. The nearest pisskan (*piss-kahn*: Buffalo Jump), Old Man Lying Butte, is only half a day away, but I think it would be too dangerous to go there. I am sure that our enemies, either the Issapó (Crow) to the southwest or the Asinaa (Cree) to the northeast, are close to this herd. So, we would be taking a chance if we drove the animals towards a pisskan that some of our enemies may also be using."

All eyes turned to Sinopáá, the warrior in charge of the hunt. "Let us smoke and pray on this," he said.

That night, all of the hunters sat around a fire and smoked four sacred pipefuls of tobacco. It was then decided that we would do a surround of the buffalo tomorrow morning. Wearing buffalo robes and wolf skins to mask their own smell, our warriors would creep up to the herd. Once they were close enough, they would attack the animals, and then more hunters would run up with their lances to finish off any that did not go down quickly.

Rather than risk a stampede, the dogs would be held back at the beginning. Knowing that the buffalo would run just as soon as the smell of blood entered their nostrils, we needed the herd to be docile for as long as possible as we crept up on them. As soon as they started to take off, we would loose the dogs and their handlers in an effort to turn the herd back to us and keep them away from the village.

"There are also many antelopes grazing among the buffalo," said Sikapínii. "We have to ensure that they do not bolt and scare the buffalo."

Several of the older boys were asked to take a group of about one hundred dogs to get the lay of the land, watch over the hunt, and guard the killing area in case a scavenging kiááyo wandered into the area. Should that happen, the dogs would be released to run it off.

One of the Elders then told the boys a story about what had happened during a hunt many seasons ago, and why it was so important that they were chosen to watch for bears.

"Many moons ago, three young men involved in a hunt watched as a grizzly bear approached where they had killed a few buffalo. Since it was a great feat to slay a grizzly, and the claws they harvested would prove that they had slain a powerful animal, they decided to try and kill the beast. The boys knew it would be difficult, because they had no dogs with them to distract and harry the bear.

"Since they had used up most of their arrows during the hunt, they were down to only two apiece in their quivers. Unfortunately, all of their shots hit the bear in non-vital areas, which only served to enrage the beast. The huge animal had tremendous speed and reached the first boy before he had a chance to run away. With a powerful swipe of its forepaw, the grizzly tore out a section of the boy's ribs and intestines.

"While the other two managed to create some space between themselves and the bear, it wasn't nearly enough. The animal quickly caught up to both of them and slashed them across the legs. One was so severely wounded that he could not walk, while the other was able to hobble away and get help as the bear turned its attention to mauling his friend.

"When the limping boy got to where the adult hunters were, he had lost a lot of blood. The warriors rushed off to find and slay the beast, but when they got there, it was already eating the first disembowelled hunter. The other badly mauled boy died in his father's arms. After we killed the bear, the wounded boy asked for the fore claws, but we denied his request and burned the animal's body until only ashes remained."

When the story was done, the Elder looked around and said, "Our people are the rulers of the plains. A hungry wolf pack may hunt down a lone hunter and kill him in certain instances, and sometimes, if they are ravenous, they will try to steal a kill from a group of hunters. But the grizzly is the only animal that will actually hunt *us* down and kill us. We have to respect these powerful animals and their ways. We always use the dogs to drive bears off now, and we never hunt one without them."

That night, all of the men who were involved in the hunt went to sstsiiy (use the sweat lodge) to pray and prepare for the next day. At the same time, our women were busy pitching the lodges close to where the hunt was to proceed. We had chosen to camp at the bend of the Milk River Valley, near the Writing-on-Stone sacred place and in sight of the Kátoyissiksi (Sweetgrass Hills).

The young boys were responsible for running all of the meat-loaded dog travois back to the camp. Upon arrival, the Elders would unload the meat, and the younger girls would cut it into strips and then dry it in the sun on racks of cottonwood. The boys would then hurry back to the women on the killing field, reload their travois, and repeat the cycle. In order for the hunt to be successful, everyone needed to know their job and do it well.

The Kanáttsoomittaa (*kan-nat-so-me-ta*: Crazy Dog) Warrior Society was chosen to police the hunt. Since it would be their task to watch out for any enemies and bears, the Crazy Dog Society would be our guardians. But they were not as experienced as the Stumikiiks (Bull) Warrior Society, who would be going out under the skins to strike the first blows of the hunt. All of our warriors belonged to a society based on their age. They would usually move up to the next tier as a group every four or five years, with the Bulls as the oldest and most skilled faction.

As the sun rose and shone that morning through the east-facing lodge entrances, the village crier went among the sweat lodges and tipis and woke everyone up for the day. It was not long before the smells of burning buffalo chips, tea, and roasting meat were wafting through the air, entering my nostrils and awakening my stomach.

People rushed to where the meals were being cooked and helped themselves. There was a nervous laughter among the gathering, since everyone knew how important this hunt was to our survival, and the day's events would determine our immediate future. The hunters took on the most important role that day, and their success or failure weighed heavily on their shoulders.

The Crazy Dogs had been watching the herd all night, and they sent one of their men back to tell us that the buffalo were starting to rise from their rest and calmly graze around. After grabbing their skins, the Bull Warrior Society followed the Crazy Dogs to the spot where they would try and creep up on the herd.

My fellow Bull Warriors and I then started to spread out and stalk our prey. As I walked through the tall prairie grass covered with a heavy buffalo robe, my bow primed and two more arrows grasped between my teeth, my back became coated with sweat. Beads of moisture dripped from my forehead and ran into my mouth, filling it with a salty taste.

Stirred up by my movement and attracted to my scent, swarms of insects rose from the tall grasses to attack the bare parts of my body. I had to endure their bites without making any sudden moves to get rid of them, because I did not want to risk spooking the animals near me. As I stalked through the tall prairie grasses, wet from the early morning dew, both my moccasins and the bottoms of my robe soon became drenched by all of the residual moisture.

Like a smooth-flowing summer river with no beginning or end, the buffalo herd drifted around the plains. They walked slowly, grazing, grunting, defecating, and urinating the entire time. The musky odours of the animals, the pungent aroma of their dung, and the sweetness of their urine mixed in with the smell of wet grass to create a powerful early morning fragrance.

As their hooves stirred up clouds of biting insects, some of the buffalo took to rolling around on the ground in wallows to ward them off. This also helped them shed fur and cool down. As soon as the bugs were airborne, the ksííniiksi (cowbirds) overhead dove down to snatch them out of the dust-filled air.

Other cowbirds bounced around on the backs of the great beasts, pecking at their shaggy, fur-covered bodies and coming up with a morning meal of juicy insects. These prairie birds were so preoccupied with keeping up with the herds that they only paused long enough to lay their eggs in the nests of other birds. By doing so, they hoped that the new parents would not notice anything out of the ordinary and raise the fledglings as their own once they hatched.

As the huge herd moved away from its evening grounds, I witnessed a grim reminder of the circle of life. I watched as a flock of vultures and a pack of wolves snarled and screeched at each other in a frenzied feeding rite as they tore chunks of meat and fur from the carcasses of three old buffalo. Their deaths would serve to keep others alive in this complicated food chain.

By now, my heart was pounding so loudly that I thought all of the nearby animals would run from the noise of it. The warm air of my breath filled the hood covering my head, adding to the sweat running down my forehead and neck. Walking slowly in the crouched position, my back started to tighten up and cramp, and I wanted nothing more than to stand up and stretch.

I passed by an antelope that was grazing on the outskirts of the herd, and the big bull raised his head up. Seeing his nostrils flare and neck muscles twitch, I assumed that the animal had detected the faint smell of my sweat and was on the verge of leaping away and startling the buffalo. I quickly knelt down and loosed an arrow, aiming just behind the animal's left shoulder blade where the heart and lungs overlapped. The arrow struck true, the antelope coughed up a stream of blood, and it fell forward onto its front knees. Wide-eyed, he slowly dropped to his side and then died a silent death.

Later on, some of the women in their own society, the Máóto'kiiksi, would come along and butcher this animal. They were involved in organizing their part in the hunt, which included sectioning up the animals, drying the meat, and tanning the hides when given the chance. Their group was also involved in organizing important events, such as the Sun Dance.

After slowly creeping up to the animal, I cut my arrow out. I would need every one for what was to come. As far as I could tell, the disappearance of the antelope had caused no perceivable distress among the buffalo. I looked around at my fellow Bulls, and they were all closing in on their prey. As soon as the entirety of the Bull Society was within killing distance, the Crazy Dog leader, Sinopáá, would blow his eagle bone whistle to signal the start the hunt.

During my approach, I skirted a pair of iiníí bulls that were fighting over some nearby cows. They were banging heads, roaring, frothing, and kicking up a small dust storm. Occasionally, they'd back away from one another and shake their huge heads in a display of masculinity.

Waiting patiently in my crouched position, I picked out as my first kill a young cow that did not appear to be carrying a calf. When the eagle bone whistle finally blew, the cow reacted to the sound by raising her head and sniffing the air, while the two big bulls gave no indication that they had heard anything. She then went back to her grazing.

With that, I tossed off my robe, scattering all of the insects that were feasting on me. I spent my arrow, and the well gauged shot dropped the animal to its front knees. It coughed and snorted up blood until a young man from the Kakkoo (*ka-koo*: Pigeon) Warrior Society rushed up and finished the beast off with his lance.

With the young Kakkoo now by my side, I quickly moved on the big iiníí bulls. I shot two arrows, striking them in the area around their heart and lungs.

One gasped up blood and instantly dropped, while the other turned, snorted, and charged at me in a full run. Amazed that I had not even staggered this animal, I ran as fast as I could off to the side to avoid its deadly horns.

I loosened another arrow as he narrowly passed by me, and it struck in just above where the first one had entered. This stopped the bull in his tracks, and he snorted, teetered, bellowed, and stomped his one good leg in the dirt. Off to the side, I caught the sight of the Kakkoo Society Warrior lunge at the animal with his spear, but the beast turned just as the boy's weapon plunged into its neck and embedded there.

The culmination of all these injuries immediately sent the iiníí into a fit of rage. The animal took one look at his closest assailant and charged, and the terror-stricken young man took off. Even though the animal was weakened by blood loss, its lungs were shutting down, and the three shafts sticking out of his body were bouncing with each powerful step, it still had enough stamina to close the gap with the boy.

I shot another arrow into the grouping of the other two. The bull caught up to the Kakkoo boy and tried to gore him with a horn, but his nimble quarry jumped up on the animal's back, laid out flat, and grasped the bull's horns with each hand. The huge iiníí shook his head violently, and the boy flew off on his backside, sliding through the long grass and causing both dust and a few chirping ksííniiksi to rise into the air.

As the bull turned and took a few steps towards me, I set my last arrow, hoping to finish him off. At the same time, a Crazy Dog Warrior rushed out of the long grass and launched a spear into the animal's withers with such force that the lance shaft broke. Blood exploded from the beast's nostrils and mouth, and it hit the ground with a huge groan. Between the final putrid breath rushing from the buffalo's lungs and the horrid smell of its bowels emptying upon its dying moment, the collective stench brought tears to my eyes.

I watched as my ally in battle rose up from the ground, covered in dust and grass. The Crazy Dog Warrior looked at him and said, "Pigeon Warrior, you have earned your name today – Oostóyi Takáá Ohkitópii Iiníí (*o-stoy tac-ah ooh-key-toki e-nee*: He Who Rides Buffalo)!"

The newly named boy stood up, wiped the debris from his nearly naked body, and glanced around with a stunned look on his face. At the sight of this, my fellow warriors and I broke out in laughter, and the young man dropped to his knees, singing a "thank you" song to the Creator. I walked over to the big bull, pulled the boy's spear out, and handed it back to him. He received it with a huge smile on his face and then continued on his way. As I bent over and cut my arrows out of the carcass, the Crazy Dog warrior went back to his designated post to watch over everything.

We spent the better part of the morning killing as many buffalo as we could get near. They were now on the run, and the imitáá (*e-me-taa*: dog packs) were let loose to turn some of the animals back towards us on the open grasslands. This meant we had to be extra cautious because once the main herd smelled blood and started to run, we had to stay clear of them or be trampled. Many a warrior has lost their life when these mighty animals suddenly decided to run from danger.

Our small group, consisting of three fellow Bull Warriors, two Crazy Dogs, and four young Kakkoo boys, were busily slaying any animal that the dogs could turn back towards us. The escaping animals were rising up in a ghostly haze of dust, which I feared might draw the attention of hunters from other nations. I took a moment to survey our hunting grounds, counted thirty-three carcasses lying on the land, and started to smile.

Suddenly, a hand grasped my left shoulder. I turned to see who it was and noticed drops of blood reddening my bare shoulders. One of the young men had an arrow sticking from the back of his throat and out the front. Instantly, I knew who our attackers were, based on the feathers and make of the arrow.

"Kotonáá'wa (*coo-ta-gnaw*: Kootenai) warriors!" I yelled, hoping to alert everyone within earshot.

11

DEFENDING OUR RIGHT TO LIVE

WITH THE YOUNG man's life swiftly leaving his body, I slowly and gently lowered him to the ground. I then reached over my shoulder to grasp an arrow from my quiver and realized that there was only one left. I slipped the notch of the shaft onto my bowstring, looked in the general direction that the boy had come from, and saw nothing.

Three young men, all armed with lances, arrived at my side. Like me, the other Bull Warriors only had one or two arrows left. The two Crazy Dogs, who had not been hunting, each had a quiverful, and they shared their arrows with me and the other three Bulls. Even then, we only had five apiece. I grasped two shafts with my teeth and knelt down on one knee, but there was still no sign of the enemy.

In the distance, I heard Sinopáá blow warnings with his eagle bone whistle, which meant that others were also being attacked. With our warriors strung across the buffalo killing fields in small groups of five or six men, the Kotonáá'wa would decimate us in batches if they attacked in force.

After our group took cover behind two kills that we had just made, we hastily cut out our arrows to supplement our meagre weapons cache. The buffalo were starting to smell, and if we did not drive these unseen warriors away soon, we would be fighting bears and wolves for our kills.

Ni'tókskaa Kiááyo (*knee-tooks-kaw key-i-yo*: One Bear), one of the Bull warriors, whispered to me, "Where are they? They slay one boy and then run? They have to be somewhere near!"

As the buffalo herd continued on its journey north, its ranks were thinning out, and many carcasses dotted the land. Among the dead animals, we spotted several downed Blackfoot warriors and many others like us taking cover. Among the casualties were some of the Crazy Dogs, taken by surprise while they were guarding us during the hunt. Clearly, the Kotonáá'wa had been slowly picking off individual warriors, which told me that they did not have the numbers to attack us in force.

Spread out like they were, our men were leery about the open distance they would need to cover in order to rally back together. I also noticed that both our dogs and their handlers, who had been tasked to turn the herd back towards us, were nowhere in sight, making us wonder if they were all dead.

Suddenly, one of the young boys pointed towards the distant mountains and said, "Look, Ííksspitaawa Kiááyo! That small hill over there, I see movement!"

All of our eyes turned towards his hand motion. In the distance, we could see about twenty Kotonáá'wa warriors emerging from the back of the hill. They started towards us at a fast lope and slowly spread out into a ragged line. As they neared us, they dropped to one knee.

"Get down as close as you can into cover!" I yelled.

A volley of arrows flew through the air and made a series of thudding noises as they hit the ground around us or embedded into the carcasses we were hiding behind. One of the Bulls failed to tuck himself close enough to a dead buffalo and took an arrow to the thigh. Without making a sound, he took his knife from its sheath and cut the arrow out of his leg. Reaching into his medicine bag, he put beaver castor on the wound and added áóhtoksóo'ki (yarrow) to it to stop the bleeding. He accomplished this quickly and without a single exclamation of pain.

Frustrated by our situation, I looked at the men and boys around me and spurred them to attack by saying: "Today we die as warriors! *Leeleeleelee!*"

As we stood up, we heard a continuous series of shrill yells off to our right, coming from the direction of our camp. The Kotonáá'wa and our group looked towards the sounds and saw women, Elders, and children all bearing weapons and running through the waist-high prairie grass. They were closely followed by a few warriors and a pack of several hundred dogs. Once they got within range, they stopped and let loose with a barrage of arrows, lances, and stones.

After several Kotonáá'wa warriors fell with arrows and lances protruding from their bodies, their companions tried to drag them off the field. They scrambled in full retreat towards their distant lands with a huge pack of our dogs harrassing any stragglers. Eventually, they were forced to abandon some of their wounded, and those poor souls disappeared under a wave of howling, slobbering dogs.

My two sister wives, Iipisówaahs and Sinopáá, approached me. They each held one of my lances and had huge smiles on their faces.

"After what happened here today, we will have to add the Máóto'kiiksi to the list of warrior societies!" I said to them.

"It was all of us," Sinopáá answered, "Elders, children, and women!"

I stood there, listening in rapt fascination as she explained what had happened.

"One of the children who came back to camp with a load of meat said that there was trouble on the hunting ground. By that time, many of the women had rushed back from the scene and the warriors running the dogs were approaching the village. So, everyone grabbed what they could and rushed to the aid of the hunters."

She paused to survey her surroundings with a grim look.

"I see, though, that we lost some of our men. There will be mourning and dancing in the next few days;

sadness over the loss of our fallen warriors and happiness over the success of the hunt."

"Yes," I replied. "The Kotonáá'wa are long gone now, and we can continue the butchering of the iiníí. This day will be remembered with a mix of sadness and happiness."

Following my two wives over to one of the iiníí I had slain, I bent down and cut out the hot liver, followed by the gall bladder. Squirting bile from the gall bladder onto the liver, I sat down to enjoy this delicacy while my mind pondered just how close I had come to dying here today.

The timely appearance of these so-called weaker members of our community on this field of death had saved many of the stronger ones from travelling on to be with their ancestors. The Blackfoot warrior has always been feared and respected by our enemies, but now stories would be told of how the women, children, Elders, and dogs drove off a war party of Kotonáá'wa warriors during a buffalo hunt. I smiled, knowing that this would contribute even more to the legend of the Blackfoot people.

After I finished my delicious meal, I looked around. Women were busy cutting chunks of meat from the huge beasts, their hands covered with blood and their clothing spotted with crimson. Periodically, they would pause to toss a piece of meat to the pacing dogs or hand a bloody chunk to a grasping child. After a dog travois was laden down with meat, their young guides would whisk it away back to the village, where an expert team of older women would cut it up into strips and dry it over the fires. This would form a hard crust on the meat and prevent flies from laying eggs on it.

I walked over to where my wives were working together on a carcass and knelt down at the head of one of the bulls that we had slain. Taking out my knife, I cut out one of the beast's jawbones. After raising it up in the air and swinging it around my head, I could tell that the heft and weight was perfect. It would become a very useful weapon in the future.

The first things that the women removed were the tongues and organs. The body was then cut up into eleven pieces for transport: four limbs, two sides of ribs, the brisket, the croup, the two sinews on either side of the backbone, and the backbone itself. After the women cut the meat from the big bones, they would smash them open with rocks and eat the delicious delicacy of marrow on the inside. As they worked away, they would share this with the children guiding the dog travois.

Flies, crows, ravens, and buzzards all decended on the area as the afternoon heat amplified the stench of the kill. Knowing that all they had to do was bide their time and wait, a few bears and wolves, along with a pair of cougars, patiently roamed the perimeter. Once the humans left, there would be enough scraps for all.

While the meat was being prepared, the women would scrape the hair off some of the buffalo robes to make sootsímaan (parfleche) bags. After this rawhide was stretched to dry, animal glue obtained from boiling buffalo hoofs was spread on the hide for protection. The women would then paint designs on them using charcoal, algae, and ochre for the colours. The bags would then be used to store meat and mòòkimaan.

The women had also placed a basket nearby to collect entrails, which were streaked with slim lines of snow-white fat. After returning to camp, Sinopáá would take them down to the river and wash them thoroughly. Then, after bringing them back to the lodge, the women turned them wrong side out to keep the fat on the inside. Nut-sized chunks of meat would then be cut up and stuffed inside. Both ends would then be tied up with sinew.

That evening, the entrails were placed on the hot embers to roast and then continually turned to keep them from burning. They were then thrown into boiling water until Sinopáá said they were ready. The delicious juices dripped down my chin as I devoured my share.

We call this delicacy *is-sap-wot-sists* (put-inside-entrail), which includes the Blackfoot name for the Crow Nation: Issapó. This made me wonder if they had taught our people to cook the entrails during one of our peace treaties with them, and that is why we included "Issapó" in the Blackfoot name.

The following evening, the community had a big feast to celebrate the success of the hunt, a hunt where many irreplaceable lives had been sacrificed in order to protect the rest of us.

After the men and boys dug two large bowl-shaped pits, they lined both of them with flesh-side-up buffalo robes to make a seal and then filled them up with water. At the same time, stones were placed into a nearby burning fire. As soon as they were glowing red-hot, we used forked sticks to move the stones into the water pits. By continually replacing the cool rocks with hot rocks, the water was quickly brought to a boil, and the meat was then added to cook. Two nights after this feast, my wives roasted buffalo udders and teats, another delicacy that the three of us shared.

We spent most of the summer camped there, hunting game and repairing the tipis with our new buffalo robes. The women and men would paint the lodges with male animal shapes on the men's side and female animal shapes on the women's side.

One mid-summer day, I walked among the tipis and thought about what needed to be done before the fall hunt. There was definitely one thing I needed to fix: a mistake that I alone was responsible for.

12

WINDS OF CHANGE

ANOKÌ

After returning from the rescue of Crazy Crow, our group of warriors stood on the knoll overlooking the village. Tears rolled down my cheeks as I studied the devastation laid out before us.

Mashkawizì Mahingan turned to me and said, "Uncle, this is how we found our home. We did not go down and disturb anything; we just sat here and looked and prayed to Kije-Manidò. Did we do the right thing?"

"Yes, you and your cousin did the right thing," I answered.

Turning to the others I said, "Let us go down and see what we can do."

Slowly, we walked down the hill. From our vantage point, it looked as if animal carcasses had been strung up throughout the village and surrounding area. Scavenging wolves, crows, ravens, and vultures were devouring as much carrion as they could gulp down, so we tossed rocks and yelled at them to scare them off. Upon closer inspection, we realized that they had been eating the same chunks of buffalo and antelope meat meant for our winter stores.

Clearly, the women had had very little time to section the meat up for the drying racks or process it into pemmican. What little they had managed to do now hung from broken trees, rocky outcrops, and the tassels of the long prairie grasses. Worse still, the people of our community had had to abandon the larger pieces, as they were now scattered throughout the grounds and the grasslands beyond the village.

Although the Wese'an (*we-say-an*: it is a tornado) had demolished just about everything, many of the skins from our lodges had been snagged in the roots of a few upturned trees. Looking out over the land, I could see a trail of articles from the village scattered along the path of this great wind after it tore through the community and spat out what remained of our lives.

The two women among us roused the men from our dazed trance, shouting orders to retrieve the lodge skins from the roots and collect as many robes, cooking items, food, and other useful things as we could. The three students of Mitigomij gathered up as many lodge poles as possible to make travois for the dogs while others crafted simple leather harnesses cut from the large skin of a destroyed tipi. Whatever we could salvage from the devastated village would be loaded onto the pole sleds to move with us.

While another group of warriors went back to the river to fill up all of our waterskins, others started searching the surrounding area to see which direction our people had gone.

Jilte'g, Crazy Crow, and the Cheyenne came back just before nightfall and said they found the trail our people had travelled. It led off to the north, away from where the big wind was headed when it tore through the village.

"We know where they will be going," said Kinepik, the younger of the two Cree warriors.

"In the spring, around this time of year, our people camp near three lakes that host many waterfowl. We call the lakes Sewitakan (*see-wit-akan*: Salt) because the water is undrinkably salty, even though the rivers that flow into them have lots of fish and good water. While camping there, they hunt all types of geese, ducks, cranes, and other waterfowl. Along with dried buffalo meat, the birds we dry over the fires are a staple food for us during the winter. After this great fall bird hunt, our people separate to our winter camps."

Zhashagi looked at me and said, "Anokì, after we rest and eat tonight, we can set off early in the morning for the area that the two Cree men have told us about. It only makes sense the community will be going there after escaping the big wind. Your wife and children brought back Cree warriors to protect our village during our search for Crazy Crow, and those warriors would take them to where they knew their people would be."

"Yes, Zhashagi, that does makes sense," I replied. "We will rest here for the night."

"Good," said Zhashagi. "I need time to mourn my brother."

Sitting around the fire, I looked at Kànìkwe and asked him how they were able to find us and how much time had passed since they had left the river of our homeland, the Kitcisìpi Sìbì.

"Anokì, we left when the ice of the Kitcisìpi Sìbì started to break up during our Omàmiwinini moon Kà-wàsadotòj (*ka-wah-suh-koh-tooj*: April). Once your mother passed, we approached Mitigomij about coming west to find you and the rest of the family, since there was nothing holding us in our homeland anymore. The twins wanted to be together with you and Crazy Crow again, and their sons wanted to see, in person, the legendary warriors they had heard about in stories since they were young.

"We paddled from dawn to dusk and ate fish for most of the trip. One day, we were able to slay a mònz (*moans*: moose) that was feeding along the shore of the river we were on, and another time we managed to take two wàwàshkeshi (*wa-wash-ke-she*: deer) who were swimming across a lake. When we camped, it was always at dusk, and there was no time to hunt. Any fresh meat we were able to slay always came by chance. Fresh meat was a wonderful break from all of the fish that we had been eating.

"When we left the big lake that the Anishinaabe call Gichigami (Lake Superior), we came upon another inland lake, where we met two Anishinaabe warriors and an Omashkiigoo (*oh-mush-key-go*: Cree) warrior fishing. They called the lake they were on Pikwedina

Sagainan (the inland lake of the sand hills — Lake of the Woods).

"After introductions, and telling the story of where we were from and where we wanted to go, the three of them all said that they knew you and your people. That night we camped and shared what food we had between us and our new friends.

"The next morning, they took us towards a river they called Miskoseepi (Bloodvein River). It took us many suns to get there, and, even after we arrived, it took another seven suns to get to the rock walls where the river drained into a big lake. It was there that they showed us a rock where you, Zhashagi, and the rest of the people had drawn pictures when you had arrived in this part of the land. We added some of our own to show that we had also been there. Our guides were very proud to show us these drawings and to tell us that they knew who you and your people were.

"The three of them led us to your village on the other side of the big lake where this river drained into what the Cree called Wīnipēk (Lake Winnipeg). We paddled across this shallow, muddy lake and portaged to another, which the Cree called Manito-wapâw (Lake Manitoba). After paddling across this larger body of water, we stashed our canoes, and the three men led us to your village.

"It was close to two hundred suns making our way to you; a real adventure! Sometimes, we were hungry, and, many times, the bugs ate away at our bodies before we could get our fires going and smudge them away.

"But it was all worthwhile, Anokì. We are now together again, like in the time of your father and uncles when they battled the Haudenosaunee and the Lakota. We have buried many friends, but our seeds have been spread, and we now have others to take our place when our ashes become part of the land. Now, my friend, when am I going to meet your son and daughter? I know that Mitigomij is also anxious to see them."

"Hopefully, Kànìkwe, you will meet them when we get to the Sewitakan Zaaga′igan (*see-wit-akan saw-ga-eh-kan*: Salt Lake) area," I replied. "Where is Mitigomij?"

"Anokì, he and the black cat are getting older, but their powers are growing, especially now that they like to stay in the darkness and keep to each other. They will show themselves when it is time, and always when the time is right!"

"Kànìkwe, I have always been of the opinion that Crazy Crow has special powers. I have heard the story of the Mi′kmaq finding him in a canoe floating down river, guarded by crows on the boat and in the air, and that Nokomis raised him. Stories of how he and Glooscap were close friends before that tall warrior and his dogs, Tepgig (*dip-geek*: Night) and Na′gweg (*na-quik*: Day), as well as his little person warrior friend, Apistanéwj (*a-bis-taw-ouch*: Marten), returned back to the land of the Mi′kmaq."

"My friend," replied Kànìkwe, "I believe that the Mi′kmaq warrior Elue′wiet Ga′qaquis, whom we call Crazy Crow, is just a very skilled combatant watched over by Kitchi Manitou's creatures, the crows. His abilities in battle are second-to-none, but unlike Mitigomij, he wears the scars of a being, like we do. Other than his fighting prowess, I have yet to see him use any special powers. I do not know why he has such an affinity for the crows; perhaps he is a shaman and they are his spirit guides. What I *do* know is that he is a great friend and warrior, and that is enough for me."

Looking from Kànìkwe towards the fires, I watched as Crazy Crow and his Mi'kmaq warrior friends, E's and Jilte'g, laughed and told stories to my sister, Pangì Mahingan, and her husband, Ki'kwa'ju. Pangì Mahingan's husband was an Eli'tuat (*el-e-do-what*: Men with Beards) warrior that had been captured by the Mi'kmaq when he was young. The Mi'kmaq community made the decision to send him to live with our Omàmiwinini band many summers ago. He married my sister, and, hopefully, a child will soon be born. When I look at him, I wonder if their children will have the light hair and blue eyes of their father.

Before building the evening fires, we erected temporary lodges to keep us dry from the rain that started just after dark. Between the steady rhythm of the raindrops and a warm dog curled up beside me, I soon fell asleep.

I woke up just as the sun broke the horizon and immediately noticed that the chilly, damp air was infused with the sweet smell of burning wood. The women, along with the three young warriors, had gotten up early to start the fires, and they were already burning brightly. The wood crackled and snapped as the tea boiled, and the smell of whatever meat was cooking drew us to their collective warmth.

Not many words were spoken in our group. Crazy Crow, Kànikwe, the Cheyenne, and the two Cree warriors ate quickly, then they left to scout the trail ahead of us. By blazing a trail and keeping a keen eye out for danger, they put considerable distance between themselves and the main party

I walked up to Kànìkwe's son, Kìnà Mòkomàn, and said, "Come with me. We will walk in the lead."

After loading the dogs' travois up with every usable item that we had scavenged from the camp, we headed out in front of the group. Following the blazed trail marked by Crazy Crow and his group, Kìnà Mòkomàn and I got quite a ways ahead of the pack by midmorning.

Suddenly, we heard the scolding screech of a diindiisi (*tchin-dees*: blue jay) – sentinels of the forest who warn of intruders in their land. It dove from the tree tops on the other side of the beaver dam that we were walking across. The dam was huge, and the pond that it was holding back was the size of a small lake.

The noise of the jay sent chills down my neck and caused my hair to stand on end. Since this jay had not seen us yet, I knew that it was not warning about our approach. Something, or someone else, had gotten his attention.

Knowing that something was concealed from our view, the faint trail we now walked along suddenly took on an ominous feel. I turned to Kìnà Mòkomàn and motioned for him not to talk. At that moment, I wished we had brought a dog along to warn us of any nearby danger and let us know what direction it was coming from. Had the jay been disturbed by something after our five scouts had passed by? Or had an enemy surprised and slaughtered our warriors, and now the jay was stalking their attackers for its own reasons?

I do not like surprises when I am alone on a trail. Sunbathing snakes and the sudden, fluttering takeoff of a partridge always gives me a start and makes my heart race. Even with Kìnà Mòkomàn accompanying me, I was still on edge.

As we neared the blue jay's relentless attack from the sky, we each silently prepared our bows with an arrow. Anxiety over the unknown caused my body to dampen with sweat, and my lips became dry from the lack of moisture in my mouth. Meanwhile, Kìnà Mòkomàn seemed undeterred by what lay ahead; a possible sign of his inexperienced youth.

Stepping off the beaver dam that we had used to cross the pond, we walked towards the long grass of the meadow. The jay was still screaming and diving towards the ground, and now I could see the shoulder-high grasses violently waving from side-to-side. Someone, or something, was moving the stalks as it came towards us.

The action of the grass was accompanied by a deep-throated growling and snarling sound. At first I thought it was a bear, but then the unmistakable, rancid smell of what is sometimes mistaken for a skunk struck our nostrils, causing both of us to sneeze, cough, and gag. The jay buzzed my head at the same time that I was almost run over by a Gwiingwa'aage (*gwing-gwa-ah-gay*: wolverine) carrying a mouse in its mouth.

As I speculated on what likely had happened, the tension drained from my body and I chuckled to myself. The Gwiingwa'aage probably outwitted the diindiisi by stealing the mouse after the jay had killed it. It was the case of one thief robbing another!

"Anokì," chuckled Kìnà Mòkomàn, "That was a lot about nothing!"

"Well, I do not know about you, but I broke out in a sweat wondering what was coming towards us through the meadow. That will be the last time I leave without a dog to accompany me!"

We continued on our way, laughing about our scare. By the time the sun dropped towards the midday sky, we had come upon an acceptable camping spot next to a small, crystal-clear stream. The river had fish in it, and there was plenty of deadfall lying around to start a fire with.

Kìnà Mòkomàn took off his moccasins and waded into the water with his spear to look for fish while I gathered wood and piled it up on the chosen site. After collecting enough wood to supply our overnight needs, I started to gather up some rocks to construct three fire pits. I also made sure to place several fist-sized rocks into the pits, which would be used as water-boiling stones to make tea and cook the smaller fish. We would roast the larger ones on sticks over the fires.

When the fire pits were finished, I retrieved a piece of leather from my shoulder bag, made a mid-sized bow from a small ash tree limb, and then entwined a pointed stick in the string. I then found a flat piece of wood and made a hole in it that was about the same size as the stick's point. Finally, after carving a "V"-notch from the edge of the wood into the hole, my fire-starter was complete!

I placed a small pile of dried grass under the notch and then pulled back and forth on the bow with my right hand, causing the stick to spin. To keep the turning stick in place, I gently held the top of it with a small, flat piece of wood in the palm of my left hand. This caused the wood to heat up, and the resulting embers immediately ignited the dry grass. I fed this with some small twigs, and pretty soon I had a fire going in all three pits.

"Anokì," Kìnà Mòkomàn yelled, "I have speared all the fish that I could see. Now we need to clean them."

I looked over and saw close to twenty fish flopping around on the ground. As we started to clean them, an eagle suddenly swooped down with a screech from out of nowhere, grasped a fish in its huge claws, and then took it skyward.

"It is always a good omen when an eagle shares our meal," I said to Kìnà Mòkomàn.

He looked up at me from his task, popped a piece of fillet in his mouth, and smiled.

It took us very little time to skin the fish, cut off the heads and tails, and then debone them for our meal. We then scattered the inedible parts around the campsite as a treat for the dogs when they arrived.

As Kìnà Mòkomàn and I prepared the fish, I could only wonder if this would be one of our last meals before we arrived at the Sewitakan lakes. After running for their lives away from the big wind, it would be a while before the deer, moose, and antelope returned to the area.

Led by the tree blazes and the smell of the fires, our companions soon arrived. As soon as the dogs were freed from their travois, they ran to the stream for some fresh water. After emerging from the river, they located and wolfed down all of the fishy snacks we had left scattered around for them and then celebrated by happily rolling around on their backs.

The young Cree warrior, Kinepik, was limping badly when he arrived. As soon as he sat down, the twins' wives, Àwadòsiwag and Ininàtig, had him remove his moccasins so they could examine his feet. They immediately chewed some tobacco, spat the juice on his toes, and then rubbed it into the wounds.

Meanwhile, I searched the travois for some buffalo stomachs to boil our water in for tea. After finding three, I hung them up on notched sticks and then filled them with water. I then used a forked tree limb to remove the red-hot stones from the fire pits and drop them into the sacks. As soon as the water started to bubble and froth, I tossed in handfuls of berries and chunks of honey to make a sweet berry tea.

Leaving the tea to boil, I found two leak-proof baskets, filled them with water, and then added more boiling stones. I then threw in some fish, along with what little meat we had left, as well as some dried roots and prairie turnip. Between this cooking stew and the remaining fish roasting away on skewers over the fire, my nostrils were alight and my mouth was watering.

The voices of men and women in quiet conversation could heard amidst the crackling sounds of wood burning. This, in turn, was punctuated by snapping and growling noises as the dogs discovered, and then promptly fought over, the remaining fish scraps. All told, it was a typically quiet Anishinaabe, Omàmiwinini, and Omashkiigoo camp site.

After scooping up a cup of stew and another of tea, I sat on a log and wondered if Osk-îskwêw, Wâpikwan, and Môso had found safe haven from the big wind. Since my family was immeasurably strong, and our devoted pack of littermate dogs would protect them to the death, I still held out hope that they had gotten to safety.

Around the fire that night, the two Cree, Kinepik and Cahcahkalow, told us that it would be eight to ten suns of travel to get to the salt lakes. At this stage, any larger animals that did not run from the big wind, like moose and deer, would now be deep in the woods for their winter protection. Because of this, fish and beaver would likely be the only food left to forage. It would take time to stop and spear them, and that would delay us from getting to our destination.

Because they were familiar with this land and knew where we had to go, it was also decided that the Cree would now be our advance scouts. Crazy Crow, the Cheyenne, and the twins, Makwa and Wàbek, would travel with them. Kànìkwe and the three young warriors would handle the dogs, and the rest of us would guard the sides and the rear. If possible, we would try and camp near water so that we might find fish, clams, or crayfish to eat.

Kànìkwe spoke up, "Hunger will stalk us on this trail!"

His words were followed by murmurs and whispered agreements. All of us knew that a warrior's path was filled with danger, and hunger was an enemy we were often forced to contend with.

Cahcahkalow then spoke, "Tomorrow we will find the well worn trail that our people took to the lakes. The travel will be easier, but the berries, roots, and nuts will have been picked clean from the trees and bushes by those preceding us. Even the streams will have very few fish. When we find the walking trail, we must decide if we continue on this easy path, where the food will be lacking, or do we branch off and make our own way through the land, where the travel will be harder but there may be more food?"

Zhashagi answered, "We will make that decision when we are forced to. Tonight, we have food and warmth, so let us enjoy this day that we have survived. When it comes time, Kitchi Manitou will guide us to make the right decision."

"Kitchi Manitou will protect us!" the group said in unison.

Zhashagi stood up and said, "I need everyone to gather up all the food they have on themselves and bring it here to the fire pits."

After everyone brought forward what could be found, Zhashagi made eight piles and then directed the three young warriors to put each one on a separate travois.

"Although this is not much for over twenty people to share, it will be our food for the next eight days. After our morning meal, we will give each person an equal portion to get us through the day. What is left from the pile will be our evening meal. Of course, we must always be alert for any game we come across during the day's walk.

"When we let them loose from their travois at night, the dogs will have to scavenge for mice, moles, and anything else they can find. Although there is a limited number of bones in our stores, the dogs can have them after we break them open for marrow. The Blackfoot might not eat dog meat or fish, but we will if it saves us from starvation. But before we start down that path, the last resort will be to boil and soften up the tipis leather to eat and drink the broth."

Many of the older warriors gathered around had eaten everything that Zhashagi had mentioned during past brushes with starvation. Even though the younger ones might turn their heads at the prospect, starvation forces us to eat anything in order to survive.

Kìnà Mòkomàn, Kigìbigomesì, and Mashkawizì Mahingan all came forward, and Mashkawizì Mahingan said, "Since we are responsible for the dogs being on this journey, we will take one of the tipis that is in very bad shape, cut it up into strips, and feed a little bit to the dogs each day to help sustain their strength. We will also search for squirrels during the day and give the guts and fur to the dogs. Should any of the weaker dogs die from starvation on this sparse diet, we will look after preparing them for our meals."

After gathering up enough stones to represent every member of our party, Zhashagi then marked three of them with charcoal. Everyone, except the Cree warriors, then drew lots. Kànìkwe, Jilte'g, and Wàbek's wife, Ininàtig, drew the black stones, so they were given extra rations and tasked to travel away from our group every day to try and find game or anything else we could eat. That night we all slept on full stomachs, knowing that this would likely not happen again any time soon.

We trudged on over the next two days, following the lead of the Cree men. Other than catching some rabbits, squirrels, and a few grouse, our hunters did not have much success. We threw everything into the boiling water, along with some leather, to make a bush stew that was not particularly tasty or filling. What little berries we found went into making tea.

By day four, our failing strength was slowing us down, and this would extend our journey by another two or three suns. Even after a dog died, it was not nearly enough to fill our stomachs. We needed to find a moose, since it would supply both us and the dogs with enough food to get us through. It wasn't just the big wind that had sent the animals into a panic and driven them far north from that danger; they would also have been spooked by our families trekking through the bush.

Midway through our fifth sun of travel, we came upon a campsite used by our escaping family. Unlike previous sites, this one had the bones of a large moose lying around. Frantically, both man and dog alike dove at these bones like a pack of ravenous wolves. We smashed them apart with rocks for the life-sustaining marrow inside and then threw the remnants into boiling water in an effort to render off anything that we could not scrape off with our knives. This would make a thin soup for us, and the dogs would get the shards. Only when bordering on starvation does a feast of bones feel like eating the choice cuts from a moose.

If not for the fact that we were all in good physical shape, many of us would already have succumbed to the darkness of starvation. I have seen communities in the troughs of hunger, and it is horrible to behold. At first, they start shivering because they cannot get warm, and they have trouble sleeping, but this eventually leads to hair loss and bodily functions shutting down.

So far, the only thing that seemed to be happening to some members of our group was difficulty sleeping and fatigue quickly setting in during our travels. Nothing too serious was breaking down yet, but I knew that we were on the verge of much worse things happening. Every day a dog died, and, although it provided some sustenance, it did not supply us with nearly enough food to bring everyone back to full strength.

Hunger pangs and exhaustion had clearly taken their toll, and there was very little conversation around the fires that evening. The Cree warriors, Kinepik and Cahcahkalow, sat across from me, my cousin Makwa, and his wife Àwadòsiwag. Out of nowhere, Makwa started to speak to me in our Omàmiwinini tongue so that the Cree could not hear what was being said.

"Anokì," he said in a low whisper, "Look at the fire-light shining on Kinepik's left leg."

"What am I looking for, Makwa?" I replied.

"Do you see the big, red bruise on his foot and above his ankle, as well as a thin, red line running up his leg from that?"

"Yes, Makwa, I do. His leg is poisoned and he must be in immense pain!"

Àwadòsiwag spoke up and said, "I have seen this before in wounded warriors after a battle. He will only last another day, two at the most. The only way he will survive is if we cut off his leg."

"Most would not give up the affected limb and would rather die a painful death than lose an arm or a leg," Wàbek turned to his wife and said. "We know that Kinepik is just such a man, and he will never let us take his leg. He will choose death and want to keep going so that he can die near his people."

Nothing was said to him, or his friend Cahcahkalow, that night. They knew what was happening and did not need to be reminded of it. If they wanted any help, they would ask.

The next day of walking was hard for all of us, since we were suffering from lack of food, and the dogs were weak from pulling the travois. Even though Kinepik was hungry, in pain, and could barely walk on his bad leg, he managed to keep pace in the front, leading our column along with Cahcahkalow.

Recognizing his pain and courage, each one of us stepped forward and walked along with him for a while, sharing any meagre rations we had with him. Cahcahkalow was softly singing Cree songs to him as they walked, which brought a smile to Kinepik's face. Even though the day was clear and warm for this time of year, hunger was still gnawing away at our insides, and a chilling weakness drifted down upon us like a morning mist. Nevertheless, we urged ourselves to walk a little bit further than normal. We would only stop when Kinepik, a true warrior, called it a day.

That evening, we cooked almost everything we had around the fires for a celebration feast to thank Kitchi Manitou for helping us get this far. We laid our tobacco down as an offering and burnt sweetgrass and sage to smudge and purify ourselves.

The following morning, we found Kinepik dead under his huge moose robe. We buried him in this robe, along with his weapons, some tobacco, and a bit of food to help him on his way to the west, where his ancestors were waiting for him. His grave was between two large pine trees, and we covered it with stones to prevent the wolves and wolverines from digging it up.

Our trail had brought us here, to Kinepik's death, in ten suns. After walking a bit in the morning, we came upon a narrow stream bathed in warm sunlight, with clear, cold, refreshing, knee-deep water running over its rocks. The dogs immediately made a beeline for this, lay down on their bellies, and lapped away at the cool water.

While sitting there, they watched intently as a fish swam by, and several of them still blessed with strength jumped into the water after it. They tumbled, yelped, snarled, and growled around in the brook until one of them came up with the scaly creature in his mouth. In an effort to devour the fish whole, the dog stood on his rear haunches and used his front paws to bat away any rival that dared to venture too close to him.

But the rest of the snarling pack would not to be denied, and they charged at the gulping champion, tearing chunks of the fish from his mouth. After this sudden burst of energy was all over, the dogs were completely exhausted. They lay down in the shallow river, with blood from both predator and prey flowing by their wet, ragged forms. A few of them took mouthfuls of water from the stream as they tried to devour small chunks of fish floating by.

Since none of us had the strength or desire to wade in among the fighting dogs to vie for that elusive fish, we all watched the unfolding bedlam from afar. A majority of us just sat in the vicinity of a small waterfall to feel the energy of the rushing stream on our sore, weakened muscles. It was very soothing, and it helped relax our undernourished bodies.

"Anokì," said E´s, one of our Mi´kmaq allies, "I could lie here all day and just soak up the life from this stream."

Ki´kwa´ju, my brother-in-law, and my sister, Pangì Mahingan, were lying beside me with their eyes closed, resting their heads against the soft bank of the stream.

"Brother, I am with child," Pangì Mahingan spontaneously announced through closed eyes and tight lips. "I need nourishment or my baby will die inside of me."

Surprised by this revelation, I asked, "How long have you been with child?"

"Three appearances of the moon," she replied.

Ki'kwa'ju suddenly rose up from his spot.

"I hear movement in the woods off to the west!"

The warrior's keen sense of hearing was a skill above the rest of us. I pursed my lips and sounded a jay's cry to warn the others. The ones that had been in the water quickly exited the stream, rushed over to the warriors who had been lying on the bank, and readied their weapons as they were handed back to them.

Seeing the quick movements of their masters, the dogs climbed out of the water and shook the cool droplets from their fur, covering everyone within range. They also turned their attention towards the sounds emanating from the dense forest shadows.

The edge of the woods was bathed in a blanket of sunlight from the eastern sun, and out of this light walked Ininàtig.

"Tie the dogs up!" she said in a commanding voice.

13

ESCAPE

WÂPIKWAN

"Mother, the warriors that our Cree families gave to us to protect our village were not very helpful. Of the four that did come with us, three of them are young men who have not yet proven their manhood, and the other is an older warrior with a crooked arm broken in battle."

"My daughter, Wâpikwan," Osk-îskwêw replied, "all four of them stepped forward to come to our aid, and that says a lot about who they are. Our Cree families are on the move to the Sewitakan Zaaga′igan area, which is an aanikegamaa (chain of lakes). There, they will hunt and then dry the meat of all the waterfowl they kill, which will help keep the starving days to a minimum during the winter months. Everyone is needed to move the camp, and they had no one else to spare. We still have seventeen warriors in camp, plus these men, who I am sure are just as brave as our men."

"Sorry, Mother, I was not in the council lodge when you asked for help, but I should have known that they had good reasons for doing what they did. Everyone thinks I am still a child, but I am not. I am as good a hunter as anyone in our community, and the only thing I have yet to prove is my bravery in battle!"

"Wâpikwan, your father has always wished that you could have met his mother, Wàbananang. He says you have her fire!"

"Her spirit follows me, Mother. I am sure of it!"

"I do not doubt you one bit."

My brother, and one of the Cree boys, went ahead with the dogs to scout out the path and prevent the pack of animals from becoming a nuisance. They had been gone for most of the morning trek when the three Cree males that were with us stopped and pointed. Bounding down the trail were the six dogs and two sprinting boys. Immediately, our Cree companions took up a fighting stance, worried that trouble might be just behind the group.

"Mother, look what my new Cree friend, Mâtinawe-kîšikâw (*matt-in-a-way geech-a-go*: Turtle), and I have killed for supper!"

The two boys raised their bloody hands up in celebration, brandishing three rabbits and four partridges. Blood from the slain animals ran down their arms and dripped off their elbows onto the ground, which the dogs eagerly lapped up.

"Môso," I asked, "tell me the truth: Did the dogs kill these animals?"

The three Cree men standing with us laughed at my accusation.

Both Môso and Mâtinawe-kîšikâw answered at the same time, "No, *we* did, using our blunt arrows to kill small game, just like we have been taught! You insult two great hunters!"

As we all shared a good chuckle, mother handed him a mashkimod (*mash-ki-mud*: bag) and said, "Put your game in here and clean it when we stop for the evening. It will be our supper."

"Miigwetch, mother."

The rest of the day was spent walking along the well worn trail that connected the two fall encampments. The honking of geese overhead warned us of the approaching cool weather. The past few days had been very warm for this time of year, and we watched as distant thunderstorms put on a lightning show against blackened skies.

We walked until we got to a campsite we had used many times over the years, which was about a half-day's travel to our lodges. It was on a bald rock in the middle of a grove of trees. There were lean-tos and stacks of dry wood, which we replaced with green wood after we took enough to start our cooking fires. The other two Cree boys helped skin the rabbits and pluck the birds while the older man scouted around the area. Everyone went to sleep with full stomachs and lots of tea to quench our thirst. As always, the dogs, our eternal protectors, slept in a circle around Mother, Môso and me.

The next morning, Mother and I arose at sunrise and got the fires burning again to boil tea and make a stew out of turnips, onions, and some meat that we had in our shoulder bags. When the morning smells of food and tea hit their senses, the men quickly got up. I gave each of the dogs a piece of fish that I carried with me, but they would have to forage for themselves for the rest of the day. The bitch was a great hunter and kept her brothers well supplied with rodents, frogs, snakes, and anything else that she could catch and kill.

From that point on, the trail to our village was well worn, and our group loped along at a ground-eating pace, arriving at the lodges well before high sun. Once we arrived, we were kept busy talking to friends, introducing the four Cree who had arrived with us, and re-settling back in our tipis.

Around midday, the far western sky became black as night, and the temperature plummeted. From out of nowhere, deer, elk, antelope, moose, wolves, foxes, and many other beasts came stampeding through our village, knocking lodges down and driving our people up into the trees and behind large rocks for safety. Looking towards the sky, there were thousands of birds trying to flee from something off to the east. It was scaring all of Kitchi Manitou's creatures, and their panicked snorts, bellows, yips, and howls filled the air.

After most of the stampeding creatures had passed by, only the odd straggling beasts, which were too old or crippled to keep up, hobbled through our midst as quickly as their broken and aged bodies would allow. Their outlook for survival was bleak.

An old woman's screams suddenly startled me, and I looked up to see a black, sky-to-ground twisting wind.

Immediately, one of our warriors yelled for everyone to grab some food and their weapons and run with him. My mother, brother, and I turned and ran back up the trail we had just come from, and it was not long before the others caught up to us. At least ten warriors had paired off and were dragging the Elders on travois.

We ran for a long time and heard a tremendously loud gale behind us. Turning to look, I saw that the sky was full of small trees, tipis, and other items from our village swirling around and colliding into one another. To keep well ahead of the powerful wind, warriors made sure that there were no stragglers, and the women carried the children.

At one point, a mother handed me her small child; she had been carrying one in each arm. The young girl never said a word; she just looked up in the sky behind us and then fell asleep as I ran with her. My mother then paused briefly to help a woman who was struggling with her three small children. Meanwhile, my brother, along with the three Cree boys and the crooked-arm man, were all helping to pull Elders along on pole sleds.

When we finally stopped just before dark, I was soaked from sweat and the pouring rain. Even though the winds were slowly dropping, we were not safe yet. We reached the camp where we had spent the previous evening, and everyone crawled into the lean-tos to get out of the rain. While the warriors and women attended to the little ones, the Elders, the older children, and I distributed the dry firewood stored underneath the lean-tos to the people in the shelters. During this time, our dogs stayed close to my brother and me, while the other thousand or so did whatever they could to get out of the rain and stay dry, including crowding in among the people and huddling under trees.

After the women settled their children down and made them comfortable, they managed to get the fires going and start an evening meal. While the women were doing this, the rest of us busied ourselves in making more lean-tos to help ease the over-crowding of people and dogs. By nightfall, the rain finally quit and the winds subsided. Everyone sat around the evening fires, wrapped in robes while their clothes dried out. Camp guards were posted, and soon the day's excitement began to abate, and everyone fell asleep, cuddled up to a dog or a loved one.

I rose with my mother before dawn, got a fire going, and boiled water to make tea and a morning stew with chunks of meat and roots. After everyone had eaten, the warriors, led by the Cree with the crooked arm, started us on the trail towards the Sewitakan Zaaga′igan trio of water bodies. There, we would gather with his village and hunt waterfowl to help get us through the winter. Our allies, the Assiniboine, would also be on the shorelines, trying to harvest as much as they could.

The first night we camped, the crooked-arm Cree, whose name was Nipahtâw (*nip a towl*: He Kills It), gathered all of us together. He then told us to make as many blunt arrows as we could during our nightly stops, reminding us that these arrows would kill the waterfowl without tearing their bodies apart, as barbed arrows would.

"When we reach the shores of these lakes, we will find plenty of options to feather our arrow shafts with," he went on to say.

It would take us several suns to reach our destination, and we could only travel as fast as the children and Elders. The Elders who could walk led the procession, and we kept pace with them. As we walked, women picked berries and roots to add to our meagre supplies, and the warriors hunted through the countryside. Unfortunately, they barely came up with enough game to keep us fed because the big wind had scared most of the animals away.

Whenever we camped near a stream or river, Môso and I and the children, including the three Cree boys — Mâtinawe-kîšikâw (*matt-in-a-way geech-a-go*: Turtle), Otema (*o-tem-a*: Dog), and Išpakocin (*is-pa-ko-chin*: He Flies High) — would spear, clean, and divide the fish up among the cooking fires. Since the three Cree boys were still too young to have proved themselves in battle, they had not yet earned their warrior names.

During our trek, the Crees, Môso, and I, along with a few of our friends, made sure that all the children were looked after and fed while their mothers were busy. We also helped the women collect berries and roots, maintain the fires, and cook. After eight suns of travelling, Nipahtâw told us that this would be our last night on the trail.

That same evening, I gathered together my brother, the three Cree boys, an Anishinaabe girl, and two other Anishinaabe boys and asked them if they would like to start a young warrior society. After each of them agreed, I told them what our warrior society would be responsible for.

"We will protect the children and women, which, you know, is already the job of a warrior. But when they meet an attacking force head on, it will be our duty to gather up the children and women and defend them if any of our enemies break through our men's line of defence. Our group will be called the Elk Whistle Warrior Society. In Anishinaabe, we will be known as the Omashkooz Gwiishkoshim Ogichidaa (*oh-mush-koos-gwish-ko-shim-o-gich-e-dah*); in Cree, Wâwâskêsiw Kwêskosîwin Nôtinkêwiýiniw.

"Two distinguishing things will set us apart. The first will be an elk antler whistle, which we can blow in times of danger. When nearby members of our society hear this, they will know to come to the aid of the whistle-blower. For this, we must hunt an elk, and, if we are successful, there will be meat for the village and antlers for our whistles.

"Tonight, each of the boys will get a tattoo of two feathers on the back of their left legs, while Gidagizi Gidagaakoons (*ged-a-gay-zay-ged-ah-ga-cones*: Spotted-Fawn) and I will get the same on the back of our right shoulders. Only after obtaining the tattoo, making our whistles, and taking a vow to protect our women and children from being stolen by the enemy will we become Elk Whistle Warriors!

"A woman will always lead this warrior society. In the beginning, it will be me, Spotted Fawn, and our daughters, and, when they have children, they will carry on after our deaths. For any women that joins after this night, their daughters will also become eligible leaders. Anyone may join if they are twelve summers old, pure of heart, and respectful of the teachings of Kitchi Manitou. They must also be willing to give their life to protect the women and children of their community and to share the spoils of the hunt with their village."

The two Anishinaabe brothers were very excited to be included in our new warrior society. Their names were Bangii Zhiishiib (*bun-ge zhe-sheep*: A Little Duck) and Animaanagidoone (*on-e-mon-gi-toni*: He Goes Away Talking). Both were a few years older than my brother Môso, but they were very good friends of his.

"I have been saving charcoal and soot from our fires over the last few nights and have enough to tattoo everyone. Who wants to be the first to get their tattoo?"

Môso immediately blurted out, "Me!"

I asked Spotted Fawn to watch carefully so she could do the tattoo on my shoulder and also tattoo a couple of the boys. After I got Môso to lie by the fire, I took a piece of charcoal and outlined the tattoo in black. Then, using my knife, I etched the two feathers onto the back of his left calf, using moss to wipe away the blood. When the shape I wanted was carved into his skin, I took the soot and dye mixture I had made up and rubbed it into the wound. When the skin healed over, this would highlight a perfect tattoo.

Spotted Fawn and I worked by the light of the fire well into the night. Once they were tattooed, the boys had big smiles on their faces, knowing that they now belonged to a warrior society that they could call their own. Even when they became adults and earned the acceptance of a man's warrior society, they would cherish the special, sacred pledge of the Elk Whistle Warrior Society for the rest of their lives.

For the time being, we would keep our numbers at eight. Eventually, we would split up to live in our own communities, but we would always make sure that each offshoot of our group had eight members: two girls and six boys. When they returned home, the Cree warrior boys would have to pick two girls or women to lead them and add three more boys to bring their numbers up to eight, but, for now, we were the beginning.

We just needed to slay an elk and use their antlers to make whistles. This had to be done before the spring, when they would shed their horns. If we were lucky, we might be able to find horns in the forest, but we would have to beat the mice, squirrels, porcupines, foxes, and bears to them, because they would devour them on sight. It would be better to hunt a live elk, not only to acquire the material we needed to make our whistles, but to gain some life-saving meat to share with our community.

"Once we arrive at the Sewitakan Zaaga′igan area, Wâpikwan, I can take you to a place where there should be elk," said Otema, one of the Cree boys. "It is near the end of their rut season, so we should be able to hear the bulls calling the females with their bellows and fighting off other males at quite a distance. With your six dogs, the eight of us should be able do this. It will be a great adventure!"

"Otema, you will lead us on this hunt when it is time," I replied.

After all of us were tattooed, we went our separate ways to get some sleep. The night was cool and the sky was clear and star-filled. Between the soothing smell of the wood fires and the security I felt from the female dog as she lay beside me, I was hastened away on my journey to the dreamlands. After a peaceful night's sleep, I woke up to my mother's hands on my shoulder.

"Time to get up and eat," she said. "Nipahtâw wants us to leave as early as possible to get to the lake by high sun."

I rose in the early dawn light and went into the woods to relieve myself. I then went back to the fire, sat beside Môso, and ate quickly.

Just as we were leaving, my mother said, "Interesting tattoos that you and Môso made last night. You will have to tell me their meaning sometime."

Môso answered, "When Father comes back, we will tell you."

He turned to me and smiled, and I grinned back at him. Mother saw our wordless exchange and also smiled.

The trail that Nipahtâw now lead us on was clearly well worn from many years of use. We made our way through fragrant forests of spruce and pine and walked across beaver dams, skirting the duck- and geese-filled ponds that had resulted from these constructs. At the sun's height, our group came upon the shores of the salty lake. Just as promised, the beach areas were covered with feathers, more than I had ever seen in one place during my short life. Everywhere I stepped, there were feathers of all shapes, sizes, and colours.

The dogs ran along the shoreline and chased the birds, stirring this plumage up into the air. It stuck to their fur, covering them in fluffy coats. The young boys in charge of the dogs immediately fell into pursuit and tried to call them back to camp. Like the dogs before them, the boys sent these immense piles of feathers up into the breeze, creating a wispy, blizzard-like storm that settled in their hair and clothes.

Watching the dogs and the boys get covered with feathers soon had everyone laughing at the spectacle. When the boys realized why everyone was laughing, they started to carry on even more for our entertainment by rolling around in all of the plumage. This seemed to irk the dogs for some reason, and they barked and darted at their foolish masters in an effort to dissuade them.

Once the laughter died down, and the boys got the dogs under control, Nipahtâw said, "While we camp here tonight, gather up whatever feathers you need to complete your blunt arrows, and then shoot some birds for our evening meal. Tomorrow, we will visit our friends, the Asinii-bwaan (Assiniboine), on the western shore, and then make our way to the Cree encampment on the northern shore."

Pretty soon every fire had two or three birds roasting away on a spit, along with a pot of steeping tea. As we feathered arrows for the immense hunt that would take place in the coming days, the evening's darkness fell upon us. The night sky was dotted with stars, and there was a constant din coming from the lake as thousands of birds talked back and forth in their varied languages.

Gathered around a fire together, our Elk Whistle Warrior Society members shared our meal and talked excitedly about the prospects of slaying an elk. The next several suns would be full of excitement. I went to sleep that night hoping that my father was safe and that he would soon appear with all our friends and family. Sleep came swiftly, and my dreams were of the coming hunts.

The next day, Nipahtâw and three of our Anishinaabe warriors visited the camp of the Asinii-bwaan. They asked to travel through their hunting grounds and offered some tobacco and sweetgrass as a peace offering. The Asinii-bwaanare were old allies of the Cree and, as such, were also friends of my Anishinaabe people. Nipahtâw returned in two days and told us that all was fine and that we would travel to the Asinii-bwaan camp, stay there for one night, and then continue on to his Cree community.

As great hunters, the Assiniboine lived by following the buffalo, much like our people. They called themselves the Hohe Nakota, and we called them the Asinii-bwaan (*a-sin-nee-bwan*: Stone Sioux). The night we stayed in their camp, we were treated to a feast of food, storytelling, dancing, and drumming. It was very late in the evening before I went to lie down on my buffalo robe to rest my body.

I slept uninterrupted until my mother woke me and my brother up and told us to get ready to move. Eating quickly, we were soon on the trail and reached our Cree friends on the north shore before high sun. This was a happy time, as old friends embraced and welcomed us back into their camps.

We set up our own camp to the east side of the Cree and, for the next several days, hunted geese, ducks, and cranes by using the blunt arrows we had made on the trail. After gathering up our kills, the women, children, and Elders plucked the birds and then dried them over the fires, which singed away any remaining feathers and down. By hunting, plucking, and smoking the birds from sun-up to sunset, we slowly built up our food stores for the winter.

After several days of this, one of the Cree boys, Otema, came to me and said, "I have found a group of elk close to where we first came upon the lake shore. The bulls are still at the end of their rut and are bellowing to the females, so we should have no problem finding them."

We promptly assembled all eight members of our Elk Whistle Warrior Society, along with our six dogs, and then set out on our adventure. I told my mother and Nipahtâw what we were doing, and they both suggested that we take some experienced hunters along with us.

"No," I said, "this is something that we must do ourselves. We will be back in three or four suns with meat for the community and antlers for what we need."

We left early the next morning while there was still a heavy frost on the ground. Running at a constant lope, we quickly covered a lot of distance. With Otema leading the way, we passed around the Asinii-bwaan village before high sun and arrived at our original campsite on those shores just as the sun was setting. After Môso and I gathered firewood, we started a blaze, made tea, and roasted some birds that we had brought with us.

"We must rise early tomorrow, because the elk are most active just before dusk," Otema said. "Their high-pitched whistles and roars carry over a long distance, and our group must follow these sounds to find the bulls."

After finishing our meals, we made sure the dogs were well fed, since they would be burning off a lot of energy as we attempted to make our kill.

Rising before dawn, we were greeted by a light drizzle of rain, which was just enough to dampen our hair and clothes. This moisture slowly drifted down from the sky and settled on the same grass stalks and pine needles that we were forced to walk through, further dampening our clothing and adding to our discomfort. The misty rain covered my face, ran into my eyes, and dripped off my chin, reminding me of the salty sweat of a hot summer's day.

Even though all six of the dogs were completely drenched, they did not convey any hint of discomfort to us. With their keen hunting senses anticipating every possibility around them, the males followed the female without hesitation.

We walked the whole morning and only heard a couple of bulls sounding off. By the time we arrived at the spot where we thought they might be, there were no more sounds. Just by observing the bent grass and broken branches of the trees, we could tell where they had been standing and where they had gone back into the woods.

When the rain stopped, we paused to build a fire, dry our clothes out, and make plans for the rest of the day. After a quick meal, we decided to stay put beyond mid-afternoon. Our plan was to try and find the bull elk just before dusk, when they became active again.

Some of the group slept for a while, but Môso, Spotted Fawn, and I kept watch and maintained the fires. Darkness was coming earlier and earlier each day, and, if we did not find an elk tonight, we would have to start all over again in the morning. I was in the process of shaking awake the sleepers when the female dog let out a low growl. The five males instantly fell in behind her; their now-dry fur rose up on their backs, and they emitted a collection of throaty rumblings.

I grabbed my bow, notched an arrow, and looked to where they were staring, upwind from the camp. Everyone around me quickly rose up from their resting spots and silently readied their weapons. After a moment of complete silence, the tranquility was shattered by the sound of a tree branch snapping, followed by an ear-shattering whistle and roar.

"A bull, right there," whispered Išpakocin.

I signalled for Môso to take the one female and two male dogs and circle behind the shadowy beast in the woods. Spotted Fawn and the two Anishinaabe boys went with him, while the others followed me and the remaining dogs. Taking care to stay upwind from our quarry, we soon located a game trail. The dogs lay down, ready to spring into action if needed, and we kept our arrows and spears at the ready. This was our chance to make a kill and prove to our village that we were now old enough to be dependable hunters.

After circling around, Môso and his companions drove the elk down the game trail. Just ahead of where we were waiting, the path flowed straight, with a small stream running across it. We could hear the barking of the bull as he ran from the yelping dogs. When he turned the corner and hit the straight run, we could see two arrows embedded in his rear quarters. The dogs were right on his heels, and the bull was spewing blood-tainted saliva in great swaths from his mouth.

As the elk splashed across the stream, his front feet and rear hooves cascaded water back onto the pursuing dogs. I put my hand out to keep the other three dogs down, since we did not want our prey to turn. Pulling the arrow back to my ear, I yelled, "Now!" and then let it loose. My arrow, and three more from my fellow hunters, all hit their marks with a series of *thumps.*

Incredibly, this failed to bring the big animal down, and he continued right at us, resulting in my split-second decision to jump into the surrounding scrub to avoid being trampled. In my haste to avoid the animal's hooves, my face and arms were scratched by branches, and my shoulder slammed into a rock, breaking my forward motion and flipping me end-over-end.

I quickly sprung to my feet and watched through blood-soaked eyes as Mâtinawe-kîšikâw drove his spear into the front left shoulder of the animal. As soon as the weapon lodged there, it struck Turtle in the waist and spun him onto the ground. I yelled, "Go!" to the dogs as the elk charged past, and they immediately jumped to their feet and tore off down the trail, joining their brethren in a fit of snapping, growling, howling, and barking. By this time, my brother and his companions had caught up to our group, and all eight of us ran off in pursuit of the chaotic mob.

After Turtle's spear snapped off on the first tree the beast brushed past, blood started spurting out of the open wound whenever the elk's left leg pushed off the ground. By this point, there were six arrows and a spear head in the animal's body. He was also being harrassed by six dogs and eight hollering, hopeful young hunters. Despite all of this, he continued to crash forward through the woods, leaving a trail of blood along the way.

It wasn't until after dark before the chase finally ended and the beast crashed to the ground with a great dying bellow. The dogs rushed at the animal, but I called them back. I did not want them ripping at the carcass, and their discipline would be rewarded later. We stood beside the animal, whooping in celebration, and the forest echoed our sounds back to us.

We all lay down up against the body, resting alongside the panting dogs. For all of us, this was our first big kill that was larger than a deer. We soon realized, however, that by failing to make a quick killing shot, we had made the animal suffer needlessly. We also knew that there was a lot of work to do before we could let ourselves sleep.

Before doing anything else, I took tobacco out of my medicine bag and offered it to the animal's spirit. Grateful to both the elk and Kitchi Manitou for this life-sustaining gift of meat, I also asked forgiveness for the suffering we had put our quarry through.

At that point, I noticed that both Môso and Spotted Fawn were staring at me with their mouths agape. In the excitement of the chase, I had forgotten about the scrapes I'd endured after jumping into the underbrush. When I wiped my hands across my face, they came away covered in blood. My arms were also scratched up and my shoulder was throbbing in pain.

Môso took some water from his waterskin and started wiping the blood away, asking, "Are you going to die, Wâpikwan?"

"No, I do not think so, brother."

Spotted Fawn sat beside us, spat tobacco into her hand, and then rubbed the chew into the gash on my head. She then covered it with moss and secured it with a piece of leather. Since the scrapes on my arms had barely broken the skin, Môso washed the dried blood off and smeared some more tobacco juice onto the cuts. After they moved my shoulder around, we all concluded that it was just bruised and not broken.

We started some fires to give us the light we needed to go about our bloody work. Since one of our main goals was to make our whistles out of the elk's horns, the first thing we did was cut the antlers off. We then segmented the meat in such a way that the dogs could pull it on pole sleds while we carried a portion on our backs. Each of us then paused to take a bite from the heart.

Spotted Fawn then cut a big chunk of meat from the beast and put it on a spit. While it cooked, we continued to butcher the animal, keeping the dogs busy by throwing the occasional piece of meat to them. By the time we finished, it was almost daylight, and we were all exhausted. We slept in shifts, posting two guards to keep an eye out for bears and wolves, which we hoped were either asleep in their dens or would be scared off by the dogs and fires.

By midday, we had slept enough. Môso and Otema stayed in camp while the rest of us entered the surrounding forest and cut the poles we needed to haul the meat. After that, we used the harnesses we'd brought along to hook the dogs up to their travois. Everyone carried a load of meat on their backs, and I pulled a pole sled bearing the elk's skin and antlers. Since it was his responsibility to lead the group and be vigilant, Môso only carried a light pack of meat.

We had to walk until dark, but we finally reached the campsite that we had used on our first night out. After a quick meal of elk, we were soon asleep, with the two Anishinaabe boys, Bangii Zhiishiib and Animaanagidoone, watching over us as we slept. When they grew tired, they woke up Spotted Fawn and me, and, later that same night, Môso and the Crees would take their turn.

Rising at dawn, we ate and then made our way back towards our camp, following the trail that had brought us here. Towards the end of the day, our scout Môso came back with one of the dogs.

"Warriors!" he reported. "Fifteen or twenty of them where we have to come out onto the beach at the far side of the forest! They have fires burning and appear to be eating. There is no way we can get by them without being noticed."

"Blackfoot?" asked Otema.

"I could not tell," replied Môso.

"We are no match for a party of seasoned Blackfoot warriors," I replied. "Our scalps will be hanging from their lodge poles this winter."

Suddenly, a voice rang out from the shadows.

"Stay where you are!"

Our dogs growled as this voice of death called out to us from the darkness of the forest. We immediately grabbed our weapons and postured for a fight.

14

STARVATION

ANOKÌ

In our weakened state of near-starvation, it became a chore just to gather the dogs up. Luckily for us, they had even less energy than we did. I grabbed a large dog by its mane to get a noosed rope around its neck, but, when the animal decided he did not want to be tied up, the two of us tumbled down the embankment into the stream.

Standing in the water, I finally got the noose around his neck, but I did not have the energy to pull him out of the stream, and he did not have the energy to climb out on his own. Ki'kwa'ju waded in to help me, and, between the two of us, we got the limp animal out and tied him up to a tree. The dog lay down, gave out a big sigh, put his head between his front paws, and moaned.

When Ininàtig saw the two of us struggling with the dogs, she came to our aid. When we had all of the animals secured, I looked around and saw that the others were no better off than me. Everyone was lying on the grass, gasping for air, waiting for Kànìkwe and Jilte′g to come back from their hunting trip.

Even in their weakened state, the dogs could sense the return of our hunters before we could see them, and they started to whimper, moan, and strain at their tethers. When the two warriors finally emerged from the woods, we all gasped. Balanced on their collective shoulders was a huge buck tied upside-down to a tree limb.

After Kànìkwe and Jilte′g laid the deer down on the ground, Zhashagi and two of his Anishinaabe warriors quickly started to skin the animal and section it up to roast. The rest of us hastily collected firewood and made spits to cook this precious, life-saving meat while Kigìbigomesì, Mashkawizì Mahingan, and Kìnà Mòkomàn collected the guts, bones, and hide from the butchering area.

During this time, the smell from this fresh kill sent the starving dogs into a frenzy of howling, whining, slobbering, and jaw snapping. The three young warriors quickly cut all of the remaining meat off the hide and fed these scraps to the dogs. They took great care portioning this up amongst the animosh, since giving them too much food after going hungry for so long would likely kill them.

To help control the food distribution and prevent the dogs from fighting, they kept the animosh tied up. Between the hide, bones, and guts, the animals eventually had a grand feast. Once they had finished eating, we untied them, knowing that their shrunken stomachs would be full, and they would be in no mood to fight, just sleep.

After starting a fire, Àwadòsiwag and Ininàtig began to heat up rocks to boil water in leather baskets. They sent their husbands, Wàbek and Makwa, into the woods to find any berries and roots they could scavenge. When they came back, the berries were dropped into one basket to make tea while the roots were mixed in with some chopped-up deer organs for a stew.

The women kept a watchful eye over these things, making sure to replace the cooled rocks with red-hot ones. They also made sure that no one dipped their clay cup into the tea and stew before they were both done. These two things would be ready to consume before the chunks of meat were finished roasting on the spits.

The lack of nourishment over these last few suns had shrunk our stomachs and thrown off our body's spirits. We had to gently bring our systems back without shocking our internal organs with a rush of food. While the stew and wood-spitted deer were cooking, many of the warriors ate small chunks of raw meat, but they all knew not to gorge themselves.

In past times, all of us had seen friends and family overeat after times of starvation, which would cause them to vomit and, in some rare cases, die. The tea and stew would be ready first, and consuming them would give us the nutrients needed to prepare our systems for the meat. Next, we ate all the fat from the animal to help slowly expand our shrunken stomachs. The meat of the animal was last, and we ate this sparingly. Everything, from the liquids to the meat, was drunk and eaten in very small portions.

When the women gave the signal, their food pots were quickly cleaned out. Even though everyone was only filling their cups up halfway, with over twenty people dipping out what they needed, the tea and stew were both quickly depleted. Àwadòsiwag and Ininàtig had planned well ahead, though, and they already had other baskets heating up.

We finished our meal just as the sun was starting to set. During that time, the air cooled off to the point where we could see our breath in puffs of steam as we talked back and forth. What meat we did not eat was hung up on tree limbs to keep the dogs, and anything that might wander out of the forest, away from our precious food.

Makwa, Wàbek, and Kànìkwe untied the dogs so that they could guard the camp from any intruders. The trio had already filled up several leather sacks with bones for the dogs and hoisted them up into a tree. Clearly, they took their responsibility of looking after the animosh very seriously.

While sitting and lying around the fire, certain sounds and smells began to indicate that our intestines were starting to work again. By making sure not to gorge ourselves, our inner organs were slowly restarting and moving towards normalcy.

Looking at Ininàtig, Jilte'g, and Kànìkwe, Crazy Crow stood up and said, "It is now time to tell my Cheyenne friend *Oak-key-whoa-a-mast*, and the rest of us, your story of the hunt for this magnificent beast, which Kitchi Manitou provided to stave off our starvation and let us continue on the journey that our Cree friend, Cahcahkalow, is leading us on."

The two men spoke up and said, "We will let the warrior woman, Ininàtig, tell the story. She was our leader on this hunt, and it is hers to tell."

Ininàtig popped a small piece of meat into her mouth, took a sip of tea, and said, "Miigwetch, my friends. Jilte′g and Kànikwe, we have been on many trails together, and this one was just as interesting and eventful as all of the past ones.

"Our hunting path took us deep into the woods. We followed a stream that took us west, hoping to find wildlife coming down to the banks for a drink. The dogs that we had with us were as hungry and weak as we were, and their lack of strength caused them to have no interest in tracking game.

"Towards midday of our second day out, the dogs finally raised their heads in the air and made a few short, mournful yips with what little strength they had left. Jilte′g, Kànìkwe and I each notched an arrow onto our bowstrings and laboured to keep up with the suddenly rejuvenated dogs. We hobbled along, following them as they held their heads up, nostrils flaring, gathering in the scent that was leading them onwards.

"The dogs stopped under a huge pine tree, looked up, and whimpered. There, hanging upside down, was a huge male wàwàshkeshi, his hind legs tied to a lower limb with spruce roots. That's when I heard a rustling of the pine needles and quickly looked up. At first glance, I thought I saw a dark form jump from the tree into the darkness of the forest floor. There, it was joined by a rabbit, and they both disappeared deep into the sun-specked woods.

"At first, I thought I was I hallucinating, but I looked back and saw the life-saving meat hanging right there in front of me. Immediately I knew that I had just watched Mitigomij, in his rabbit form, and his panther, Makadewà Wàban , vanish into the woods. That big cat was many summers old, and I remembered it clearly from my childhood.

"At this late stage of their lives, I speculated that the two of them were more of the spirit world now, caught between their shape-shifting bodily transformations and doing Kitchi Manitou's bidding. They moved around like spirits and reminded me of the Little People, the Memegwesi (*me-me-gwes-ah*), who look after lost children. Just as they had always done in the past, Mitigomij and Makadewà Wàban had saved our lives, and hopefully they would continue to do so well into the future.

"We cut just enough raw meat off the carcass to help us regain our strength and also slowly gave some to the dogs. We sat there with the wàwàshkeshi still hanging from the tree, slowly drinking some tea from berries that we had scavenged from the woods and eating very small portions of meat. We did not want to gorge ourselves and risk getting sick and lying there in a weak state while the meat in the tree rotted.

"Starvation pangs did not awaken us that night and we had the best sleep in many suns. That morning, we cooked some of the meat over a fire and, once again, ate our small portions very slowly. Because of their size and history of food deprivation, the dogs regained their strength back much faster than we did. One sun after reaching this area, we were finally strong enough to shoulder the animal and make our way back to you.

"By taking turns carrying the deer and walking in the lead with the dogs, we made good time, especially in light of the condition we were in. We stopped frequently to rest, change responsibilities, and eat small portions of meat until our bodies and spirits evolved back to our pre-starvation days.

"As we walked through the woods, I had a sense that we were being watched and could feel a hovering spirit around our small group. I did not mention my thoughts to Jilte′g and Kànìkwe until we stopped later on in the day. After expressing my concerns, they said that they were experiencing the same feeling, which made me smile and think to myself, 'Mitigomij … our constant protector!'"

Zhashagi turned to me and said, "Anokì, your uncle never ceases to amaze both me and my people. He has come to our rescue more than once, and, for that, we are grateful. We can only thank him by remaining friends with you, your family, and the people from your community."

"Thank you, Zhashagi," I replied. "The Anishinaabe people are valued allies."

Rising from my sitting position, I thanked Ininàtig for her story of how they obtained the deer. As I sat back down, I wondered why Mitigomij was staying away from our communities and remaining in his shape-shifting spirit form. Perhaps his bad leg was giving him grief as he got older, and he could get around much easier while in the form of the Great Trickster Hare, Michabo. He also had Makadewà Wàban to protect him when he was in this form.

The one thing that I *did* know for sure was that I was very happy he was alive and close to us at all times, even though we could not see him. My inner spirit could always feel his presence, as well as that of the big cat.

Talking amongst ourselves, we decided to stay put and try to regain as much strength as possible. Cahcahkalow told us that it might be another two suns or less before we arrived at our destination. We let the dogs loose for the night and selected people to stand watch, asking them to change whenever they became drowsy.

The next day was cool, and we kept the fires going in front of the lean-tos, which we had built for shelter. Tea, stew, and roasting meat were made available all day, which we still ate in small portions.

I took the first watch the following evening, waking Ki′kwa′ju up when I started to nod off. My sister's husband had grown into a huge man. He had a full, sun-coloured beard and braided hair down to his waist, but his skin was dark like the rest of us.

As he neared me, he said, "I feel well rested and will be able to do this watch until sun-up. Between the dogs for company, the other watchers to talk to, and keeping the fires going, I will have plenty to do. So go sleep and dream about your ancestors!"

"Miigwetch, Ki′kwa′ju! You are more like us now than the people who birthed you. What did the

Mi'kmaq people call them, the Eli'tuat? Yes, I am proud to call you my friend and husband of my sister."

"Miigwetch, also, my friend. We have grown up together and fought side by side many times. My past was put behind me when I left my shield, sword, and axe in the forest near where we slew the big wàbidì (*wah-bi-dee*: elk). I am now an Omàmiwinini (Algonquin), and you and yours are my family and my future!"

I smiled, went over to where my nephews, their wives, and my sister were all sleeping and joined them. During this time, I dreamt of my father and mother, Mahingan and Wàbananang, and was completely at peace.

The next morning, I woke up to what I thought was a dog licking my face. I instinctively pushed the animal away and wiped away the wetness with my hands. But, as it turned out, it wasn't dog slobber at all; it was a smear of stew that had been boiling on the nearby fire. Opening one eye, I could see Makwa and Wàbek, along with Àwadòsiwag and Ininàtig, all laughing with their hands over their mouths.

Before opening the other eye, I could sense someone beside me. Looking up, I saw my sister, Pangì Mahingan, standing nearby with stew dripping from her fingers and a dog licking her hand. I sat up, looked around at everyone, and joined in the laughter.

"The five of you will have to sleep with one eye open from now on," I chuckled. "I will be out for revenge."

Looking at Ki'kwa'ju, I said, "I thought you were on watch duty?"

"Yes," he answered, "but I was only watching for danger from *outside* our camp, and this came from *inside* the camp."

"Well, in that case, I will accept your apology for being inattentive to your surroundings. Now that I've tasted what was on my face, I'm hungry. Where is my cup?"

With our stomachs full and our destination only a few suns away, the people were in a joyful mood. We made sure to douse our campfires with lots of water and bury the cold embers, since the last thing we needed was a forest fire following our trail. Embers may look out, but a little bit of wind and a small hot spot can lead to a disaster.

The three young warriors in charge of the dogs soon had them hooked up to the pole travois. With food back in our depleted systems, we expected to make better time today. Each of us had a few chunks of meat in our bags, along with a freshly filled water bladder. During our midday stop, we would give the dogs a bit of bone, some fat, and guts. The fat was a particularly important part of our post-starvation diet, but we had to share it with the dogs to keep them alive.

The Cree warrior, Cahcahkalow, led the way at a constant, quick walk, accompanied by Àwadòsiwag and Ininàtig.

"Zhashagi, do you think that this area has as many birds as Cahcahkalow is telling us?" I asked.

"I do not think he is telling a tall story, since others have said the same thing, that there are many different birds there and piles of feathers. If it is true, then it will be nice to have newer feathers to trade and to wear in my hair and on my clothes. Hopefully, I can find some large Zhashagi (Blue Heron) feathers."

"Ah, yes! Let's hope that we *both* find some of those beautiful feathers," replied Zhashagi.

When we stopped for our midday rest, the boys grabbed the leather bags containing the assorted meat and bones to feed their dogs. But as soon as they untied them, a terrible stench instantly permeated the air, nauseating everyone but the dogs.

Crazy Crow started to cough and gag, saying, "*Whew!* Buffalo killing fields do not smell that bad! The bags will retain the smell and will be of no use to anyone, so, when they are empty, cut them up and feed them to the dogs. That is definitely a smell that only a dog, wolf, or wolverine could appreciate!"

Kànìkwe, Wàbek, Makwa, Àwadòsiwag, and Ininàtig looked at their sons and started to laugh. Between chuckles and hoots, Kànìkwe said, "Boys, do not forget to save a piece of the bag for Crazy Crow to snack on later."

"Feel free to bury my portion," he shot back. "Leave it for the wolves to dig up."

The whole group was now laughing and gagging over the smell, and the only ones who genuinely seemed to be enjoying this event were the dogs.

After Cahcahkalow stood up and announced that we would be at our destination by this time tomorrow, we gathered up our things and followed his lead. The air was crisp, the sky was blue, and my legs were starting to feel stronger with every step. Until the deer carcass appeared in our camp, the long stretch without food had taken me frighteningly close to certain death.

I had suffered hunger many times before, but never to that extent. Thankfully, we hadn't killed our dogs to eat, because we would now be carrying their loads and draining away the precious little strength we had.

That evening, we camped on a river that Cahcahkalow said would take us to the middle lake. As we finished off our deer meat next to the brightly burning camp fires, we hoped that tomorrow would bring us a harvest of waterfowl. The dogs were given what was left for them, leather bags included.

As we finished our meals, a cold rain started to fall, inspiring both humans and dogs to seek shelter in the lean-to that we had erected. After finding a dog to lay my head on, I pulled my fur robe up to my chin and listened contentedly to the rain as it pattered onto the dry ground and the spruce- and cedar-bough roof overhead. In no time, the comforting sounds lulled me to sleep.

I woke up that morning to the sputtering and spitting sound of flames trying to eat away at the outer bark of wet wood. The smell of freshly cooked venison awakened my senses on this damp, windy day. After stepping to the edge of the woods and relieving myself, I pulled my robe tight around my body to keep the wind out and sat beside the fire. I then dipped my cup into the boiling tea container and cut off a dripping piece of meat from the spit.

Cahcahkalow walked around to each of our groups nestled among our fires and said, "There will be no fresh water in this lake system, so fill your water containers from the river here. Also, do not let the dogs drink from the lake without flushing their system with fresh water from the nearest river. If they drink too much salty water, they will vomit, have diarrhea, and die. Although, more likely, they will be too busy chasing birds when we arrive!"

After enjoying our typically small portion of food, we had our tea and broke camp. Now that we were fed and rested, walking was a lot more pleasant, and, once again, I found myself acutely aware of my surroundings and keen to the smells of the forest. We only stopped once for a quick lunch and rest before pressing on to our final destination.

At sunset, we walked out onto a beach that was carpeted with thousands of feathers. The sun was dropping on the western horizon, casting a bright red trail on the white, salty lake and making colourful, sparkling images dance off the water's surface. Thousands of birds, unperturbed by our intrusion, were squawking, eating, and preening. As the dogs instinctively ran up to them, the birds reacted by spreading their wings in a menacing pose and charging back at the bewildered canines, causing them to slink away. Looking off into the distance, I thought I could see a line of camp fires slowly being hidden by the setting sun.

Cahcahkalow walked around, handing out lumps of white salt and saying, "When you eat, hold this above your meat and roll it between your thumb and forefinger. It will enhance the taste."

As we ate and drank tea, the night was filled with the sounds of laughter. Because our lives are so often touched by starving days, we always celebrate whenever we have lots to eat. Now that the darkness had surrounded our campsite, I could see the faint glow of many fires off to the west across the lake on the distant shoreline. As our group sat by the light of our own blaze, we hoped that it was our friends and families tending those fires, and that they could also see ours. Tomorrow, scouts would be sent forth to confirm whether or not that group was friend or foe.

15

REUNIONS

ANOKÌ

That first day on the lake, everyone was kept busy filling leather sacks to overflowing with colourful feathers, which we would later use to magnificently adorn our clothes, hair, and weapons. Thanks to several geese that we took from the lake, our fires burnt especially bright that night. Roasting on wood spits over the flames, the birds dropped beads of melting fat onto the fire, causing the hot embers to snap and crackle. The sweet aroma of the birds cooking intermingled with the smell of the surrounding pine forest and the salty lake made everything right and helped erase the memory of the starvation days that we had just barely lived through.

The next morning, I, along with Crazy Crow; E´s; Jilte´g; the Cheyenne, Ókôhkevó'omaestse; and the Cree, Cahcahkalow, left the group to walk around the lake and find out who had built the fires that we had seen the night before.

The water's edge was crowded with shore birds, all pecking for insects, worms, and seeds. The lake itself was populated with hordes of ducks, geese, herons, and many other types of waterfowl, most of which were craning their necks deep underwater to gobble up anything within reach. We were constantly stepping in bird droppings, and soon our moccasins were white from all of the stinking excrement.

Not only were the birds undisturbed by our presence, some even challenged us when we walked too close to them. After discovering that the birds were not easily intimidated, the dogs now largely ignored the feathered nuisances.

CRAZY CROW

"Cahcahkalow, who do you think will be hunting on that shoreline? Blackfoot?"

"No, the Blackfoot do not come this far north so late in the year. By now they will be in their winter camps, with lots of stockpiled buffalo meat to ward off hunger. I think we will find our friends, the Asinîwipwât (Cree name for Assiniboine), hunting there, hoping to build up their food reserves for the coming months."

Following Cahcahkalow's lead, the five of us kept up a quick pace along the shoreline. When our destination came into view well before the midday sun, we stopped running and slowly walked towards their camp. We did not want to alarm anyone into thinking that they were being attacked while they were busy hunting and preparing the birds. It was obvious that their base had been there for a while, and the stench from their butchered successes intermingled with the cool, crisp air.

As we neared their camp, several young men walked out from the forest and trailed us, holding their weapons at their sides in a state of complete readiness. Cahcahkalow held up his hand and approached a tall warrior with numerous scars on his chest. They talked for a short bit, and the Hohe, which the Assiniboine call themselves, said something to the warriors behind us. They nodded their heads in approval as they walked past us and stood by his side.

Cahcahkalow said, "They want us to stay the night and go back to our people tomorrow. The Cree community is on the north shore of the other adjoining salty lake, where a river empties into it. He says your people came through six suns ago and are with them now."

We spent the rest of the day hunting water birds with blunt arrows and wading into the shallows to pick them up while young boys in canoes diligently retrieved any carcasses that drifted out into deep waters. Conveniently, the Hohe were camped by a river where they could get fresh water whenever they wanted it and also rinse the white, salty residue off their legs and feet every day.

Our time with these wonderful people was well spent. They were friendly and always laughing as they hunted and went about plucking and cleaning their kills. They kept the meat-drying fires constantly fed, and the young women were always in motion, preparing the birds for winter storage and making sure everyone was well fed during the day.

That evening, before we went to sleep, the Hohe leaders expressed their desire for our two communities to join together in a buffalo hunt this coming spring in the Cypress Hills. Upon hearing this, the five of us looked at each other, and Cahcahkalow said, "But, my Asinîwipwât friends, that is Blackfoot territory!"

"We know that," answered the one with the scars on his chest. "The Hohe are warriors; are the Cree and Anishinaabe not the same?"

"Yes, we are," answered Jilte′g. "Send a messenger to us in the spring to let us know where to meet you."

"No need for that," replied the Hohe warrior. "When we all come out of our winter camps, we will meet at the north end of what the Cree call Kinookimaw (*kah-nook-a-mow*: Long Lake). There, we will hunt birds and fish for our journey south to the Wazíȟe (Assiniboine name for Cypress Hills)."

Cahcahkalow replied to the Hohe, "The buffalo also come to that area during the bird flight time!"

"*Ah*, my friend, so they do … but the Blackfoot do not," replied the Hohe warrior.

As we all looked at each other, the real motivation for the Hohe dawned on us: *war!*

The next morning, as we left for our camp, Crazy Crow turned to me on the trail and said, "Anokì, I have never been afraid of an enemy in my life. I have looked death square in the face many times and have lived to tell about it. I have travelled to many enemy territories and fought the bravest warriors of the Haudenosaunee and the Lakota. I have lost friends, whom I still see in my dreams.

"I have no fear of war, but I fear war just for the sake of it. It is clear to me that the Hohe are picking a fight. They know that the Blackfoot will be on the west side of what the Cree call Manâtakâw (*mun-a-tuh-gow*: sacred land, beautiful upland; now known as Cypress Hills). Anokì, I have fought these warriors and they are both battle-hardened and numerous. If we end up in a conflict with them, I do not like our odds. It is a feeling I have."

"Crazy Crow, I respect your thoughts. We will decide in the spring. The Asinii-bwaan people are our allies and I want to keep it that way."

"I am going to scout ahead, Anokì. I must be alone with my thoughts."

I watched as Crazy Crow walked off into the shadows of the forest. I knew he was right, but I also knew that Kitchi Manitou would guide us to do what needed to be done.

After walking through the forest for the better part of the morning, Crazy Crow approached the site where the remainder of our group was staying along the shoreline. He first smelled the elk meat, then he heard twigs snap and a voice.

Spying several figures and dogs, he crept up on the group of warriors and peered through the woods just as the midday sun cascaded down through the trees and covered the forest floor in ribbons of light. After recognizing the intruders, he smiled, silently notched an arrow and then popped up from out of the bushes.

"Stay where you are!" he yelled, revelling in the resulting shock and surprise.

Content that he had just taught a very valuable lesson, Crazy Crow emerged into the small clearing and said, "Do you not have any out-guards?"

"Crazy Crow!" yelled a young woman, who immediately ran to embrace him in a big hug. "Is my father near? Is he still alive? I thought you were dead … I thought my father was dead! We thought the Blackfoot had slain all of you!"

"*Whoa*, there, young Wâpikwan, my mind reels from all of your questions! Everyone is safe and your father is just behind me back on the trail. Unlike you, we always make sure to post out-guards."

Wâpikwan quickly changed the subject.

"These are all of my friends, Crazy Crow! We call ourselves the Elk Whistle Warrior Society. Look, we have slain an elk by ourselves!"

As she breathlessly introduced the veteran warrior to her fellow hunters, the dogs started to growl. Everyone looked up to see Anokì, E′s, Jilte′g, and the Cheyenne, White Crow, emerge into their midst. Recognizing Anokì, the dogs trotted over and tried to jump up and lick him.

Upon seeing their father, Wâpikwan and Môso rushed over and gave him a big hug.

"Father, you are back!" they both yelled in unison.

"Wâpikwan and Môso," I replied, "If you are not careful, you are going to accomplish what the Blackfoot were not able to do!"

They looked at me and laughed, sending the entire group into a fit of chuckling. Concerned that the people in the main camp nearby might hear all of this activity and misinterpret it as a sign of danger, I sent E's and Jilte'g off to announce our presence and calm any fears they might have.

That evening, we ate elk meat, told stories of our recent ordeals, and thanked Kitchi Manitou for looking after us with an offering of tobacco. Later on, we immersed ourselves in our cozy robes and slept with smiles on our faces.

The next morning, we left to join up with our families on the opposite shore. I was particularly anxious to reunite with my beloved wife, Osk-îskwêw, to show her that I was still alive and hold her tight. Travelling through the Hohe village, we stopped for a short time to rest and eat. Before leaving, we agreed to meet with them in the spring at Lake Kinookimaw.

It took us another sun to arrive at the Nehiyawak (Cree) camp, whom the Anishinaabe called the Omashkiigoo. Ever since we first entered this land, the Nehiyawak had been our most loyal and trusted allies, so it made sense for our people to go here for protection after the great wind storm.

As we walked towards the camp, Wâpikwan and Môso never left my side. Along the way, my daughter told me about the Elk Whistle Warrior Society that she and the others had started up, and both of them proudly showed me their impressive tattoos.

We arrived at the Omashkiigoo camp well before sunset. As we entered the outskirsts of the village, a Cree woman whom I recognized as Osk-îskwêw's cousin came up to me and the children. Her hair had been shorn off and she was wailing a death song.

Immediately, I knew that my wife had died. Wâpikwan and Môso also started to wail, and Wâpikwan used her knife to cut her hair and then slash at her arms. I was stunned.

After we were led to where my wife's body lay, they told us how she died. She had gone by herself to get fresh water from the river that flowed into the salty lake, not far from where they were camping. It had rained, and the river bank was quite muddy. The men who discovered her body said that it looked as if she had slipped and fallen into the exposed root system of a large tree.

Osk-îskwêw was found hanging upside down among the roots and the weight of her body had very nearly snapped her left leg off at the knee. They said that there was a lot of blood from the fracture point, plus her head was under the water line, so she either drowned or bled to death.

The following day she was buried with enough clothes and food to help her on her journey to join our ancestors, while the rest of her belongings were burnt in a fire. We had to start our lives over again, so Wâpikwan, Môso, and I gave away all of our possessions, including our clothes. After this, we covered ourselves with whatever rags we could find.

Losing Osk-îskwêw was a great loss for us as a family. After the burial, the children and I started to make new weapons and clothing, replacing everything that we had given away during our time of mourning. And although the fall bird hunt had been very successful, and the community dried a lot of meat to help get us through the starving months, the winter would only be a time of tremendous sadness for the children and me.

That fall after our hunt, we went west to Manitou Lake to heal our sick in the restorative waters there. After staying there for a week, we continued west to winter along the forested shoreline of a lake (present day Pike Lake, Saskatchewan) that teemed with ginoozhe (*kin-nose-shay*: pike).

The following winter was snowy and cold. Our hunters were kept busy trying to feed over four hundred mouths and supplement our stored food with fish, deer, elk, and moose. Despite their best efforts, we still lost many Elders, children, and weaker members of the community during the late winter months when food was particularly scarce. At the height of these starving days, we were so weak from hunger that the bodies of the dead lay in the lodges for many suns until we found the strength to move them.

As spring's warmer temperatures lured the deer, elk, and moose back out of the deep woods, our hunters managed to kill just enough of them to help us slowly regain our strength. The end of the Snow Bushing Moon (April), Iskigamizige-giizis (*is-ki-gamo-azing-a-gee-zas*), led us to travel to Last Mountain Lake over the course of eight suns, where we would meet the Hohe and other Cree bands.

With four hundred people and thousands of dogs all travelling in a scattered column, the sight was something to behold. For our one hundred warriors, it was a constant vigil to protect all of the Elders, women, and children from wild animals and enemies, while our huge pack of camp dogs kept bears and wolves at a distance.

Our destination would be the lake known as the Kinookimaw, which the Cree said was formed when the Great Spirit shovelled dirt out of the valley to form the mountains to the east. Once there, we would hunt and fish in preparation to travel with the Hohe. As soon as we were all together, we would then make our way to the Cypress Hills to hunt the buffalo, hopefully avoiding the Blackfoot in the process.

The Hohe may have wanted buffalo and war, but our people had to respect the wishes of our allies. As we travelled to the land of the feared Blackfoot, I could not help but wonder if the Zaagibagaa-giiziz (*zaa-gi-ba-ga-gee-sus*: Budding Moon, May) would bring death to my people.

16

THE COLLISION OF THE PRESENT AND FUTURE AND THE SORROW OF DEATH

ANOKÌ

As the days grew longer and the blooming wild flowers began to blanket the ground around us, the Hohe arrived at our campsite. We had been there for many suns, and we were enjoying the bounty of the readily available ducks, geese, and fish to fill our stomachs. We had also slain seventy-eight buffalo from a huge herd that had travelled through the area near our camp, which let us feed our visitors without immediately tapping into our own food stores. Nevertheless, we now had over a thousand people to feed, so Zhashagi was soon forced to take his hunters out to try and cull even more from the buffalo herd.

There were also more than three thousand animosh now roaming the site, all fighting, whelping, and breeding. When the smell of dog feces, smoke from the cooking fires, and the stench of dead animals being butchered mixed in with everything else, it created a disgusting odour that made me long for the fresh air out on the land, away from the village.

Mni'ódųwą (Looks in the Water) was the Hohe leader that we had met at the Sewitakan salt lakes. We were told that the scars on his back and chest came from his participation in many Sun Dances.

"Anokì," Mni'ódųwą said, "we, the Hohe, have come with over six hundred people, of which one hundred and fifty-two are warriors and hunters. The journey to Wazíȟe (Cypress Hills) will take twenty to twenty-five suns. We have to leave two suns from now, because we want to get there when the buffalo grass is high. As soon as the green grass is dry enough, the Sihásaba (Hohe name for Blackfoot) will burn the prairie, the spring rains will bring on new growth, and this will lure the pté (buffalo) back to the sacred hills."

"My relatives of the Omàmiwinini and the Mi′kmaq warriors will go," I replied. "We have always fought together, and that will not change. Zhashagi himself is not going, but he is giving his people the choice. He told me that there is plenty of buffalo and game to hunt and feed his people here without fighting the Blackfoot. Many of the Cree warriors will go, and their women will follow them to help with the hunt.

"Zhashagi said that any Elders and children of the Cree and Anishinaabe who do not go will be welcome and that both he and his people will watch over them. He has also said that any Hohe Elders, children, mothers, and anyone else too sick or weak to travel are also welcome to stay. Our communities will be able to add about forty Cree and Anishinaabe warriors to your hunting party."

"Forty warriors will have to do," replied Mni'ódųwa. "I will ask our Elders and the parents of our children what they want to do."

As Mni'ódųwą walked back to his people, I heard the sounds of barking and snarling and the screams of a girl and her mother. I ran over to the scene, saw two dogs engaged in a vicious fight, and noticed that there was a little Cree girl caught up in the middle. After wading into the fray, I was forced to club the dogs to death when they refused to halt their mindless assault on one another.

I could see that the girl had sustained serious wounds on her legs and arms as well as a torn cheek, so I picked her up and took her to the nearest tipi. As soon as I scooped her up in my arms, I was instantly covered with a mixture of blood from the girl's wounds and from the two dogs I had killed. I now looked like a crazed Windigo, scaring children as I walked past them.

Before entering the lodge, I yelled to my children,"Wâpikwan and Môso, I need your help! Gather up your Elk Whistle Warriors and get them to bring back as many leeches as they can from the lake and also some maggot-covered meat from the refuse piles! I need you to be especially quick with the leeches ... they are very important!"

After entering the tipi with the frantic mother, I saw that there were two women inside. The three of us immediately set to work to try and stop the bleeding. The little girl had finally stopped screaming, and the only sounds coming from her were deep sobs and choking sounds. Not long after, two of the Cree boys in Wâpikwan's group rushed into the tent with handfuls of leeches. We started applying the slimy creatures to all of the cuts and tears on the girl's body, knowing that they would stop the bleeding and help heal the wounds. After the Cree boys left, Spotted Fawn and Wâpikwan came in with more leeches, and soon the girl's body was practically covered with the wriggling, black creatures.

While the leeches did their job, the two women sewed up her wounds with sinew and bone needles. They removed the leeches wherever they sewed, then put them back on after the wound was sutured. The girl was still alive but very weak from loss of blood. Her mother, now relatively calm, was stroking the girl's hair and singing a song to her about birds and flowers. In the meantime, I boiled water and used it to wipe the blood from her body. After the girl's wounds were sewn up, the many threads of sinew crisscrossing her body made her look like a stitched shirt.

Môso and his friends then arrived with two bags filled with maggots and the debris they were feasting on. We had to keep them alive while waiting for the leeches to gorge themselves on the blood. After the leeches were finished with their grim handiwork, we popped them all off. Once that was done, we laid tobacco down and thanked Kitchi Manitou for supplying us with these helpful creatures.

While Wâpikwan's friends took the leeches back to the lake, we added the maggots to her injuries, which the women immediately wrapped up in moss to keep them in place. Over the next two or three suns, they would eat away all of the dead skin and help cleanse the wounds. Between these creatures, the healing man, songs sung in her presence, and smudging, I hoped that this otherwise young and healthy girl would live.

Two suns later, just as we were preparing to leave, I came by and was relieved to see her sitting up, eating soup, and drinking tea prepared by the medicine man. It looked like she would survive!

Around that same time, Zhashagi came up to me and said, "Anokì, I cannot put my people at risk by looking for a battle. We will always defend ourselves, as well as our allies and friends. My warriors and I have never backed down from a fight, and you need not look any further than the Lakota and Haudenosaunee Wars for an example of that. But right now, I need any warriors that survived those battles to hunt for and protect our women and children. They are the future and we must provide for them. If we are to become powerful again, we must grow."

Crazy Crow answered, "Zhashagi, you will always be our friend, and, if we survive this hunt, I hope that we will still be welcome to share your lodges."

"The fires of our people will always be kept burning to welcome you. I will pray to Kitchi Manitou for your safety and ask our women to honour you and your people with a Sun Dance upon your safe return."

Everyone exchanged handshakes and hugs, along with gifts of tobacco and sweetgrass. As we left, we could not shake the distinct feeling that we would not see each other for quite some time, *or ever again.*

With a combined force of over one hundred and fifty warriors, around the same number of Elders and women, about fifteen children, and close to two thousand dogs, we started out for the Cypress Hills. Many of the Hohe left their children with Zhashagi's people, under the care of a group of Elders who made the decision to stay behind.

Wâpikwan, Môso, and their Elk Whistle Warrior Society took the job of looking after the remaining children during the trek.

Even though the days and nights were still cool, it became progressively warmer as we marched south. We made good time, and Wâpikwan's group would watch out for stragglers and help guide them along. Even though we had taken sufficient food to keep us going, hunters were still sent out every day to forage. What they were able to slay was cooked up each night, and the dried meat that we had brought along with us was saved for leaner times. Every night, guards were posted to sit up and watch for danger. Everyone took their turn, including women and Elders.

About ten suns into our trip, it started to rain, and the walk became miserable. The following day, the rain and wind were so strong that it became unbearable to walk. We were able to find shelter in a grove of cottonwood, along the south fork banks of what the Cree called the Kisiskāciwani-sīpiy (*kisi-skaci-wan sipi*: Saskatchewan River). We speared fish and dried our clothes there until the weather broke a day later. It was also here that one of our Elders died, and we buried him along the river bank.

On the fifteenth day of our walk, a husband and wife were off hunting prairie dogs amidst a patch of long grass when they stumbled upon a slithering group of zhiishiigwe. Several lunged at them, and the man cut off the heads of the snakes that bit them. Taking care to walk very slowly back to within earshot of the group, they quickly informed some women that they had both been poisoned.

The four women immediately sprung into action, gathering up enough plantain to chew and apply to the bite wounds in an effort to reduce the swelling. After the man and his wife were placed on their own travois, four dogs were hooked up to each sled to pull them. Keeping them off their feet was critical, since it prevented the venom from spreading.

The next day, the four women helped the shaman apply a salve of black cohosh to their wounds. For most snake bites that I have seen, the victim is dead by sunrise of the second day, so, if they survived two suns, they would most likely live. Fortunately, because the women were so quick to apply the plantain, the husband's and wife's lives were saved, and they were up walking again within three suns. Both of them were very lucky, and they did not stray from the main group again.

As it turned out, the area we were walking through was teeming with snakes. For the most part, our immense group was noisy enough to scare them out of our direct walking path, but we did lose seven dogs to bites, since we did not have the time or resources to treat them all.

By the twenty-seventh day of our journey, we were running very low on dried meat. Our hunters were having a tough time finding enough prey to feed so many people. When we camped that night, Mni'ódųwą told us that we were very close to our wazíȟe destination and that we would be able to see the outline of the hills in the morning sunrise.

Rising with the sun the next day, my friends, family, and I stood in awe of the distant hills breaking the horizon. We walked towards them and got close enough to discern details in the surrounding area just after high sun. To our amazement, there were thousands upon thousands of buffalo as far as the eye could see, more than I had ever seen in one place before.

Môso walked up to me and said, "Father, this takes my breath away. In all my life, I have never seen so many of these animals on the land!"

"They are a gift to us from Kitchi Manitou, and, for that, we must always be grateful," I answered. "Tonight, when we prepare for the hunt, we will burn sweetgrass, lay down tobacco, and enter our sweat lodges with pure hearts. There, we will ask Kitchi Manitou to guide us to make our arrows and lances fly true in tomorrow's hunt."

17

THE BLACKFOOT CAMP

ÍÍKSSPITAAWA KIÁÁYO

I stood on a bluff overlooking Powakiksi (Cut Bank Creek), where my people had wintered. With the coming of spring, the snow was starting to melt, and the days were bringing longer times of sunlight and warm weather. Thankfully, our band had come through the starving moon of late winter with only a few deaths. My wife Iipisówaahs had given birth to a son three days earlier, and we named him Mai'stóó (*may-stew*: Crow) because, just as he was born, a crow flew through the open flap of the tipi, walked around, and then left.

My second wife, Iipisówaahs's sister, Soota, cared for her older sister and made her sweetgrass tea to stop the residual bleeding from the birth.

While all of this was going on, I pondered our options. In order to gain the strength we needed to join up with the other bands at their summer camp in Buffalo-Bulls Head near the Cypress Hills, the people needed a surplus of food from a successful spring hunt. We also needed healthy dogs to move the camp, but there were now over four thousand of them, and they were also on the verge of starvation. Unlike other plains tribes, we Blackfoot didn't use our dogs for food, but now the animals were starting to kill and eat the weaker members of their packs.

A day after my son's birth, several hunters came back with two buffalo they had slain, but after it was divvied up amongst the forty families in camp, it proved to be barely enough. More food would be needed, and quickly. So, I turned towards the intimidating-looking leader of the Black Catchers, an elite group tasked with policing our camp. Their faces painted black with yellow zigzags below their mouth and eyes, these warriors were a fierce and imposing sight.

I told the Black Catcher, "Send your warriors out to any camp within a sun's walk from here. Take them tobacco and sweetgrass and ask them to gather their best buffalo runners and callers to join us at Estipahskikikini-kots (Head-Smashed-In) as soon as the snow melts. We will meet them there in eight to ten suns."

"The sun is gathering strength each day, and the snow is disappearing quickly," he replied. "By the time my warriors get to the camps, it will be time to hunt."

I walked back to my tipi and passed through the entrance, which we always faced east to welcome the new day. Walking through the flap, I was greeted by my two wives. While Iipisówaahs nursed our son, Soota tended the fire and prepared a meal from our share of the buffalo that had recently been brought in.

"Soota, will your sister be able to travel in two days?" I asked.

"She is a Blackfoot woman; she could have travelled right after giving birth. We will be ready when the time comes!"

Two days later, the Black Catchers arrived back in camp. They had contacted three bands who were all ready to move. The next morning, the women took down the tents, and, by high sun, we were already travelling. There were two hundred and eleven people, of whom only twenty-two were warriors, plus thousands of dogs pulling our possessions on travois.

It would be eight or nine suns before we arrived at Head-Smashed-In. There, we would camp below the cliff, near the fresh water of the Náápi Otsíí'tahtaan (Old Man River). When the other bands arrived, there would be eight or nine hundred people and enough warriors to run the buffalo. After everyone helped to repair the many wa'kihtaki (cairns) lining the run lanes, our runners would dress up in the skins of coyotes and wolves and approach the buffalo herd grazing in the nearby Porcupine Hills. Then, they would guide the iiníí into the run lanes.

During each day of the trek, our hunters managed to slay some antelope and the odd wandering buffalo, which kept our group fed and strong. My son, Crow, travelled in a kapimáán (cradle board), which kept him safe on his mother's back while travelling and when she was doing chores. He would be in this board until he learned to walk and would only be free of it when someone could watch over him. That way, he would never venture unattended too close to the fire or to the dogs.

We reached Old Man River after walking for nine suns. While the camp was being set up by the women, the Black Catchers scouted for the herd. They found them close by, and plans were immediately made to begin the hunt the following day. The Black Catchers would patrol the camp all night long to prevent anyone from starting the pursuit on their own. Anyone caught doing this would be whipped with sticks, their weapons would be broken, and they would not be allowed to participate in the hunt.

Early the following day, the runners were sent out, and around midmorning, we could hear the dogs driving the buffalo towards us. Snorting and bellowing with rage, they came in on thundering hooves amidst choking clouds of dust, closely pursued by the barking dogs. Everyone lined up along the run lanes waved their robes to keep the animals racing towards the cliffs. As they neared me, I could see the fear in their eyes.

Over a thousand animals cut out from the huge herd were now pouring over the cliff in a suicidal wave. The resulting sound of breaking legs, crashing bodies, and terrifying death screams sent shudders up my arms and back as they struck the bottom of the gorge. For some of the luckier beasts, their fall was broken by the mound of bodies down below. Miraculously, they tumbled down the side of the pile, rolled out onto the ground, and then escaped.

Warriors, myself among them, armed with spears and clubs climbed up amidst the entanglement of bodies and efficiently put the beasts out of their misery. Since the dead and dying buffalo were covered in urine, blood, and excrement, it was a slippery and dangerous area for us to navigate. We men and our weapons were soon covered in blood as we went about our gruesome task.

The snorting and grunting of the floundering, suffering animals, the cracking of clubs against skulls, and the grunting of the warriors as we drove our lances home created a din of noise that dulled my senses. Like everyone else, I was completely covered in blood. At one point, I slipped into a hairy crevice between several bodies and turned my ankle, but I was left uninjured. The buffalo-jaw club that I had made last winter was holding up very well during this intense and bloody work.

Any hobbled buffalo that emerged from the bloody stack was promptly chased down by the young boys and finished off with their arrows. Meanwhile, the older boys, Elders, women, and other warriors tied ropes to the buffalo's legs and pulled them down from the gooey pile to the ground, where they could be butchered. It started to rain, turning the whole area into an entanglement of mud, blood, and pools of water, which actually made the job of dragging and sliding the carcasses around much easier.

It wasn't until dawn the next day before all of the animals had been slain and the carcasses were spread around. Three warriors had been lost during the hunt: one in the stampede, one was gored by a big bull in the pile, and another fell into an opening between bloody bodies and smothered before we could get him out.

Even though many animals had escaped during the run, it was still a successful hunt. The final count was seven hundred and seventy-nine buffalo slain. Adept at cutting up the carcasses, the women had all of the meat drying on racks by the end of three suns. During the grand feast that followed, we laid down tobacco and prayed to A'pistotooki for our good fortune. The people had regained their strength and the dogs were now fat and lazy, with hardly enough energy to keep the flies off their bodies. They were splayed out all over in groups, with young children dozing up against their warm, furry bodies.

The smoke from the curing fires caused the women's eyes to turn red and constantly tear up. Between this smoke and the pungent hint of rotting meat being scraped off the hides, my senses were constantly alight. While the buffalo meat was being cut, smoked, and mixed in with berries from the surrounding area to make pemmican, our out-guards were forced to slay eleven grizzlies that were attracted to the alluring scents. Once we left the area, they were welcome to scrounge whatever remained, but, for now, they posed a big danger to all of us, particularly the children and the dogs.

Half a moon later, we were ready to travel to our summer camp near Einiotoka'nisi (Buffalo-Bulls Head) on the western edge of Aiiyimmikoi (*i-kim-e-kooy*: Cypress Hills). Once there, we would hunt the massive herds of buffalo that travelled through the region all summer long. When our long, strung-out line of over eight hundred people and several thousand dogs camped at night, our fires could be seen stretching towards the night horizon.

Attracted by the smell of fresh meat, packs of wolves followed us on the fringes during the day. Thankfully, because of our large number of camp dogs, they kept their distance. One day, a huge, hungry grizzly decided to take a run at a travois laden with meat at the rear of the column. He was eventually overwhelmed by dogs, but it was not an easy kill for the pack. The desperate bear was massive, and its paws were the size of a man's head.

As the dogs charged at him, he would grab one in his immense jaws, snap the animal's back, and then toss it off to the side. It took over thirty dogs to pull the beast down, and, when it was all over, nine were dead and another five had to be put to the knife because of their injuries. The animal's claws were awarded to the families who had lost imitáá in the battle, the meat was divided up among the dogs, and the huge skin was given to the warrior whose travois was destroyed by the beast.

When we arrived at Buffalo-Bulls Head after nine suns of travel, we could see that the area was covered with the tipis of other bands. There were now close to fifteen hundred people, three hundred lodges, and three hundred and sixty-one warriors. Even though this was a very large group to feed, we now had plenty of brave men to protect the camp and hunt for the entire community.

18

ANISHINAABE, CREE, AND HOHE CAMP

ANOKÌ

The combined force of the Anishinaabe, Cree, and Hohe arrived at their planned camp site on the east side of what the Hohe called Wazíȟe and the Cree called Manâtakâw. Once there, the allies quickly started to erect over eighty lodges to shelter the community.

The sky was blue and the wind was warm that day. In the distance, I could see that the valley was populated by a herd of antelope.

"Let's take the dogs and try to slay some antelope to fill our stomachs," I said to my family.

As we headed out, the Hohe dispatched scouts to find the best place to begin their own hunt. With the help of our dogs, we were able to bring back a dozen antelope, which the Cree and Hohe women quickly cut up and prepared for the large camp. Some of the Cree men also came back with a lame buffalo cow that had been straggling near the herd. In order to secure their kill, they had been forced to run off a substantial pack of stalking wolves.

On our first night there, the sky was clear and there was a full moon. Crazy Crow came to my camp and asked me to follow him over to a large hill off to the west.

"Anokì, we have to make a plan for our children to survive. I am going to show you why I am so leery of this Hohe and Cree buffalo hunt. They have come for much more than the buffalo; they have come for Blackfoot blood."

When we reached the top of the hill, Crazy Crow pointed off to the northeast.

"Look there, my friend!"

I stared into the distant moonlight horizon and was astounded by what I saw. There were campfires ... hundreds of them! Although they were probably about a sun's travel away from us, I felt as if I could reach out and touch them. This land has an odd way of making things look closer to you than they really are.

"Crazy Crow, you are a great warrior, and I know that you would never run from a fight. However, if our children are to survive whatever happens in the coming days, I will need you to protect them."

"Anokì, only because you ask, I will do this."

The next morning, the Hohe leader, Mni'ó'du̜wa̜, sent a crier through the camp to announce that it was time for the hunt!

"I wonder if he means Buffalo or Blackfoot?" I wryly said to Crazy Crow, who nodded in solemn agreement.

"I have talked to your friends, Jilte′g and E′s," I continued, "and they agree with my suggestion that you should be in charge of protecting the children. Makwa and Wàbek, along with their wives, Àwadòsiwag and Ininàtig, and their sons, are going to stay with us. Kànìkwe and his son are also going to be by our side. Wâpikwan and Môso have a group of young people that call themselves the Elk Whistle Warrior Society, and I believe that they will also be of tremendous help to you.

"My sister, Pangì Mahingan, is with child, and I have asked Ki′kwa′ju to stay with his wife and help you. There will be nearly thirty Cree and Hohe young ones, plus a few mothers, who will want to be with their children. We only have about one hundred and fifty warriors, but I will try and position them between the herd and where you will be. Even with that, you will have a huge responsibility protecting everyone."

Crazy Crow answered, "I will die defending them. I had a dream last night, Anokì, where there was blood everywhere on the ground and on the grass. A blood-covered buffalo ran through my dream, followed by warriors with their weapons all dripping red. We will meet on the other side, Anokì, along with our fallen friends and family."

Crazy Crow then called out for Wâpikwan to gather up her friends.

My daughter came forward and said, "Crazy Crow, one of the Cree boys, Otema, said that his grandfather showed him a place where we can go to. He said that no other tribe, including the Blackfoot, will camp near this mysterious, sacred place of strange rocks. Otema's grandfather told him that so long as he was a young person or a warrior watching over children, he could go to this spot and be protected."

"Wâpikwan, you and your friends have to gather up all the children," replied the veteran warrior. "Tell Otema that it is his responsibility to get us to this place.

"Crazy Crow," a voice called from behind him. "I owe you my life … and I will be coming with you!"

The legendary fighter turned around and saw his Cheyenne friend, White Crow.

"I am honoured by your presence, White Crow. *Come.*"

I watched as Crazy Crow and his followers were led away by the young Otema. Looking into the distant hills where they were travelling, I saw something that sent a chill up my back and tears to my eyes. I smiled and turned back to the task at hand, content in the knowledge that all would be well with Crazy Crow and the children.

Jilte′g, E′s, Makwa, Wàbek, Àwadòsiwag, Ininàtig, Kànìkwe, and their sons, Kigìbigomesì, Mashkawizì Mahingan, and Kìnà Mòkomàn, followed me into the Cree camp of my wife's relatives. Although there were only eleven of us, most of us had fought in, and come home from, many great battles over the years.

We entered the Cree leader's tent and watched them prepare. During the feast of antelope, each of the selected warriors was given a piece of meat to eat. They then talked about what they would accomplish during the hunt and how they would fight on the battlefield if the

Blackfoot interfered. They donned their armour, made from layers of moose, bison, or caribou hide wrapped around a wooden slab. Some carried shields with sand or pebbles affixed to them to help deflect blows, while others had breast plates made from the wide antlers of moose.

The experienced warriors put eagle feathers in their hair, indicating how many enemies they had slain, and past wounds were marked in red. They tucked bone and flint knives into their breeches, hung them around their necks, or slid them into high-topped moccasins. Bows and quivers were gathered up, wood-and-stone war clubs were hung on leather belts, and lances were grasped. Clearly, they were preparing for war as much as the hunt.

When all was ready, we approached the herd. The buffalo caller used his best injured calf cry, and we were able to slay forty of them without having to run for or corral them. There were thousands and thousands of the animals, and the land was black with them from one horizon to the other.

As the women started to butcher the animals, the killing field was suddenly bathed in a brilliant crimson sunset. Was this a sign of the blood that might be spilled in the coming days?

The next morning, I arose with the sun shining from the east and looked towards the nearest western hill, which was awash in sunlight. Basking in this radiant glow, hundreds of warriors stood out on the slope of the hill, outnumbering us three to one.

Crazy Crow's dream was being laid out in full.

BLACKFOOT CAMP

"Ííksspitaawa Kiááyo, this morning our scouts discovered a group of Anishinaabe, Cree, and Hohe hunting this huge herd. They are now butchering the animals on the east side of the hills," said the head of the Black Catchers.

"Call out the warriors and tell them to equip themselves for war. It is time to slaughter the enemy as we would the buffalo. They are in our lands for only one reason: to attack us. Gather our medicine bags and paint our bodies, for we will feast and dance tonight and show them the fury of the Blackfoot at dawn tomorrow."

ANOKÌ

As I looked up on that hill covered with Blackfoot warriors, my body became chilled to the bone. It was as if a winter wind had suddenly enveloped my spirit. They charged down the hill, parting the massive herd. The deafening sound of the buffalo's thundering hooves and their bellows mixed in with the sinister war "whoops" of the enemy.

As our camp police raised the alarm, our warriors formed a line with their bows. They released their arrows and over twenty charging foes dropped with feathered shafts sticking from their bodies. They kept coming, and we ran for whatever cover we could find behind buffalo carcasses, rocks, and tipis. Over one thousand of their war dogs were also set upon us, and they were immediately met head-on by our own dogs.

The rival animals tore away at each other with their sharp teeth, and this terrible sound was punctuated by the screams of warriors from both sides as they were caught up in a vicious melee.

I looked around and saw my family closing in beside me, firing arrows as quickly as they could. I felt warm blood splatter onto my cheek and turned to see Jilte′g die beside me with an arrow through his throat. As the battle progressed to hand-to-hand fighting, I saw Àwadòsiwag go down next with a lance through her chest.

Enraged, I turned and drove my spear into a warrior whose face was painted black with yellow lightning bolts. As soon as I realized that the lance was stuck in his chest, I abandoned it, drew a knife from my belt, and grasped my war club in my other hand. Swinging and slashing, I downed two more enemy warriors while dogs spilled over our position and engaged us in mortal combat.

I watched helplessly as a tall Blackfoot warrior dispatched Makwa with a huge war club made from a buffalo jawbone. As he turned to me, I could see that the man's arms and chest were covered in gore and that the jawbone weapon was slick with my cousin's blood. The sight sent me into a rage, and I screamed, raised my club, and charged towards my enemy.

Taking a mighty swing at him, he instinctively raised his left arm, which I heard shatter as my weapon struck true. But this was to be the last sound I would ever hear. I felt a crashing blow as the jawbone club struck my face. The last sensation I felt was that of my teeth flying from my mouth as I hit the ground. Seconds later, I received a fatal blow to my neck.

It was then that I saw a bright light, and, from it, my father, Mahingan, and my mother, Wàbananang, came towards me with their arms outstretched.

CRAZY CROW

"Crazy Crow!" exclaimed White Crow. "Look over there on the hill … there is a man and a panther, a black panther!"

"Do not worry; it is a friend."

I raised my hand and waved. He waved back but then pointed behind us. In the distance, I could see about a dozen Blackfoot warriors running to catch up to us.

"Otema!" I yelled, "how far away are we from your mystery rocks?"

"See that ridge with the line of trees? Right there!" he replied.

"Môso, you and your sister must guard our rear. Today, you will prove that you are indeed a brave warrior!"

"White Crow, we have to get this group of children and women to that ridge!"

Both White Crow and I paused momentarily to grab one of the small children and tuck them up under our arms. Môso, Wâpikwan, and their six dogs came up behind our group and urged the stragglers on. Once we got the women and children among a cluster of trees on the ridge, we were ready to make our stand. The Blackfoot were closing in fast.

"Wâpikwan, come quickly!" I yelled. "We have to make our defence here!"

As the Blackfoot started up the hill, two of their stragglers suddenly disappeared from view. One was taken down by a black streak that seemed to fly through the air, and the other's face exploded from a direct hit with a well aimed slingshot stone. It happened so quickly that their allies never even noticed that they were gone.

Just as the remaining Blackfoot crested the hill, a shrill, ear-piercing sound began to emanate from the tree line. The enemy warriors instinctively stopped, turned to face it, and immediately started dropping to the ground, their bodies bristling with small spears and arrows.

"Memegwesi!" I yelled. "The protectors of children! No wonder the Blackfoot and the other tribes were afraid to come near here!"

After killing all of the Blackfoot, the Memegwesi were now coming up the hill, with Mitigomij and Makadewà Wàban among them.

One of the Memegwesi came to me and said, "I need you and the Rabbit Man with the limp and his panther to follow me. My men will look after your people."

Mitigomij said, "Trust him."

I turned to look back at the women and children and saw Ki′kwa′ju kneeling beside Pangì Mahingan.

"She is going to give birth," I said to the little man.

"All will be fine on this side," he replied. "Come with me immediately!"

He led us into a cave entrance so small that we had to get on our hands and knees to crawl in. Once inside, we could stand up, and, in the distance, we saw a light towards the end of the cave.

The Memegwesi pointed and said to me, "You and the shape-shifter and his cat have to go towards that light. Once on the other side, you will find a man and a woman who can speak your language. Follow their instructions carefully, and, when you have finished what they ask of you, leave by the same way you entered their world. It is very important that you obey them. Only the three of you can accomplish this. Now, go towards the light, and take your weapons with you."

Without pause, we walked towards the light.

19

WINNIPEG, AUGUST 20, 2011

"BUTCHER, WHAT THE hell is pecking on the damn window?"

"Shit, I don't know, Boss."

"Well, go look!"

"Boss, what are we going to do with the boy?"

"Who cares? We're sending the girl to the house in Vancouver … just get rid of him!"

Four huge gang members stood in the office of an abandoned warehouse, with two guards stationed just outside the door. Nearby, a bound and gagged seventeen-year-old boy and a girl around the same age were laid out on a ratty, old couch.

"Butcher, check the window … that pecking noise is drivin' me nuts."

"It's just a crow, Boss."

At that moment, there was a knock on the door.

"Shit, now what? Hammer, go answer the door and see what those two morons want."

Just as Hammer tore the door open, the window shattered, and Butcher turned back into the room with a dazed look on his face. The boss gagged when he noticed that Butcher's left eyeball had suddenly been replaced by a round stone, and blood was gushing out of the vacant eye socket in a stream.

The big man grabbed for the Boss, pleading silently for help and leaving a trail of blood behind as he slid down the kingpin's outstretched arms. Momentarily distracted by this, Hammer turned back to the door just as the two guards stationed outside tumbled inward with arrows protruding from their open mouths. Even before the bodies hit the floor, the biggest panther imaginable leapt into the room and immediately flew into Hammer's stunned face.

The Boss and Koshaon, the only other remaining man, just stood and stared in amazement as two fur-clad figures with long, braided hair calmly followed the panther into the room. Koshaon reflexively charged at the limping man, only to be struck down with an arrow to the throat. Like a spectator watching everthing play out on a distant stage, the Boss impassively stood there as the man with one eye drove a large spear into his stomach. The very last thing he saw was a knife slitting his throat.

Frozen in stark terror, the two teenagers on the couch stared wide-eyed as the big, black cat curled up by the door and started licking his paws over the bloody mess of a man. The strange-looking duo walked over to the two captives, removed their bonds, and spoke Anishinaabe to them.

"You are safe now," they said. "Follow us ... there are two members of the Bear Clan waiting just outside. They will look after you."

"Who are you?" the teens managed to ask.

"Friends of the Memegwesi!" they answered.

Crazy Crow, Mitigomij, and Makadewà Wàban left this strange world the same way they had entered: through the cave, into the sunlight, and towards the sound of a newborn baby crying.

20

WINNIPEG PRESS, SUNDAY EDITION, AUGUST 21, 2011

WINNIPEG: LATE NEWS report from Saturday night. Winnipeg Police found the bodies of six members of a known human-trafficking gang slain inside an abandoned warehouse in the north part of Winnipeg. Unconfirmed reports from an anonymous source said that the men had been killed with arrows, a spear, and a rock from a slingshot. The same source claims that one of the six men appeared to have been torn apart by a wild animal. More information in Monday's edition.

ACKNOWLEDGEMENTS

ALGONQUIN LEGACY IS the fourth and final book of the Algonquin Quest series. It is an adventure based loosely on the travels of the Anishinaabe people from the East Coast of Turtle Island to what is now known as the Canadian Prairies, where they are called the Saulteaux.

By writing these four novels, I have educated myself about the lives of my ancestors. Even before putting pen to paper, I read over 120 non-fiction books and travelled many kilometres from Newfoundland to North and South Dakota, to Manitoba, and many places in between, visiting every major museum in these areas.

I am proud to say that the collection of books that I read in order to write these novels is now in the Granite Ridge School Library in Sharbot Lake, Ontario, under the name of the Algonquin Quest Resource Centre. From junior kindergarten to grade 12, the school has around 220 students, 40 percent of whom identify as Indigenous. In fact, this school has the highest Indigenous student population in the Limestone District School Board, followed by Napanee District Secondary School in Napanee, Ontario.

If you ever have a chance to visit the NDSS library, you will find a one-of-a-kind, twelve-panelled Medicine Wheel in their circular library. This amazing work of art and act of reconciliation only saw the light of day because of Karen Randall Blancher, who was a Native Studies teacher in 2016–2017. After obtaining funding for the project from the Limestone Learning Foundation, the Limestone District School Board, the Napanee Community Foundations (Canada 150), and the Napanee Alumni Association, she brought in three amazing artists from the community. They included Kirk Brant, a Mohawk artist; Morris Blanchard, an artist and storyteller; and a Settler artist named Maureen Walton. Under the guidance of Karen, Kirk, Morris, and Maureen, the students drew the pictures and helped paint them. It was an amazing undertaking that produced wonderful results. Karen also made up plaques for the people involved and recounted the stories behind the paintings.

When I first set out to write *I Am Algonquin*, I wanted to find out who my people were and where I came from. I accomplished this, and, in the end, it resulted in four novels that I am very proud of. Having my first book, *I Am Algonquin*, published at the age of sixty-one was a surprise to me, and, hopefully, it will inspire other people to remember that it is never too late in life to write.

Algonquin Sunset was supposed to be the last of the series, but, due to my discovery of an online talking dictionary of the Blackfoot language (blackfoot.atlas-ling.ca), I was inspired to continue, and then finish, the journey. Indeed, *Algonquin Legacy* would not have been written if not for the cultural knowledge of the Blackfoot Elders who made the Blackfoot Languages and Resources Digital Dictionary, based at the University of Lethbridge.

I am forever grateful to the following people who lent their voices to the Blackfoot Talking Dictionary: Joanne Yellow Horn, Kim Black Water, Shirlee Crowshoe, Jessie Black Water, Carl Singer, Noreen Breaker, and Beverley Hungry Wolf. Keeping these ancient languages alive through the 1960s and the residential school era has been a challenge, and we are lucky to have these aforementioned people who are still fluent in these languages.

You can drive to and visit all of the places I talk about in every one of my books. The legends I mention are real, and only the characters are fictional. The ways the people lived, hunted, warred, and celebrated are all based on researched fact. For example, the Mystery Rocks are actually located in the Cypress Hills on private land.

The lake mentioned in the latter part of this book, called Sewitakan by the Anishinaabe, is part of a chain of three saline lakes called Big Quill, Middle Quill, and Little Quill. The Quill Lake names are a colonial name for these bodies of water, so given because of the immense number of bird quills that the

British found along the shorelines. Many of these quills were sent back to England to be used as quill pens.

The Sewitakan (Quill) Lake area in Saskatchewan is the largest grouping of saline lakes in Canada, covering 635 square kilometres. This group of three lakes is an important breeding site for tens of thousands of shorebirds during the spring and fall migrations.

I would like to thank Senator Bill Strongman of the Touchwood Agency Tribal Council of Saskatchewan for giving me the Anishinaabe name for Quill Lake(s), Sewitakan, as well as the Cree Name for Last Mountain Lake. It took me three days, and more than a dozen phone calls around the Quill Lake area of Saskatchewan, to finally get a lead on someone who could authenticate the place names I was writing about.

Three weeks later, I phoned Bill to find out the name of Last Mountain Lake, which the Cree call Kinookimaw (*kah-nook-a-mow*: Long Lake). The lake was made by the Great Spirit when the soil from the valley was used to make the hills east of Duval. People like Bill possess a wealth of information, and he knew both names immediately when asked. Miigwetch, Bill, for preserving close to your soul the names that our ancestors gave their surroundings.

Thanks to Kirstyn from the Cypress Hills Visitor Centre for her time in answering my questions about Bullshead, Alberta, a Blackfoot summer camping ground both before and during contact.

I would like to thank the people who read my first manuscript in its most raw form.

To Al Whitfield and Will Gurnsey, two passionate men who still use the old ways to hunt: with bow and arrow. I am forever grateful to them for answering my questions.

For Karen Randall Blancher, who has travelled many learning paths with me.

To my wife, Muriel, who is always the first person to read my chapters, give thumbs up or down, and fix the obvious errors.

And also to Anne Holley-Hime, my Kingston editor, who gets it right all the time. She is a key part of this small team that helps me craft my stories.

Finally, thanks to my son, Andrew (Anokì), who actually reads my books, which is always a step in the right direction for any millennial!

PRE-CONTACT

No Homeless
No Laws
No Jails
Shared with All
Respect for Two-Spirited People
Women Held in High Esteem
Children Were Gifts
Land Was Pristine

Then they came. They traded guns and alcohol to us. Gave us diseases we had never experienced before. Then they took our children and our souls.

For all that, they left us with "treaties" that we have to fight in their courts just to keep our lands and try to obtain the treaty money owed us.

If you want to know more about Native people, take the time to talk to us. Ask us about what we are trying to do with our lives. Get to know us and understand us. Our ancestors and your ancestors made treaties in this land that is now called Canada. Try to research and understand what these treaties are about. If I can leave you with just one thing to ponder, it would be this: Whenever someone says, "What are those Indians doing with all of our tax money!" always remember that *it is not your tax money that Native people are receiving*. It is "treaty money" owed to them.

Remember the Memegwesi are always watching!

Miigwetch,
Rick Revelle
Mashkawizi Mahingan Inini

GLOSSARIES AND PRONUNCIATION GUIDES

ALGONQUIN (OMÀMIWININI) GLOSSARY

hilaroad.com/camp/nation/speak.html

Àbimì – (*ah-bih-mee*) – defend, guard
Àbita – (*ah-beh-ta*) – half
Achgook – snake
Àgimag – (*ug-ga-mug*) – snowshoes
Agingos – (*uh-gihn-goes*) – chipmunk
Agwanìwon – (*uh-gweh-nee-won*) – Shawl Woman
Akwàndawàgan – (*a-kwon-da-way-gan*) – ladder
Amik – (*ah-mik*) – beaver
Àmò-sizibàkwad – (*ah-mow-siz-zeh-baw-kwad*) – honey
Àndeg – (*un-deck*) – crow
Anìbìsh – (*ah-ne-bish*) – tea
Anìbimin – cranberries
Animosh – (*an-ney-mush*) – dog

Anokì – (*uh-noo-key*) – hunt
Asab – (*a-sab*) – net
Asin – (*a-sin*) – stone
Asinabka – place of glare rock – (Chaudière Falls)
Asinii-bwaan – (*a-sin-nee-bwan*) – Stone Sioux
Asticou – boiling rapids – (also Chaudière Falls)
Awesìnz – (*uh-way-seehns*) – animal
Àwadòsiwag – (*uh-wa-dow-she-wag*) – minnow
Azàd – aspen
Binaakwe giizis – (*be-nack-que-we gesus*) – October Moon
Enàndeg – (*en-nahn-deg*) – colour
Esiban – (*ez-sa-bun*) – raccoon
Gichi-Anami'e-Bizhiw – the Fabulous Night Panther
Guhn – snow
Haudenosaunee – Iroquois
Ininàtig – (*e-na-na-dig*) – maple
Ishkodewan – blaze
Kabàsigan – stew
Kàg – (*ka-hg*) – porcupine
Kànìkwe – No Hair
Kà-wàsadotòj – (*ka-wah-suh-koh-tooj*) – April
Kekek – (*kay-kayk*) – hawk
Kigìbigomesì – (*kih-gee-bih-goh-may-see*) – lark
Kìgònz – (*key-gounz*) – fish
Kije-Manidò – the Great Spirit
Kìjik – (*key-jick*) – cedar
Kijìkà – (*kih-juh-ka*) – to go
Kìnà Mòkomàn – (*key-na mow-ko-mahn*) – Sharp Knife
Kìnà Odenan – (*key-nah o-de-nan*) – Sharp Tongue
Kinebigokesì – cricket
Kishkàbikedjiwan – waterfall
Kitcisìpi Sìbì – Ottawa River
Kitcisìpiriniwak – People of the Great River
Kòkòkòhò – (*ko-ko-ko-ho*) – owl

Kòn Tibik-Kìzis – (*cone ti-bick key-zizz*) – Snow Moon (February)
Lenepi – Delaware
Magotogoek Sìbì – Path That Walks – (St. Lawrence River)
Magwàizibò Sìbì – Iroquois River – (Richelieu River)
Makadewà – (*ma-ka-de-wa*) – black
Makon – (*mah-koon*) – bear cub
Makwa – (*muck-wa*) – bear
Maliseet – Malècite
Mandàmin – (*man-dah-min*) – corn
Manidò – spirit
Mashkawizì Mahingan – (*mash-ka-wizi mah-in-gan*) – Strong Wolf
Mazinaabikinigan – Lake Mazinaw
Memegwesi – (*me-me-gwes-ah*) – dwarfs or little people
Me'hiken – Mahican
Michabo – the Great Hare, trickster god, inventor of fishing
Mìgàdinàn – (*mee-gah-dih-nahn*) – war
Migiskan – (*mi-gi-skuhn*) – hook
Mikisesimik – wampum belt
Mikiziw – (*me-kiz-zee*) – eagle
Minoweziwin – war dance
Mishi-pijiw – (*mih-she-pih-shoe*) – panther
Miskomini-Kìzis – (*mih-skoh-mih-nih-kee-zihs*) – July
Mitig – (*mi-tig*) – tree
Miskoz-i Wàgosh (*mis-ko-zee wa-gosh*) – Red Fox
Mitigomij – (*mih-tih-go-mesh*) – red oak
Mònz – (*moans*) – moose
Nàbek – male bear
Name – (*nu-me*) – sturgeon
Namebin – (*nu-me-bin*) – sucker
Nasemà – (*na-sem-mah*) – tobacco
Nigig – (*neh-gig*) – otter
Nìj – (*kneesh*) – two

Nìj Enàndeg – (*neesh en-nahn-deg*) – Two Colour
Nika – goose
Nitàwis – (*knee-tah-wis*) – cousin
Nòjek – (*now-shek*) – female bear
Nukumi – (*no-ko-miss*) – Mother Earth
Odàbànàk – (*oh-dah-nahk*) – toboggan
Odawàjameg – (*oh-duh-wah-shaw-megg*) – salmon
Odenan – tongue
Odìngwey – face
Odjìbik – root
Odjìshiziwin – (*oh-jee-sheen*) – scar
Ogà – (*oh-gah*) – pickerel, walleye
Omàmiwinini – (*oh-mam-ih-win-in-e*) – Algonquin
Omìmì – (*oh-me-me*) – pigeon
Onagàgizidànibag – plantain
Onigam – portage
Ouendat – Huron
Pakìgino-makizinan – (*pa-kee-gun-no muh-kih-zih-none*) – moccasins
Pangì – (*pung-gee*) – little
Pashkwadjàsh – (*posh-kwah-josh*) – coyote
Pênâ-kuk – Pennacook
Pibòn – (*pi-bou*) – winter
Pikodjisi – black fly
Pikwàkogwewesì – (*pick-wa-go-gwes-e*) – jay
Piminàshkawà – chaser
Pimizì – (*pim-me-zee*) – eel
Pine – partridge
Pìsà – (*pee-shah*) – small
Sagime – (*suh-gi-may*) – mosquito
Shangweshì – (*shan-gwe-she*) – mink
Shàwanong – (*shah-wuh-noong*) – south
Shigàg – skunk
Shìshìb – (*she-sheeb*) – duck

Shìbàskobidjige – set a net under ice
Tendesì – (*ten-des-see*) – blue jay
Wàban – (*wah-bun*) – dawn
Wàbanaki – Abenaki
Wàbananang – (*wa-ba-na-nang*) – morning star
Wàbek – (*wah-bek*) – bear
Wàbidì – (*wah-bi-dee*) – elk
Wàbigon Kìzis – (*wah-bi-gon key-zis*) – May
Wàbine-Miskwà Tibik-Kìzis – Pink Moon (April)
Wàbìsì – (*wah-bee-see*) – swan
Wàbòz – (*wah-bose*) – rabbit
Wàginogàn – lodge, home
Wàgosh – (*wa-gosh*) – fox
Wàwàshkeshi – (*wa-wash-ke-she*) – deer
Wàwonesì – whip-poor-will
Wegimindj – mother
Wese′an – (*we-say-an*) – it is a tornado
Wewebasinàbàn – (*way-way-buh-sih-nah-bahn*) – slingshot
Wìgwàs chìmàn – (*we-gwahs chee-mahn*) – birch bark canoe
Wolastoqiyik – Maliseet

ALGONQUIN PRONUNCIATION GUIDE

native-languages.org/algonquin_guide.htm

CHARACTER			
We use	**Sometimes also use**	**IPA symbol**	**Algonquin Pronunciation**
ALGONQUIN VOWELS			
a		ʌ	Like the *a* in *what.*
à	á, aa	aː	Like the *a* in *father.*
e		e~ɛ	Like the *a* in *gate* or the *e* in *red.*
è	é, ee	eː	Like the *a* in *pay.*
i		ɪ	Like the *i* in *pit.*
ì	í, ii	iː	Like the *ee* in *seed.*
o	u	ʊ	Like the *u* in *put.*
ò	ó, oo	oː	Like the *o* in *lone.*

CHARACTER We use	 Sometimes also use	 IPA symbol	 Algonquin Pronunciation
ALGONQUIN DIPHTHONGS			
aw		aw	Like the *ow* in English *cow*.
ay		aj	Like the English *eye*.
ew		ew	This sound does not really exist in English. It sounds a little like saying the letters *a* and *o* together.
ey		ej	Like the *ay* in *hay*.
iw		iw	Like a child saying *ew!*
ow		ow	Like the *ow* in *show*.
ALGONQUIN CONSONANTS			
b		b	Like the *b* in *bill*.
ch	č	tʃ	Like the *ch* in *chair*.
d		d	Like the *d* in *die*.
dj		dʒ	Like the *j* in *jar*.
g		g	Like the *g* in *gate*.
h		h~ʔ	Like the *h* in *hay*, or like the glottal stop in the middle of *uh-oh*.
j	zh, ž	ʒ	Like the *ge* sound at the end of *mirage*.
k		k^h~k	Like the *k* in *key* or *ski*.
m		m	Like the *m* in English *moon*.
n		n	Like the *n* in English *night*.
p		p^h~p	Like the *p* in *pin* or *spin*.
s		s	Like the *s* in *see*.
sh	c, š	ʃ	Like the *sh* in *shy*.

CHARACTER We use	Sometimes also use	IPA symbol	Algonquin Pronunciation
t		t^h~t	Like the *t* in *take* or *stake.*
w		w	Like the *w* in English *way.*
y		j	Like the *y* in English *yes.*
z		z	Like the *z* in *zoo.*

ANISHINAABE GLOSSARY

ojibwe.lib.umn.edu

Aabita-niibino-giizis – (*a-bi-ta-knee-bino-gee-sus*) – Berry Moon (July)
Aagask – (*ah-gust*) – grouse
Aandeg – (*on-deg*) – crow
Aanikegamaa – chain of lakes
Adik – (*a-dick*) – caribou
Adikameg – (*a-dik-a-meg*) – whitefish
Adiko-wiiyaas – (*a-day-ko-we-as*) – caribou meat
Animaanagidoone – (*on-e-mon-gi-toni*) – He Goes Away Talking
Animbiigoo-zaaga'igan – Dog Waters Lake (Lake Nipigon)
Animosh – (*an-eh-moosh*) – dog
Anishinaabewi-gichigami – Lake Superior
Apiitendang Makwa – (*a-pete-tan-den muck-wa*) – Proud Bear
Asemaa – (*as-say-maa*) – tobacco
Ashkaakamigokwe – Mother Earth

Asinii-bwaan – (*ah-sin-nee-bwan*) – Assiniboine people
Asinii-bwaan Ziibi – (*ah-sin-nee-bwan zee-be*) – Assiniboine River
Ayaaj-inini – Blackfoot people
Baaga`adowewin – lacrosse
Baapaase – (*baa-pa-say*) – woodpecker
Baawitigong – present-day Sault Ste. Marie
Babaa-ayaa Animosh – (*ba-baa-ay-ah an-e-moosh*) – Wanders Around Dog
Bangii Zhiishiib – (*bun-ge zhe-sheep*) – A Little Duck
Bikwak – (*be-kwak*) – arrow
Boozhoo – (*beau-show*) – hello
Diindiisi – (*tchin-dees*) – blue jay
E-bangishimog – West Wind Spirit
Gaagaagiwigwani-ziibi – Crow Wing River
Gibichii-adik – (*gah-bich-e-ah-dik*) – pronghorn antelope
Gichi Bizhiins – (*gich-e be-zeans*) – Big Cat
Gichi makwa – (*gich-e muck-wa*) – grizzly bear
Gichigami – (*gich-e-gam-e*) – Lake Superior
Gichigami Zibi – (*gich-e-gam-e see-bee*) – Great Lake River (now present-day St. Louis River)
Gichi-Ziibi – (*gich-e zee-be*) – Mississippi River
Gidagizi Gidagaakoons – (*ged-a-gay-zay ged-ah-ga-cones*) – Spotted Fawn
Giiwedin – (*gee-wid-en*) – north
Giizhig Animosh – (*gii-zig an-e-moosh*) – Sky Dog
Giizhizekwe Ikwe – (*key-zee-zay-kway e-kway*) – She Cooks Woman
Ginoozhe – (*kin-nose-shay*) – pike (fish)
Gizhiibatoo Inini – (*giz-e-baa-too in-in-e*) – Run Fast Man
Gwiingwa'aage – (*gwing-gwa-ah-gay*) – wolverine
Ininishib – (*eh-nay-nish-hip*) – mallard
Iskigamizige-giizis – (*is-ki-gamo-azing-a-gee-zas*) – Sugar Bushing Moon (April)

Jiimaan – (*g-mawn*) – canoe
Jooweshk – killdeer
Kababikodaawangag Saaga'igan – Lake of Sand Dunes – (Lake of the Woods)
Kagawong Zibi – (*kag-a-wong zee-bee*) – where mists rise (Kagawong River)
Keewaynan – (*kee-wi-wai-non-ing*) – Keewaynan Peninsula, on Lake Superior
Ma'iingan – (*ma-een-gun*) – wolf
Makadewaagami Zibi – (*mak-a-day-eh-wa-gami zee-bee*) – Blackwater River
Makadewigwan – (*mak-a-day-eh-we-gwan*) – Black Feather
Makizin Ataagewin – (*mak-e-zin a-tash-win*) – Moccasin Game
Makwa – (*muck-wa*) – bear
Manidoowaaling Minisi – (*mana-do-wah-ling men-eh-si*) – cave of the spirits, Manitoulin Island
Manoomin – (*man-oo-men*) – wild rice
Manoominike – (*man-oom-inik-gee-zas*) – Ricing Moon (August)
Mashkimod – (*mash-ki-mud*) – bag
Mashkode-bizhiki – (*mush-ko-dee-bish-eh-ka*) – buffalo
Mayagi-bine – (*my-a-gay-bee-neh*) – pheasant
Memegwesi – (*me-me-gwes-eh*) – dwarfs or little people
Miin giizis – August
Mindido Animosh – (*min-di-dough an-ney-moosh*) – Big Dog
Mishaabooz – Great Rabbit
Mishibizhi – (*mish-a-bish-e*) – panther
Mishigami – Lake Michigan
Misi-Zagging – Lake Michigan
Misi-ziibi – Great River (Mississippi River)
Misko – red
Misko Zhiishiib – (*mis-ko zhe-sheep*) – Red Duck
Miskoseepi – Bloodvein River

Miskwaabik – (*miss-kwa-bic*) – copper
Mitaawangaagamaa – Big Sandy Lake
Mooz – (*moans*) – moose
Mooningwanekaaing – Madeline Island
Naadawe – Huron
Naadowewi-gichigami – Lake Huron
Nadowessioux – snake (Lakȟóta)
Negawi-ziibi – Sandy River
Nenaandawi′iwed – (*ni-na-an-da-wi-e-wed*) – healer
Ningaabii′anong – (*nin-gah-be-a-nung*)– west
Nii`inaweshiiwii – Cheyenne
Niswi Nishkaadizi Ma'iinganag – (*nis-we nish-ga-da-zay na-ing-ga-nag*) – Three Angry Wolves
Nitaage Niibiwa – (*ni-ta-gay knee-be-wa*) – Kill Many
Odaabaan – (*ou-da-bah*) – sled
Ode′imin-aniibiish – (*oh-day-eh-men-an-e-bish*) – strawberry tea
Odishkwaagamii – Algonquin and/or Nipissing
Ogichidaa-nagamon – (*oh-each-e-da-na-ga-mon*) – Warrior Song
Omashkiigoo – (*oh-mush-key-go*) – Cree
Omashkooz – (*oh-mush-goes*) – elk
Omashkooz Gwiishkoshim Ogichidaa – (*oh-mush-koos gwish-ko-shim o-gich-e-dah*) – Elk Whistle Warrior Society
Onishkaa – (*un-shkaa*) – get up
Oshkiniigii Gookooko′oo – (*osh-kin-eh-gee goo-koo-koo-oh*) – Young Owl
Ozaawaa-memengwaa – (*o-zaa-wah-me-mean-gwa*) – yellow swallowtail
Ozhaashigob – (*ooh-sosh-eh-ga-a*) – slippery elm
Pikwedina Sagainan – inland lake of the sand hills (Lake of the Woods)
Sewitakan Zaaga′igan – (*see-wit-akan saw-ga-e-kan*) – Salt Lake

Waabanong – (*wah-ba-nung*) – east
Waabishki – (*wah-bish-key*) – white
Waabiski zhingos – (*wah-bish-key ching-gwas*) – white weasel
Waa-miigisagoo – wampum
Waawaatesiwag – (*wah-wah-tea-see-walk*) – fireflies
Wanagekogamigoon – (*wan-a-gay-ko-ga-me-goon*) – lodges
Wajiwan – (*wa-chew-wan*) – mountains
Waawaabiganoojiinh – (*wa-wa-big-a-no-gee*) – mouse
Wiikwandiwin – (*wick-wan-de-wan*) – seasonal ceremony
Wiininwaa – nourishment
Wiipem Makwa – (*we-pem muck-wa*) – Sleeps with a Bear
Zaaga'igan – (*saw-ga-eh-kan*) – lake
Zaagibagaa-giiziz – (*zaa-gi-ba-ga-gee-sus*) – Budding Moon (May)
Zhaawanong – (*sha-wah-noon*) – south
Zhashagi – (*sha-sha-gee*) – blue heron
Zhingibisiwashk – (*shing-ibisi-washk*) – turnip
Zhiishiib – (*zhe-sheep*) – duck
Zhiishiigwe – (*she-she-gway*) – rattlesnake
Zhiiwaagamizigan – (*zhe-wa-ga-miss-e-gan*) – maple syrup
Ziibiins – (*see-peace*) – creek

ANISHINAABE PRONUNCIATION GUIDE

ojibwe.lib.umn.edu/about-ojibwe-language

SOUNDS AND ORTHOGRAPHY

Double-Vowel Alphabet

The Ojibwe People's Dictionary uses the double-vowel system to write Ojibwe words. This alphabet has become the standard writing system for Ojibwe in the United States and in some parts of Canada. Users unfamiliar with spelling in the double-vowel alphabet should consult the Search Tips page on the website above for help in getting the best search results.

The Ojibwe alphabet is as follows:

a, aa, b, ch, d, e, g, h, i, ii, j, k, m, n, o, oo, p, s, sh, t, w, y, z, zh

Note that the double vowels are treated as standing for unit sounds and are alphabetized after the corresponding single vowels. The doubled consonants *ch*, *sh*, and *zh* are also treated as a single letter unit. This is important to remember.

Each vowel is given below, along with a phonetic transcription, Ojibwe words containing it, and one or more English words containing roughly equivalent sounds. The letters standing for the sounds focused on are in bold.

Ojibwe letter	Phonetic	Ojibwe examples	English equivalents
a	[ə]~[^]	***a**gim* – "count someone!" *n**a**m**a**d**a**bi* – "sits down" *baashkizig**a**n* – "gun"	about
aa	[a:]	***aa**gim* – "snowshoe" *m**aa**j**aa*** – "goes away"	father
e	[e:]~[ɛ:]	***e**mikwaan* – "spoon" *aw**e**n**e**n* – "who" *anishinaab**e*** – "person, Indian, Ojibwe"	café
i	[I]	***i**n**i**n**i*** – "man" *maw**i*** – "cries"	pin
ii	[i:]	*n**ii**n* – "I" *goog**ii*** – "dives"	seen
o	[o]~[U]	***o**zid* – "someone's foot" *an**o**kii* – "works" *nib**o*** – "dies, is dead"	obey, book
oo	[o:]~[u:]	***oo**dena* – "town" *an**oo**kii* – "hires" *g**oo**n* – "snow" *bimibat**oo*** – "runs along"	boat, boot

NASAL VOWELS

Nasal vowels are indicated by writing the appropriate basic vowel followed by *nh*. Before a *y* or a glottal stop ′ the *h* may be omitted in writing. There are no direct English equivalents.

Ojibwe letter	Phonetic	Ojibwe examples
aanh	[ã:]	banajaanh – "nestling"
enh	[ẽ:]~[ɛ:]	nisayenh – "my older brother"
iinh	[ĩ:]	awesiinh – "wild animal" agaashiinyi, agaashiinhyi – "(someone) is small"
oonh	[õ:]~[ũ:]	giigoonh – "fish"

NASALIZED VOWELS

Vowels are nasalized before *ns*, *nz*, and *nzh*. The *n* is then omitted in pronunciation. A few examples are:

*gaawiin ingikend**an**ziin* – "I don't know it"

*jiimaan**ens*** – "small boat"

*oshk**an**shiin* – "someone's fingernail(s)"

Long vowels after a nasal consonant *m* or *n* are often nasalized, especially before *s, sh, z,* or *zh*. It is often difficult to decide whether to write these as nasalized vowels or not. For example, while we write the word for "moose" without indicating the phonetic nasalization, many prefer to write it with an *n*:

mooz or *moonz* – "moose"

ASSINIBOINE – HOHE GLOSSARY

indigenousknowledge.indiana.edu
/resources/dictsearch/index.html

Hohe Nakato – Assiniboine name for themselves

Mni'ó́duwą – Looks in the Water

Pté – buffalo

Sihásaba – Blackfoot

Wazíȟe – Cypress Hills

BLACKFOOT GLOSSARY

dictionary.blackfoot.atlas-ling.ca/#/results

Ááattsistaa – (*aah-tist-ta*) – rabbit
Aiiyimmikoi – (*i-kim-e-kooy*) – Cypress Hills
Áísopowa – (*a-so-poe*) – It Is Windy
A'pistotooki – (*ah-piss-toh-toh-kee*) – Creator
A's Imitáá – (*as e-me-tah*) – Young Dog
Asinaa – Cree Nation
Áóhtoksóo'ki – yarrow
Einiotoka'nisi – Buffalo-Bulls Head
Estipah-skikikini-kots – Head-Smashed-In
Ííksspitaawa Kiááyo – (*iik-sspitaa-wa key-i-o*) – He Is Very Tall Bear
Iiníí – (*e-nee*) – buffalo
Iinísskimm – (*i-nis-kim*) – the Buffalo Stone
Iipisówaahs – (*ipi-so-wa-ahs*) – Morning Star
Imitáá – (*e-me-taa*) – dog
Imitáá Nínaa – (*e-me-ta knee-nah*) – Dog Man
Issapó – Crow Nation

is-sap-wot-sists – put-inside-entrail
Kakkoo – (*ka-koo*) – Pigeon Warrior Society
Kanáttsoomittaa – (*kan-nat-so-me-ta*) – Crazy Dog Warrior Society
Kapimáán – cradle board
Kátoyissiksi – Sweetgrass Hills
Kiááyo – (*ke-i-yo*) – bear
Káínai – (*kay-nay*) – Blood
Kíítokii – (*key-toe-ki*) – prairie chicken
Kináksisahtai – Milk River
Ki'somm Áwákaasii – (*key-som ah-wah-ka-see*) – Moon Deer
Kotonáá'wa – (*coo-ta-gnaw*) – Kootenai Tribe
Ksííniiksi – cowbirds
Mai'stóó – (*may-stew*) – crow
Mai'stóó Nínaa – (*may-stew knee-nah*) – Crow Man
Máóhkataatoyi – (*mook-ka-ta-toe-aye*) – Red Fox
Máóto'kiiksi – Women's Society
Ma's – turnip
Miiyíkssopoyi – strong wind
Mòòkimaan – pemmican
Nááapi – (*naa-pee*) – Old Man
Nááapi Otsíí'tahtaan – Old Man River
Niitóyiistsi – (*ne-toy yis-seas*) – tipis
Niitsítapi – (*knee-tisit-ta-pee*) – the people
Ni'tókskaa Kiááyo – (*knee-tooks-kaw key-i-yo*) – One Bear
O'mahkssa'áí – (*oomps-saw-ah*) – Big Duck
Oostóyi Takáá Ohkitópii Iiníí – (*o-stoy tac-ah ooh-key-toki e-nee*) – He Who Rides Buffalo
Piikáni – (*pea-con-knee*) – Peigan
Piinotóyi – (*pin-ot-toy*) – wolverine
Pinaapisinaa – Sioux
Pisskan – (*piss-kahn*) – Buffalo Jump
Ponoká'sisaahtaa – (*ponoka-si-sahta*) – North Saskatchewan River

Powakiksi – Cut Bank Creek
Sawómmitsiki'somm – (*sa-om-mi-tsi-ksi-som*) – The Deceiving Moon (February)
Sik Makóyi – (*sik ma-koy-yea*) – Black Wolf
Sikapínii – (*six-a-pee-nee*) – Dark Eyes
Siksiká – (*six-sah-ka*) – Blackfoot
Sinopáá – (*see-no-paw*) – Swift Fox
Soota – (*soo-ta*) – Rain
Sootsímaan – parfleche
Sstsiiy – use the sweat lodge
Stumikiiks – Bull Warrior Society
Wa'kihtaki – cairn

BLACKFOOT PRONUNCIATION GUIDE

native-languages.org/blackfoot_guide.htm

CHARACTER We use	Sometimes also use	IPA symbol	Blackfoot Pronunciation
BLACKFOOT VOWELS			
a		a~ʌ	Like the *a* in *father.* Before a double consonant or long consonant cluster, it sounds more like the *a* in *what.*
aa	â, a:, á	aː	Like the *a* in *father,* only held longer.
ai		e~ɛ~æ~aj	Varies between the vowel sounds in *bate, bet, bat,* and *bite.*
ao		ɔ~aw	Like the *aw* in *caw.* Sometimes it sounds more like the *ow* in *cow*

CHARACTER We use	Sometimes also use	IPA symbol	Blackfoot Pronunciation
i		i~I	Like the *i* in *police*. Before a double consonant or long consonant cluster, it sounds more like the *i* in *pit*.
ii	î, i:, í	iː	Like the *i* in *police*, only held longer.
o		o~ʊ	Like the *o* in *note*. Before a double consonant or long consonant cluster, it sounds more like the *u* in *put*.
oi		oj	Like the *oy* in *boy*.
oo	ô, o:, ó	oː	Like the *o* in *note*, only held longer.
BLACKFOOT CONSONANTS			
ts	c, ch, č	ts	Like the *ts* in *tsunami* or *cats*.
h	x, ch	h~x	Before a vowel, it is pronounced like the *h* in *hay*. Before a consonant, most Blackfoot speakers pronounce the *h* more raspily, like the *j* in Spanish *jalapeño*.
k	g	k	Like the soft, unaspirated *k* in *skate*.
ks	x	ks	Like the soft *ks* at the end of *asks*.
m		m	Like the *m* in English *moon*.
n	ñ	n	Like the *n* in English *night*.
p	b	p	Like the soft, unaspirated *p* in *spin*.
s		s	Like the *s* in *see*.
t	d	t~d	Like the soft, unaspirated *t* in *star*.
w		w	Like the *w* in English *way*.

CHARACTER We use	Sometimes also use	IPA symbol	Blackfoot Pronunciation
y		y	Like the *y* in English *yes.*
'		ʔ	A pause sound, like the one in the middle of the word *uh-oh.*

BLACKFOOT DIALECT VARIATION

Blackfoot/Siksika people from different nations pronounce their language little differently, just as English speakers from different regions speak with different accents. The most noticeable dialect difference is the diphthong *ai*. Most Blackfoot speakers pronounce this sound like the *ay* in *way,* with a shorter sound like the *e* in *wet* before double consonants or long consonant clusters. But on the Kainai (Blood) reserve, they usually pronounce this sound like the *a* in *bag.* And on the Piikani reserve, many people pronounce it more like the English word *eye.* There are some other pronunciation differences as well — Kainai people pronounce many words with extra *s*'s, for example. These are minor differences, and Blackfoot speakers don't have any more trouble understanding each other than English speakers in Canada and the U.S. do.

BLACKFOOT DOUBLE CONSONANTS

When a Blackfoot word is spelled with double consonants, like *nisskán* (my younger sibling) or *mottaka* (shadow), the consonant must be pronounced with double length. For an English speaker, the easiest way to pronounce a consonant with double length is to imagine a word break between the two consonants. The *s* sounds in "dress suit" are pronounced like the ones in *nisskán*, and the *t* sounds in "hot tub" are pronounced like the ones in *mottaka*.

BLACKFOOT STRESS

In English, a stressed syllable is primarily pronounced louder than other syllables in a word. In Blackfoot, a stressed syllable is pronounced a little louder but also higher pitched than other syllables surrounding it. In Blackfoot, as in English, there is no way to predict which syllable of a word is stressed. You just have to learn it when you learn the word. Many Blackfoot language teachers try to help their students by placing accent marks over the stressed syllable, like this:

nínaawa (the man)

aakííwa (the woman)

We have also done this on our site. However, when native speakers of Blackfoot are writing, they do not usually write down accent marks. Just like fluent English speakers, they automatically remember where the stress in each word is and do not spend their time marking it on every word.

One other important note about stress: In English, an unstressed vowel is often shortened or weakened to a schwa. (An example of this is the word "rebel." When "rebel" is a noun, the stress is on the first syllable, and the word is pronounced REH-bəl. When "rebel" is a verb, the stress is on the second syllable and the word is pronounced rə-BELL.) In Blackfoot, it is important not to shorten or change the sound of an unstressed vowel. The difference between a long and short vowel often changes the meaning of a word in Blackfoot, and changing a vowel sound to a schwa can make the word incomprehensible.

CHEYENNE GLOSSARY

cdkc.edu/cheyennedictionary/index-english/index

Amėstó'eeseo'o – (*um-stow-as-see-oh*) – travois
Éháesenove – (*e-has-a-nuff*) – He Has a Temper
É'ometāā'e – (*eh-oh-my-da*) – Missouri River
Haȧahe – (*haa-aah*) – hello
Háhnomápano'ėhasēō'o – (*ha-toe-ma-pa-no-ha-say-o*) – honey
Hó'nehe – (*hoat-nay*) – wolf
Ho'néhevotoomáhe – (*hoat-nay-a-doe-ma*) – Wolfrobe
Hotamétmâsêhao'o – (*ho-dam-map-saw*) – Dog Men
Hotóá'e – (*ho-toe-why*) – buffalo
Mȧhaemenȯtse – (*ma-mints*) – corn
Ma'hēō'o – (*ma-hay-oh*) – supreme being
Mȧhōō'o – (*ha-ah*) – squash
Monėškeho – (*mons-skech*) – beans
Mo'ôhtávêhahtátaneo'o – (*mo-a-taf-a-tet-a-knee-o*)
 – Blackfoot
Oenenéeše'he – (*on-a-nay-shea*) – Harvest Moon (August)
Ókȯhkevó'omaestse – (*oak-key-whoa-a-mast*) – White Crow

Óoetaneo'o – (*ooh-ooh-ten-yah*) – Crow
Tse'némoo'o – (*set-knee-moor*) – tobacco
Tsétsėhéstaestse – (*tih-dis-dus*) – Cheyenne person
Vóhkeesá'e – (*wak-is-saw*) – Crooked Nose Woman
Vóhpåhtse-náhkohe – (*whoop-say-knock-a*) – grizzly bear
Vó'kaa'e – (*vok-ah*) – antelope

CHEYENNE PRONUNCIATION GUIDE

native-languages.org/cheyenne_guide.htm

CHARACTER We use	Sometimes also use	IPA symbol	Cheyenne Pronunciation
CHEYENNE VOWELS			
a		a	Like the *a* in *father*.
aa	a:	aː	Like the *a* in *father*, only held longer.
e		I~ɛ	Like the *i* in *pit* or the *e* in *pet*.
ee	e:	eː~ɛː	Like the *e* in *get* or the *ai* in *gait*, only held longer.
o		o	Like the *o* in *note*.
oo	o:	oː	Like the *o* in *note*, only held longer.

CHARACTER We use	Sometimes also use	IPA symbol	Cheyenne Pronunciation
CHEYENNE DIPHTHONGS			
ae	ai, ay, ï	aj	Like English *eye*.
ao	aw, au	ɔ	Like the *aw* in English *saw*.
oe	oi	oj	Like the *oy* in English *boy*.

CHEYENNE VOICELESS VOWELS

Voiceless vowels (also known as whispered vowels) don't exist in English. If you've ever heard Japanese, the soft breathy *u* in the middle of names like Asuka or Satsuki is an example of a voiceless vowel. Pronouncing a syllable with a voiceless vowel as if you were stage-whispering that syllable (but not the other syllables around it) will help you say it correctly.

Note: With very few exceptions, vowels at the end of a word are always pronounced voiceless, even when they are not written that way.

Character we use	Sometimes also use	IPA symbol
ȧ	å, â	ḁ
ė	e̊, ê	i̥
ȯ	o̊, ô	o̥

CHARACTER We use	Sometimes also use	IPA symbol	Cheyenne Pronunciation
CHEYENNE CONSONANTS			
h	x, ch	h~x	Before a vowel, it is pronounced like the *h* in English *hay*. Before a consonant, most Cheyenne speakers pronounce the *h* more raspily, like the *j* in Spanish *jalapeño*.

CHARACTER We use	Sometimes also use	IPA symbol	Cheyenne Pronunciation
k	g	k	Like the soft, unaspirated *k* in *skate.*
m		m	Like the *m* in English *moon.*
n	ñ	n	Like the *n* in English *night.*
p	b	p	Like the soft, unaspirated *p* in *spin.*
s		s	Like the *s* in *see.*
š	sh	ʃ	Like the *sh* in *shy.*
t	d	t~d	Like the soft, unaspirated *t* in *star.*
ts	c, z	ts	Like the *ts* in *tsunami* or *cats.*
v	w	v~w	Like the *v* in *vine* or the *w* in *wine.*
x	kh	x	Guttural sound that doesn't exist in English. Like the *ch* in German *ach.*
'		ʔ	A pause sound, like the one in the middle of the word *uh-oh.*

CHEYENNE TONES

Unlike most Algonquian languages, Cheyenne is a tone language. Some syllables are pronounced with higher pitch than others. In English, the last syllable of a question is pronounced with high pitch, so you can hear the difference between sentences like "You see a man." and "You see a man?" In Cheyenne, such high and low tones are used in nearly every word, giving the language a lively sound.

Vowels with high tones are marked with acute accents in Cheyenne:

á é ó

The pronunciation of Cheyenne tones is actually slightly more complicated than this — vowels without high tones can be pronounced with either medium or low tone, and overall pitch starts out higher and becomes lower over the course of any Cheyenne sentence. But the difference between high and low tones is the most important part to get right, because that can change the meaning of a Cheyenne word:

he'e – liver

hé'e – woman

CHEYENNE VOICELESS VOWELS AND *H*

A voiceless vowel before an *h* collapses into the syllable following it. A word like "o'kȯhome" is actually pronounced [oʔkhomi̥]. A word like "mȧeo'o" is actually pronounced [majoʔo̥].

This can make words with these letter combinations difficult and unintuitive to read, and some Cheyennes are working on simplifying this part of the orthography.

CREE GLOSSARY

talkingdictionary.swarthmore.edu/moose_cree

Âhkolawew – (*ah-ko-lo-will*) – it is a violent wind ᐋᐦᑯᓚᐧᐁᐤ+
Asinîwipwât – Assiniboine ᐊᓯᓃᐃᐧᐹᐧᐟ
Cahcahkalow – (*cha-chak-a-loo*) – blackbird ᒐᐦᒐᐦᑲᓗᐤ
Išpakocin – (*is-pa-ko-chin*) – He Flies High ᐃᔥᐸᑯᒋᓐ
Kaskitêwaýasit – Blackfoot Tribe ᑲᐢᑭᑌᐊᐧᔭᓯᐟ
Kinepik – (*kin-a-peck*) – snake ᑭᓀᐱᐠ
Kinookimaw – (*kah-nook-a-mow*) – Long Lake (present-day Mountain Lake)
Kisiskāciwani-sīpiy – (*kisi-skaci-wan-ipi*) – Saskatchewan River
Mâtinawe-kîšikâw – (*matt-in-a-way-geech-a-go*) – turtle ᒫᑎᓇᐧᐁᑮᔑᑳᐤ
Nēhiyawēwin – Plains Cree ᓀᐦᐃᔭᐁᐧᐃᐧ
Nīhithawīw – Woods Cree ᓀᐦᐃᖬᐁᐧᐃᐧᐤ
Nipahtâw – (*nip-a-towl*) – He Kills It ᓂᐸᐦᑖᐤ
Paskwâwi-mostos – buffalo ᐸᐢᑳᐧᐃᐧᒧᐢᑐᐢ
Manâtakâw – (*mun-a-tuh-gow*) – sacred land (Cypress Hills)

Manito-wapâw – strait of the spirit (present-day Lake Manitoba)

Môso – (*moo-so*) – moose ᒨᓱ

Osk-îskwêw – (*os-kee-is-kwee*) – Young Woman ᐅᐢᑮᐢᑵᐤ

Otema – (*o-tem-a*) – dog ᐅᑌᒪ

Sâkahikan – (*sak-ka-he-gan*) – Wînipêkohk (Lake Winnipeg) ᓵᑲᐦᐃᑲᐣ ᐐᓂᐯᑯˣ

Wâpikwan – (*wah-pi-kwan*) – flower ᐚᐱᑿᐣ

Wâwâskêsiw Kwêskosîwin Nôtinkêwiýiniw – Elk Whistle Warrior Society

Wīnipēk – Lake Winnipeg ᐑᓂᐯ`

Wînipekw – (*win-a-peg*) – James Bay ᐑᓂᐯᐠ

CREE PRONUNCIATION GUIDE

native-languages.org/cree_guide.htm

CHARACTER			
We use	**Sometimes also use**	**IPA symbol**	**Cree Pronunciation**
CREE VOWELS			
a		ʌ~ʊ	Like the *a* in *what*. After *w* it sounds more like the *au* in *taut*.
â	aa, á	aː~ʊː	Like the *a* in *father*. After *w* it sounds more like the *aw* in *saw*.
e	ê, eė	eː	Like the *e* sound in Spanish, similar to the *a* in *gaze*.
i		ɪ	Like the *i* in *pit*.
î	ii, í	iː	Like the *ee* in *seed*.
o	u	ʊ	Like the *u* in *put*.
ô	oo, ó	oː	Like the *o* in *lone*.

CHARACTER We use	Sometimes also use	IPA symbol	Cree Pronunciation
CREE DIPHTHONGS			
aw		ʌw~aw	Similar to the *aw* in *awake*. In some dialects it's pronounced like the *ow* in *cow*.
âw		aw	Like the *ow* in English *cow*.
ay		aj	Like the English *eye*.
ew		ew	This sound doesn't really exist in English. It sounds a little like saying the letters *a* and *o* together
ey		ej	Like the *ay* in *hay*.
iw		uw~ow	Like the *oe* in shoe. In some dialects it is pronounced like the *ow* in *show*.
îw		iw	Like a child saying *ew!*
iy		ij	Like the *ee* in see.
ow		ow	Like the *ow* in *show*.
oy		oj	Like the *oy* in *boy*, especially the way it's pronounced in Australian English.
CREE CONSONANTS			
c	ch, ts, č, dj	ts~tʃ~dʒ	Like the *ts* in *tsunami* or the *ch* in *chair*, or like the *j* in *jar* (see Voicing, below).
h		h	Like the *h* in English *hay*.
k	g	k~g	Like the *k* in *skate* or the *g* in *gate* (see Voicing, below).
kw		kw~kw	Usually it is pronounced like the *qu* in English *queen*, but at the end of a word, it is pronounced more like a *k* with a puff of air after it.

CHARACTER We use	Sometimes also use	IPA symbol	Cree Pronunciation
l		l	Like the *l* in English *light.*
m		m	Like the *m* in English *moon.*
n	ñ	n	Like the *n* in English *night.*
p	p	p~b	Like the *p* in *spill* or the *b* in *bill* (see Voicing, below).
s		s	Like the *s* in *see.*
sh	š	ʃ	Like the *sh* in *shy.*
t	d	t~d	Like the *t* in *sty* or the *d* in *die* (see Voicing, below).
th		ð	Like the *th* in English *this.*
w		w	Like the *w* in English *way.*
y		y	Like the *y* in English *yes.*
'		ʔ	A pause sound, like the one in the middle of the word *uh-oh.*

CREE DIALECT VARIATION

Cree is spoken all throughout Canada, so there are multiple dialects of the language. The main difference between Cree dialects is that the consonant that is pronounced *l* in Moose Cree is pronounced *th* in North Cree, *y* in Plains and Eastern Cree, and *n* in Swampy Cree. So the word for "wind" is pronounced *lôtin* in Moose Cree but *yôtin* in Plains Cree, *nôtin* in Swampy Cree, and *thôtin* in Northern Cree. Also, speakers further to the west pronounce *s* instead of *sh*, and speakers to the east and north pronounce *î* or *â* instead of *e*. Nonetheless, speakers of different Cree dialects are able to understand each other, just like English speakers from America, Canada, and Australia can (despite significant differences in their accents).

CREE CONSONANT VOICING

Some pairs of consonants that are distinct in English are merged in Cree. These pairs of consonants are:

k and *g*

p and *b*

t and *d*

c and *j*

When they come between two vowels, these consonants are always pronounced voiced (as *g*, *b*, *d*, and *j*). Anywhere else in a word, these consonants are pronounced voiceless (as *k*, *p*, *t*, and *c*).

For example:

pâkân is pronounced *pâgân*

sohkan is pronounced *sohkan*

kaskatin is pronounced *kaskadin*

There are some exceptions to this rule, but they're complicated. Since the same consonant is always pronounced the same way in the same position, you can never make an error with voicing that could confuse a Cree word's meaning. The worst it can do is make your accent sound bad.

STRONG *H*s

In Cree, unlike in English, the letter *h* is pronounced before a consonant as well as between vowels. For some Cree speakers, it is pronounced like any other *h* here (you can get the hang of pronouncing an *h* before a consonant by practicing the sound you make breathing on glass to fog it up). But for other Cree speakers, *h* becomes a stronger sound when it is pronounced before a consonant:

1) Before a *k*, *h* can be pronounced gutturally, like the *ch* in the German word *ach*. So *sohkan* is pronounced [*sohkʌn*] by some speakers and [*soxkʌn*] by others.
2) Before a *t*, *h* can be pronounced like the *th* in *think*. So *mahti* is pronounced [*mahti*] by some speakers and [*maθti*] by others.
3) Before a *c*, *h* can be pronounced like the *sh* in *sheep*. So *kihci* is pronounced [*kihtʃi*] by some speakers and [*kiʃtʃi*] by others.
4) Before a *p*, *h* can be pronounced like the *f* in *feel*. So *pâhpowin* is pronounced [*pa:hpʊwin*] by some speakers and [*pa:fpʊwin*] by others.

This is the rarest of the four.

Not all Cree speakers pronounce their *h*'s this way, and you don't have to use these pronunciations yourself, but it's good to be aware of them.

MI´KMAQ GLOSSARY

mikmaqonline.org

Apalqaqamej – (*a-bach-caw-a-mitch*) – chipmunk
Apigjilu – (*a-beech-ge-lou*) – skunk
Apistanéwj – (*a-bis-tan-ouch*) – marten
Apji´jgmuj – (*a-pa-cheech-go-mooch*) – black duck
Apli´kmuj – rabbit
Apsalqigwat – (*ap-sal-fee-quet*) – have small eyes
Ap´tapegijit – (*a-tap-ge-a-jit*) – turkey
Atu´tuej – (*a-do-do-etch*) – squirrel
Bootup – whale
Eli'tuat – (*el-e-do-what*) – Men with Beards
Elue´wiet – (*el-away-we-it*) – crazy
E´pit – (*eh-beet*) – woman
E´s – (*s*) – clam
Gajuewj´j – (*ga-ja-we-o-geech*) – kitten
Ga´qaquis – (*ga-ah-gooch*) – crow
Gaqtugwaw – (*goth-to-go*) – thunder
Gesga´t – (*guess-got*) – lost

Gespe′g – Land's End
Gespe′gewa′gi – People of the Last Land
Gisu′lgw – (*geese-oak*) – Creator
Gitpu – (*geat-pull*) – eagle
Giwnig – (*gee-o-nick*) – otter
Glmuej – (*glum-o-wetch*) – mosquitoes
Gomgwejg – (*gum-quetch*) – sucker fishes (plural)
Gtantegewinu – (*ook-dat-the-guy-we-new*) – hunter
Guntew – (*going-dell*) – rock
Imu′j – (*all-mooch*) – dog
Jenu – (*jah-new*) – giant
Jilte′g – (*jil-teg*) – scar
Ji′nm – (*gee-num*) – man
Jipji′j – (*jip-geech*) – bird
Ki′kwa′ju – wolverine
Lentug – (*len-took*) – deer
Lentug′ji′j – (*len-took-geech*) – fawn
L′nu′k – (*key-kwa-ju*) – the People
Magisgonat – (*ma-hes-hoe-nut*) – big nose
Matnaggewinu – (*mot-not-gay-we-new*) – warrior
Matues – (*ma-to-s*) – porcupine
Matueṣuei – (*ma-to-s-away*) – porcupine meat
Megwe′g – (*meg-weg*) – red
Mg′sn – (*unk-ka-sin*) – shoe
Midewiwin – Grand Medicine Society
Migjigi – (*mic-chich*) – turtle
Mui′n – (*moe-in*) – bear
Musigisg – (*moo-see-kisk*) – sky
Na′gweg – (*nah-quik*) – day
Natigòsteg – Forward Land (Anticosti Island)
Negm – bloody
Nukumi – grandmother
Penamuikús – birds lay eggs (April moon)
Puglatm′j – a little person

Sabawaelnu – Half Way People
Saqpigu'niei – (*soft-be-go-knee-it*) – I am shedding tears
Siggw – (*sick* or *sook*) – spring
Stogon – (*as-stow-hon*) – balsam tree
Tagawan – (*dah-ha-one*) – salmon
Ta's'ji'jg – (*daw-saw-geetch*) – little bit
Tepgig – (*dip-geek*) – night
Tia'm – (*de-hum*) – moose
Tmawei – (*duh-ma-way*) – tobacco
Wikuoms – wigwams
Wookwiss – fox

MI´KMAQ PRONUNCIATION GUIDE

native-languages.org/mikmaq_guide.htm

CHARACTER We use	 Sometimes also use	 IPA symbol	 Mik´kmaq Pronunciation
MI´KMAQ VOWELS			
a		ɑ	Like the *a* in *father.*
á	a', a:	ɑː	Like *a* only held longer.
e		e	Like the *e* sound in Spanish. In English, the Mi´kmaq pronunciation sounds like a cross between the vowel sounds in *met* and *mate.*
é	e', e:	eː	Like *e* only held longer.
i		i̞	Midway between the vowel sounds in *hit* and *heat.*

CHARACTER We use	Sometimes also use	IPA symbol	Mik´kmaq Pronunciation
í	i', i:	iː	Like the *i* in *police*, only held longer.
i	‘, ê, ŭ	ə	Schwa sound like the *e* in *roses*.
o	ô	o	Like the *o* in *note*.
ó	o', o:	oː	Like *o* only held longer.
u	o	u	Like the *u* in *tune*.
ú	u', u:	uː	Like *u* only held longer.
MI´KMAQ DIPHTHONGS			
aw	au	aw	Like the *ow* in English *cow*.
ay	ai	aj	Like English *eye*.
ew		ew	This sound does not really exist in English. It sounds a little like saying the letters *a* and *o* together.
ey	ei	ej	Like the *ay* in English *hay*.
iw		iw	Like a child saying *ew!*
MI´KMAQ CONSONANTS			
j	c, ch, tj	tʃ~dʒ	Like the *ch* in *char* or the *j* in *jar*.
k	g	k~g	Like the *k* in *skate* or the *g* in *gate*.
kw	kw	kw~kw	Usually it is pronounced like the *qu* in English *queen*, but at the end of a word, it is pronounced more like a *k* with a puff of air after it.
l		l	Like the *l* in English *light*.
m		m	Like the *m* in English *moon*.
n		n	Like the *n* in English *night*.
p	b	p~b	Like the *p* in *spill* or the *b* in *bill*.

CHARACTER We use	Sometimes also use	IPA symbol	Mik'kmaq Pronunciation
q	x, ĝ, kh	x~ɣ	Guttural sound that does not exist in English. Like the *ch* in German *ach* or the *g* in Spanish *saguaro.*
qw	xw	xw~xw	Guttural sound that does not exist in English. Usually it is pronounced like a *q* and a *w* together, but at the end of a word, it is pronounced more like a *q* with a puff of air after it.
s		s~z	Like the *s* in *Sue* or the *z* in *zoo.*
t	d	t~d	Like the *t* in *sty* or the *d* in *die.*
w		w	Like the *w* in English *way.*
y	i	j	Like the *y* in English *yes.*

SELECTED RESOURCES

Archibald-Barber, Jesse Rae. *Kisiskâciwan: Indigenous Voices from Where the River Flows Softly*. Regina, Saskatchewan: University of Regina Press, 2018.

Banks, Sarah H. *The Way Was Through the Woods: The Story of Tomo-Chi-Chi*. Roberts Rinehart Publishers, 1993.

Bourrie, Mark. *Bush Runner: The Adventures of Pierre-Espirit Radisson*. Biblioasis, 2019.

Brumwell, Stephen. *White Devil: A True Story of War, Savagery, and Vengeance in Colonial America*. Weidenfield & Nicolson, 2006.

Carrington, Margaret Irvin. *Absaraka: Home of the Crows*. University of Nebraska Press, 1868.

Daschuk, James. *Clearing the Plains*. University of Regina Press, 2013.

Dempsey, Hugh A. *The Amazing Death of Calf Shirt and Other Blackfoot Stories*. Fifth House Publishers, 1994.

Dempsey, Hugh A. *Red Crow: Warrior Chief.* Western Producer Prairie Books, 1980.

Dempsey, Hugh A. *The Vengeful Wife and Other Blackfoot Stories*. University of Oklahoma Press, 2003.

Doering, Ronald L. *Defending Our Home*. Borealis Press Ltd., 2012.

Grinnell, George Bird. *Blackfeet Indian Stories*. Charles Scribner's Sons, 1913.

Grinnell, George Bird. *The Fighting Cheyennes*. Charles Scribner's Sons, 1915.

Grinnell, George Bird. *Two Great Scouts and Their Pawnee Battalion*. University of Nebraska Press, 1973. Reprinted from the original 1928 edition by the Arthur H. Clark Company.

Hamilton, William Thomas. *My Sixty Years on the Plains: Trapping, Trading, and Indian Fighting*. Skyhorse Publishing, 2015. First published in 1905 by Forest and Stream Publishing Co.

Hart, Michael L. *Wilderness Empire: A Story of the Iroquois Confederacy*. Tellwell Talent, 2017.

Hutton, Paul Andrew. *The Apache Wars*. Broadway Books, 2016.

Hungry Wolf, Beverly. *The Ways of My Grandmothers*. Harper, 1980.

Katz, William Loren. *Black Indians: A Hidden Heritage*. Atheneum Books for Young Readers, 1986.

Lehman, Herman. *Nine Years Among the Indians: 1870–1879*. Acadia Press, 2018. First published in 1927 by Von Beockmann-Jones Company.

Lowe, Percival Green. *Five Years a Dragoon (1849 to 1854) and Other Adventures on the Great Plains*. The Franklin Hudson Publishing Co., 1906.

Mann, Charles C. *1491: New Revelations of the Americas Before Columbus*. Vintage Books, a Division of Penguin Random House, 2011.

Middle-of-the-Sky Woman (Nah-Wah-Gki-Shi-Ekkwe-O-Beek). *Indian Stories of Long Ago (May-Whin-Shah-Ti-Pah-Chi-Mo-Win).* Echo Printing Company, 1984.

Nelson, John Y. and Harrington O'Reilly. *Fifty Years on the Trail.* Fredrick Warene & Co., 1889.

Portman, Dale. *The Green Horse: My Early Years in the Canadian Rockies — A Park Warden's Story.* Rocky Mountain Books Limited, 2017.

Rasky, Frank. *The Taming of the Canadian West.* McClelland and Stewart Limited, 1967.

Schultz, James Willard. *My Life as an Indian.* Skyhorse Publishing, 2010.

Schultz, James Willard. *Running Eagle: The Warrior Girl.* Houghton Mifflin Company, 1919.

Schultz, James Willard. *With the Indians in the Rockies.* Constable and Company Ltd., 1912.

Shoalts, Adam. *Alone Against the North.* Penguin Random House Canada, 2015.

Sides, Hampton. *Blood and Thunder: The Epic Story of Kit Carson and the Conquest of the American West.* Anchor Books, a Division of Penguin Random House, 2007.

Symington, Fraser. *The Canadian Indian.* McClelland and Stewart Limited, 1969.

Tanner, John. *The Falcon.* Penguin Books, 1994. First published by G. & C. & H. Carvel in 1830.

Thorp, Raymond W. and Robert Bunker. *Crow Killer: The Saga of Liver-Eating Johnson.* Indiana University Press, 1958.

Underwood, Lamar. *Tales of the Mountain Men.* The Lyons Press, 2004.

Weidensaul, Scott. *The First Frontier.* Houghton Mifflin Harcourt Publishing Company, 2012.

Zinovich, Jordan. *Gabriel Dumont in Paris.* University of Alberta Press, 1998.

WEBSITES

dictionary.blackfoot.atlas-ling.ca/#/results
cheyennelanguage.org/words/lists.htm
ojibwe.lib.umn.edu/
translateojibwe.com/en/dictionary-english-ojibwe/great+lake
zia.aisri.indiana.edu

ABOUT THE AUTHOR

RICK WAS BORN in Smith Falls, Ontario. He worked for Nortel for thirty years, retiring in 2002. He belongs to the Ardoch Algonquin First Nation. His early years were spent in Wilton and Odessa, Ontario. He lived for thirty-two years in Glenburnie, Ontario, and since 2019, has lived in Napanee, Ontario, with his wife, Muriel. He has a black belt in judo, and in the '70s and early '80s, he coached softball, winning two Intermediate and one Junior "A" Ontario Championships. He also coached at three Canadian Championships. Rick is in the Loyalist Township Sports Hall of Fame. He is also an avid golfer, golfing every day, and belongs to two golf courses.

I Am Algonquin (2013), *Algonquin Spring* (2015), and *Algonquin Sunset* (2017) were published by Dundurn Press. The series takes place between 1320 and 1350 on both sides of the St. Lawrence River Valley and the Great Lakes and in the Rocky Mountains. It follows an Algonquin family unit as they fight to survive the harsh climate of warfare, the elements, and the constant quest for food in this pre-contact era. Rick's readers are introduced to the Algonquin, Anishinaabe, Lakota, Mi'kmaq, Mohawk, and Lakȟóta languages as they are used in the vernacular in the four novels.

Rick's books are read in Native Studies classes across Canada. Rick is also a Knowledge Keeper for the Algonquin Lakeshore Catholic School Board and the Limestone District Public School Board, both in the Kingston, Ontario, area. During the school year, Rick visits these boards with his Native Tickle Trunk and Tickle Bag full of furs, weapons, and artifacts. He makes presentations from JK up to grade 12 and also reads his novels to intermediate and high school classes.